T0149581

THE
MADMAN

MICHAEL AIELLO

-H.Bsc University of Toronto
-M.A. Wilfrid Laurier University

THE MADMAN

iUniverse books may be ordered through booksellers or by contacting:

iUniverse
1663 Liberty Drive
Bloomington, IN 47403
www.iuniverse.com
1-800-Authors (1-800-288-4677)

ISBN: 978-1-5320-1287-7 (sc)
ISBN: 978-1-5320-1286-0 (e)

Library of Congress Control Number: 2017900447

Print information available on the last page.

iUniverse rev. date: 01/10/2017

To Frank, Lydia, and Jonathan.

CHAPTER 1

THE MADMAN

I SIT ON THE DOCK, GAZING across the lake at the setting sun, which still warms my skin and glistens beautifully off the delicate crests of the waves. With each pulse in my direction, a delicate gust cools my face, and I sense a life-force in the watery expanse, an infinite and unadulterated power, which, paradoxically, is able not only to heal the wounds of a time-worn spirit, but also to incite chaos from deep within the soul. I find myself experiencing calm like never before, as the sparkling reflections work their magic, battling the pressures and stress of urban routine, and encouraging the peace and tranquility that usually accompanies refuge at the lake. Those who are lucky enough to get away to the cottage would attest to the magically-nostalgic power that stems from only one source, the water. Lakes, rivers, streams, and oceans all radiate a sovereign spirit that, for those who can sense it, awakens a passion within the soul. As the waves continue to spank the shore with a certain cadence, that both pacifies and aggravates me, I detect its spirit. The rhythm is quieting, I have to admit, but I am frustrated by the idea that the waves will only ever be waves and will continue their mockingly-slow movements long after people are out of sight. I feel a fiery annoyance toward the useless, slow-moving waters that, with each slap of advance and moan of retreat, remind me of their pathetic attempt to matter. I'm disgusted with their lack of purpose. I close my eyes to avoid the irritation.

This is my first time on the dock since its construction. Although Miranda and I have owned the cottage for a few years, we began building it mere months ago. My wife is the one who argued strongly in favour of the purchase, claiming it would provide the perfect sanctuary from busy city life whenever we needed a relaxing escape. Her reasoning included the fact that her parents have a home nearby, and she wanted to spend more time with them, as they enter their golden years. They are decent people, and I have always gotten along with them relatively well, despite the reality that, in my opinion, they have a lot to be desired as nurturers. Miranda's a mess. My parents raised me properly. They made it known that I would be worth only what I could produce and that no one held preordained entitlement. "Nothing comes easy, my boy," they would say. "Work hard and you'll get where you want to go, but be grateful when you get there." As a result, I have a very reasonable ego, and only rarely do I act arrogantly. I postulate that if the rest of the world were as astute as my parents, and as humble as I, it would prosper much more abundantly than it is. Miranda, on the other hand, can do no wrong. Her parents view her as perfect. They spoiled her and told her she was attractive, talented, and smart, and still do! They tell her she has value, potential, and worthiness. What swines! Her inflated ego, intolerable at times, makes me so angry that I often consider ending our marriage. Don't misunderstand me. I love my wife, who, by and large, is a very sweet and beautiful woman. We share a charming bond, but it is evident how her parents' constant coddling continues to weaken her personality and strengthen their mutually-parasitic relationship. I don't consider myself an angry person, but, whenever I think about my in-laws' distorted perspective of their daughter, and how they diverged from the proper and just course of nurturing, I become so enraged that I feel compelled to correct the wrongs of an overindulgent upbringing. Of course, being the type of humble and considerate person that I am, I would never confront or blame Mr.

and Mrs. Cranston. They would, undoubtedly, reject my ideas, and respond with hostility. And so they should, I suppose.

With my head resting against the back of the chair, a cool breeze kisses my sun-swept skin, bringing me back to the reality of my surroundings. I open my eyes to the startling sight of thick, dusky clouds, rolling in from every direction, and quickly making the recently-bright, clear day, dark and ominous. A mysterious fog spills over the now dead-calm lake, and a brisk chill stings the air like a rebellious swarm of poisonous wasps. An intensely eerie shudder runs down my spine, goose bumps explode over my body, and my hair stands up on its ends like an army of soldiers alerted to battle. The sudden reversal in the weather appears as though the universe is preparing to show me something, in dramatic fashion, and Mother Nature, herself, is retracting the curtains. My senses are heightened, my attention, fervent, and my posture, defensive. Not a sound is made during this entire pre-show, but the view overwhelms with greys, whites, and deep charcoals, flooding the scene. The wind picks up for a swift minute, assigned to blow the fog off the water. All of nature is perfectly still; even the distant trees look like background props, their leaves, rigid, as if too afraid to move. I stand up, walk to the end of the dock, and strain to focus on something across the water. There is a man, on the island across the lake! He glares in my direction and our gazes lock. He stares at me with an unwavering stoic expression that penetrates my protective façade and permeates the depths of my soul. It's a frightening glare; his eyes are bloodshot like that of a wolf on the prowl. I struggle to break free of their magnetic hold, only to observe his rugged, battered body, rippling with muscular fortitude. His hair is long and matted, and he is wearing only a pair of tattered, khaki shorts. He is just standing there, motionless, gripping a long, wooden staff with both hands. Somehow, once again, against my will, my eyes fix on his. I shudder with uneasiness. What is he doing now? He moves! He widens his stance and thrusts his staff into the ground. The long, wooden rod begins to bend as he persists to push it deeper and deeper into the ground. With each attempt, his muscles flex and move, in response to his demands. Suddenly, the staff snaps, spraying a bloom of splinters into the air. Quickly, he chooses one of the jagged pieces of wood and stabs it, repeatedly, into the water before him. Such an exhibition of raw savagery parallels the uninhibited expression of deep primordial tendencies that every man conceals behind his mask of social normativity and refined intellect. He is liberated, he is unrestricted, and he is insane. He jerks his wooden weapon out of the water to showcase the erratic flails of his speared victim, a rather large fish that is desperately trying to cling to life. As it shakes violently, it splashes water in every direction. Throughout the entire production, the man's countenance has not changed. His ruthless, feral countenance never changes! He stands rigid, motionless. Eventually, the fish follows suit. The climax has been reached, the madness subsides, and with a final soul-piercing glare, the wild man turns and disappears into a small, dilapidated structure, an old fishing hut, situated off to one side of the island. The play ends, and I am speechless. The physical tension, that has been an unconscious constant throughout the show, is now dissipating, and I feel my muscles expand and blood flow, naturally, to my extremities again. Never before, in my whole life, have I witnessed such a spectacular performance.

CHAPTER 2

HELEN

I AM AWAKENED BY A WARM breeze drifting through the bedroom window. It caresses my shoulders with the silky, soft touch, like that of a lone wildflower stroking the neighbouring grasses, as it sways in the gentle wind. I look over at Miranda, lying next to me, and take a few minutes to relish the attraction, as has been my routine for the last six years. Her naked chest, half-covered by the white, satin bed sheet, rises and falls with the tender cadence of her breathing. She is most certainly an angelic vision, as her brown hair frames her pristine face, ever so softly, as if to point out its portrait-worthy quality. I struggle with my longing to fondle her, but history, however, reminds me how grumpy Miranda can be when her sleep is disturbed. I manage to carefully slip out of bed without waking her, and tiptoe my way into the bathroom. The morning rituals begin.

When I finish showering and return to the bedroom, I find the bed empty. I hear two sounds. Miranda and her mother are conversing in the kitchen downstairs, and Alaska, our dog, anxious for her morning walk, is barking at the bedroom door. I dress quickly and open the door to find our precious family member in obedient sitting position, her furry tail, wagging in keen anticipation, and her eyes, wide with excitement. Alaska is a beautiful, blue-eyed Siberian Husky with the kindest, gentlest, most caring heart of any dog you could ever meet. Her silky coat is exquisite with its greys and whites, interwoven in the most charming way. She is a very well-behaved, compassionate creature who loves Miranda and me very much. I am quite fond of Alaska, too. She is the best of companions, with an attentive ear, that, for me, provides the soothing antidote to the anxiety and disquiet that stems from the obligations, tribulations, and affairs of life and living; my canine therapist, you could say. I am beginning to get irritated by the incessant, high-pitched voice of my mother-in-law, echoing up through the floorboards, so, like two thieves in the night, Alaska and I escape through the back door, fortunate to go unnoticed.

"Let's go, Alaska," I whisper.

The dawning sun works its magic, as it awakens the wildlife, warms the flora, and lights our path. The air is fresh and filled with the sounds of crackling twigs, as they snap beneath our steps, and birds, chirping their good morning greetings. Mother Nature can certainly excite the senses and facilitate an appreciation for the great outdoors, more so in cottage country than in the city. Alaska and I are in no hurry to cut our walk short. A chipmunk, suddenly, darts across the trail and, instinctively, Alaska succumbs to the temptation, giving my shoulder a painful yank.

"Ow! Shit!" I chastise her out of anger and pain.

I decide it's time to turn around and head back to the cottage, even though I'm not looking forward to what awaits me in the kitchen. I begin to think about the madman I saw last night, and his scary image becomes vivid once again, in my mind. I realize, now, that thoughts of him kept me awake for a few hours last night. His presence was very off-putting but has sparked my curiosity. I wonder if Helen knows who he might be. It's likely she will have some answers for me because, after all, she has lived in this area for more than thirty years.

Miranda's mother always manages to aggravate me in some way or another, and having a conversation with her is never easy. When we interact, she cloaks herself in a robe of niceties, so as to maintain the illusion that she is prim and polite, speaking only to me in reverent tones. Out of respect for Miranda, and solely in her presence, does she pay me proper esteem, but I know the truth! My eyes are able to rip through that deceptive façade and see her for who she really is. The old woman is a fraud! Her "sweet-old-lady" routine may fool others, but not me! Nevertheless, I need to find out just who the savage man is, and Helen is my best option. Oh, how I dread that my query will give Helen the opportunity to grate upon me, with her condescending tones and pejorative attitude.

Alaska and I find our way back to the cottage just as the sun is beginning to present its full potential across the clear, blue sky. Its reflection dances off the shallow waves, twinkling from all possible angles, dictated by the will of the tide. As we approach the cottage, I set Alaska free of her leash and enter through the back door. I take a deep breath in preparation for the guise and pretence that lurk in the kitchen.

"Hey, there!" Helen says, excitedly, and with a big smile. She immediately gets out of her chair, totters over, and gives me a big hug. "How are you?"

"I'm doing well, thanks," I reply.

"That's wonderful. Beautiful day, isn't it? How was your walk?"

"Oh, can't complain," I say. "The sun is especially beautiful today."

"Yes, it is lovely," she replies. "Oh, and I just want to say that you've really done a beautiful job on the landscaping around the house. Miranda tells me that you spent the last few weeks working on it, and it looks amazing. Great job!"

Oh, how that cunning woman strikes with such efficacy! Can you not hear the quanta of hatred spewing from her mouth? Her words, cloaked in all their sensationalized merriment, attack me with sinister intent, like hot embers on my skin, meant to singe my masculinity.

"Thanks," I reply. I give nothing more.

"You're welcome, Brian!" she replies, with a bright smile, a hypocritically-exuberant smile, meant to blind Miranda from the slights and attacks she aims at me. She fails to conceal anything from me! Her latent assaults are like a pack of wolves on the hunt, hidden by the shadowy glow of the night moon. The floodlight may blanket the view, but the wolves are still backstage. Underneath the smokescreen lies the heart of a woman who has never accepted me into the family, nor ever will. She despises my being with Miranda and has never once entertained the thought that I might be good enough for her. She hates me. I am sure of it. She, then, rushes up, throws her arms around me, and gives me a zealously-tight hug, once more.

"We really love you, Brian! Jim and I are so very happy to have you as our son-in-law!"

Do you not see it? Do you not see the palpable hue of abhorrence executed in perfect concealment, like a swelling mist that obscures the oncoming car, which becomes visible only seconds before the crash. Oh, how her lies seep into my veins, and poison me with her toxic disgust for my very being. Like a decorated thief, she uses my name as if it belongs to her, as if *I* belong to her. Helen's acts of benevolence toward me are as sly as jackals, and every time Helen and I speak, I can hear them laughing. Do not insult my intelligence with your flimsy attempt at counterfeit kindness!

"We love you guys, too," Miranda says, after a subtle silence. "We're happy that you and dad are coming over for dinner tonight."

Dinner!? Tonight!? Her words echo violently in my mind. Oh, how not ready am I to face the two-headed monster that will undoubtedly feast on my bones like a starving lion that stumbles upon an injured zebra! You see, my father-in-law, Jim, is no different. In fact, he is probably worse. His hatred for me, in all of its masculine glory, holds a more explicit character. He is far more open about his displeasure of Miranda's choice of life partner and can be far more cunning and deceptive. Tonight should play out like a carefully-strategized chess match, unfairly, two against one. So be it. Bring on the Cranston tag team. I am up for the challenge.

"Yup, great!" I offer. "Oh, Helen, before you go, I want to ask you something. Do you know who lives across the lake from us? On the island?"

"No one," she answers, confidently. "That island lot has been vacant for years."

"Are you sure?"

"Quite sure. The last person to live there was old Mr. Hawkins, but he has long since left this area. In fact, he died around the time when most of the residents here, moved in. Jim and I were here for only three months before he died. We didn't know him very well, but would occasionally wave to him."

"Oh, really?"

"Yes," she replies. "I think he had a son, but we haven't seen him around in a long time, and I'm fairly sure he doesn't own the lot, anyway. Why do you ask, Brian?"

"Well, I saw a man there, yesterday. He was a very peculiar man who looked rather menacing. I just wondered if you knew who he might be."

"Not too sure. Jim might know. You can ask him tonight. Well, I'd better run. Bye, Brian!"

She hugs me, for a third agonizing time, and then, quickly scurries out, as Miranda holds the door open. She leaves with such haste that I toy with the suspicion that she is intentionally concealing the identity of the madman, but this presumption lasts for only a second. Even though I have thorough knowledge of her sinister feelings toward me, I do not believe that she can engage in this sort of domestic espionage, nor do I have any reason to believe that the madman has any connection to Miranda's family, or that he is a sinister figure himself. I do, however, have every intention of asking Jim about him at dinner, tonight.

CHAPTER 3

MIRANDA

"So, MY LOVE," MIRANDA SAYS. "Who is this man you speak of?"

"Oh, just someone I saw yesterday when I was relaxing on the dock. Honey, have you ever seen anyone there before?"

"Uhh---no, never. But relax. Dad should know something about him." All of a sudden, Miranda throws her arms around my neck and kisses me. My thoughts of the madman instantly melt away into lighter things. "So, what can I make you for breakfast, sweetie?" my wife asks.

"Oh, maybe, just some oatmeal."

"Ok, love. Go sit down and I'll bring it to you."

She hands me the newspaper and directs me to the chair in the living room. It is our Saturday morning tradition. I sit in my chair and work on a crossword puzzle while Miranda makes me breakfast. Although I very much enjoy this routine, I can't help but wonder if this monotonous ritual contributes, simply and directly, to the sort of general malaise that has plagued me for so long, and plagues me still. These occasional fits of despair and disquiet seem to sour my desire to smile, suck away my longing to laugh, and shroud the existence of any delight. Of course, at times, I am still able to have fun, and be happy, and even have hope, but these ideals have been corrupted over time. I can remember as a child, I had a very jovial demeanour. I exuded a free, happy-go-lucky spirit, and enjoyed making others laugh. I was rarely without a smile on my face, a smile that brought with it, no pretence; an expression of my true, inner self. Later, during my teenage years, I recognized a particular sentiment that crept ever so softly into my consciousness. Like a parasite, this feeling soaked into the very core of my being. It was sorrow, so to speak, like a chronic, dull ache, that has remained with me ever since. I recall trying to fight off the random bouts, sometimes in anger, the way an aggressive immune system works to fight off invading bacteria. I used to try to out-think my new tenant by employing a mind-over-matter strategy, convincing myself that I could be cheery and fun-loving once again. It was to no avail. No matter how hard I tried, and despite several successful escapes along the way, the war was lost, so to speak. By my mid-twenties, the infection had completed its invasion, producing the sporadic unrest that I speak of. I'm sure everyone, who thinks back to his youth, can relate.

I know that carefree, young boy of the past was me, and that I have the same body as that young child, but I know I am no longer the same soul. If the spirit of that boy is not dead, it has certainly taken a long, reclusive leave of absence and has not been seen or heard from by anyone, especially myself, in many, many years. I am now a shell of the joyful, young man I once was, crippled not by some sensational event involving excruciating pain, but by the slow, lingering pollution of a lifeless mourning that has, perfectly and completely, penetrated my inner core. Naturally, I have often wondered if, for me, or for anyone else who shares this affliction, the stagnation of routine and ritual facilitated the conversion. I also wonder if, had I been perhaps more impulsive and spontaneous, it would have, at least, slowed down the transformation, and allowed me a few years free from total parasitic domination. Alas, I do not know the answer; I am merely speculating.

Even the should-be-happy moments of my past were rinsed in a bittersweet wash that eroded the possibility of total unadulterated bliss. My wedding day, for example, supposedly the best day of my life, was marred by a ubiquitous feeling of hopelessness, that no matter what I was to do in this life, I would be cursed and headed towards inevitable doom. Periodically, a small portion of my tainted inner being would find its way into the realm of delight, and for a few fleeting moments, triumph, putting a smile on my face and a warmth in my heart. Throughout the festivities of that day, I often gazed at Miranda, in her exquisite, white dress, and I relished in her beauty, which, still today, boosts my disposition. However, even now, the beauty of my soulmate can offer me only short respites from my sadness, and, invariably, my being slips, ever so sheepishly, back into the depths of its dark and vile coating, returning me to the despair which is bonded, ever so tightly.

It was on the day that I got married that I realized why people perform weddings with such grandeur. You see, my wedding was the most beautiful, most elegant, most boundless, and most perfect event one could ever imagine. The decorations, the music, the food, the people, and, of course, the bride, were all perfectly elegant and stunning. Everyone and everything seemed touched by the spirit of love, herself, which was present, in no small quantity, that day. All components of my wedding contributed to the creation of a hopeful spirit, one that mimicked the spirit of that small boy of yesteryear. Yet, my perfect day was marred by my sickness. Weddings are not about the future, they are about the past. They are representations, symbols that stand for love and love's ability to revive the dormant spirit of a young boy, to retrieve the irretrievable, and to make possible the impossible. I thought then, and I still think now, that love might be the cure to the condition that ailed me. For most people, this remedy succeeds in keeping the parasite at bay, however, for reasons unknown to me, my particular malady is winning the battle, even against love. I am sure that I am not like others who could be saved from the parasite by love's enduring benevolence. As I sat, that night, at the head table, looking around at my friends and family, who seemed to be enjoying themselves, I recognized that

I was a member of a different breed, a flawed breed, doomed and destined for sadness, as my soul rejected the remedial attributes of love.

"Here's your oatmeal, my love."

The interruption startles my introspective examination. I am able to think normal thoughts again. I know that I love Miranda with all my heart. Since our first meeting, I have never been attracted to another woman. Come to think of it, my skin has never even touched the skin of another woman, and I am pleased by the thought. I could never cheat on her, nor could I, even, lust after other women. My affections are only for her. She is everything I have ever wanted. In my eyes, celebrities, models, actresses, and the like, all pale in comparison to my gorgeous Miranda. She is all that is good in this world, and my heart belongs to her, entirely.

"Thank you, my dear," I reply.

Miranda acknowledges my gratitude with a subtle nod. Her modesty is an integral part of her beauty, and it only makes me love her more. Then, she picks up a basket of neatly-folded towels and heads upstairs. Her absence leaves me alone with my ponderings, once more. Loneliness, as one might expect, does not become me, and I am old and wise enough to fear the feeling. I fight the urge to crawl back inside my sickness by focussing on my crossword puzzle and keeping my thoughts void of self-loathing. Just then, I recall that I have to head into town to pick up a few things at the hardware store. I'll take Alaska with me. She'll enjoy the change of scenery. I finish my breakfast, crossword, and clean up.

CHAPTER 4

CHUCK

I FIND ALASKA IN THE BACKYARD, running around, ever so playfully. Her beautiful blue eyes glisten in the sun. She waits, calmly and obediently, as I put the leash on her. We make our way to the front of the garage and, as I open the door of my truck, she jumps in, eagerly. As we drive toward town, she sits upright, perched on the front passenger seat, like royalty, chest out, head held high. She is pristine but alert, taking her eyes off the road only once in a while, to poke her nose out the window to enjoy the warm breeze, filtering into the truck. She seems to maintain a protective eye over me, as though I am her child and she is prepared to give her life for mine, if need be. Nevertheless, she remains as refined and as beautiful as ever. Her heartbeat is steady, her breaths are consistent, and there is a serene joy on her face. I wish I knew what she is thinking so that I, too, might enjoy that natural happiness. At this moment, I realize I can't possibly love her any more dearly than I do. She is the perfect quantum of joy, illuminating dark pockets of sadness everywhere she goes. Her temperament is devoid of fear, and I am resolutely envious.

It isn't too long before we pull into the parking lot of the hardware store. I need some light bulbs and a good shovel to unearth a small tree that is dying in the yard. I park the truck, cue Alaska out, and head into the store; Smith & Sons Hardware Company, the most trusted place in the entire town. Owned and operated by good ol' Charlie Smith, the man with the sweetest, most trustworthy face on the planet. Everyone in town loves this charming elder. He has been the town's unofficial handyman for decades and there isn't a finer choice anywhere in the world. He is an honest man, whose sincerity is matched only by his ability to bring warmth and comfort to those around him. He typically operates wrapped in a blanket of levity, making him a very easy person to deal with. He stands about 5 feet 8, has a soft, burly laugh that is more of a giggle than anything else, and he demonstrates it often. He has a thinning beard that is clinging to the memory of younger days. His semblance to Kris Kringle is matched by his propensity for lighthearted kindness, and I often consider the notion that this man can very well be jolly Saint Nick, himself. Of course, I doubt anyone who knows Chuck would consider it shocking, in any way, to learn that he really was Santa Claus. Most likely, they would greet the news with pleasant confirmation and then, go about their days, as if nothing had changed.

Chuck and his loving wife, Dotty, opened the business before I was born, and he is slowly giving more authority to his three sons, especially since the passing of their mother. Dotty, too, beloved by the entire town, was greatly mourned when acute lymphoblastic leukemia took her from this world. For weeks after her funeral, for most people, it felt like there was an oppressive, muggy darkness, clinging to the particles in the air, in place of joy. Dotty was the unofficial mom of the town, frequenting the homes of the townspeople with a tray of cookies in one arm and a loving hug in the other. Miranda and I hardly spoke for a few days afterwards, supposing that breaking the silence would have lasting and devastating effects on the universe. The whole town was quiet. People were more reserved and proper for the first few weeks after her death. Children, who were typically ornery and vociferous, became the absolute models of solemnity and proper behaviour. I was a younger man when this happened, and I experienced a loss, like the others. It was a universal loss, if you will, one that struck deeply into the hearts of those around me, resulting in a widespread sadness, blanketing what seemed to me, the entire world. It was like when fans mourn the passing of a beloved celebrity, and people all around the world are connected by the loss. When the coma of sadness subsided in our town, we awoke to face an even harsher reality; sadness gave way to pain and anger. I remember a distinct hatred growing inside of me; a hatred for death, cancer, and for sadness, too. The idea that the human body can be corrupted from within was maddening. For a while, it felt as if the whole human race was doomed, and, at any moment, our bodies would turn on ourselves and self-destruct, without warning or merit. We were without hope, having accepted the Trojan horse of death.

However, the small, remaining ember of hope fanned into flame when Charles and his three young boys emerged from their reclusion and reopened the business. The store had been closed since Dotty's funeral, and no one in town had seen or heard from the Smith family for three weeks. It was mid-summer and, to revive the community connection, the town decided to have a bonfire on the local beach. Chuck and his boys appeared toward the end of the event, holding their emotions together, as if with scraps of duct tape and paper clips, but their courage resonated loudly, and it was their courage that infiltrated the blanket of solemnity that encased the town, and hence, illuminated all of human hope. The darkness began to dissipate, but I noticed something else, something more sinister. The remnants of the Smith family were not the same. They had not escaped their nightmare unscathed. They were different, they were weaker, and although their courage was remarkable, their frailty spoke loudly, to me. It spoke of a coming storm, one of no escape. It spoke of the downpours of death that would rain, invariably, until their existence washed away from all memory in the universe.

During the time after the bonfire, the town's original equilibrium and routine was gradually restored. With the hardware store open again, people began to function with playfulness and optimism. Miranda and I returned to our frisky relationship, full of laughing and silliness, typical of the young, in love. Miranda returned to her original self, her charming positivity filling our house, once again. I, on the other hand, carried a weight upon my shoulders, a weight of confusion. I could not reconcile the fact that someone, Dotty, was lost, lost to the flaws of the human condition, and memories of her would, eventually, waste away. It took quite a while for a certain amount of levity to return to my spirit. Charlie's recovery mirrored mine. I often noticed how the joys of his spirit had been replaced with anguish and confusion, as if a certain part of him had been ripped from his very core. Since that time, I've wondered how Charlie, and all those who had experienced that kind of loss, could maintain a civility about them and refrain from raging against the deafening silence that was once filled by a wife, a mother, or a child. I think about the rage that can come as a result of losing a loved one, and my thoughts are, immediately and ferociously, consumed with the man I saw across the lake. Now that was rage! Perhaps, the feral part of him was born out of irreparable loss. Perhaps, long ago, he wore Polo golf shirts and cheap khakis while walking hand in hand with his high school sweetheart, only to end up consumed by a poisonous darkness that replaced what he had lost. There was certainly a rage in his eyes that could be the result of such a wrenching past. Perhaps, the ferocious stabbing into the lake was his way of dealing with the pain of his emptiness and solitude. I recall how, with each strike of his spear, I trembled with terror. I've got to ask Charlie if he knows of such a man living on old Mr. Hawkins' property.

As I walk into the hardware store, Alaska trotting energetically by my side, the clanging of cow bells, hanging on the door, signals my entrance. Alaska follows obediently. My senses are overwhelmed with data, but my eyes pan the aisles, searching solely for Charlie, until they land on him, standing behind the counter.

"Hey there, ol' buddy, ol' pal," Chuck shouts, in a playful manner. He has always had a liking for me.

"Charlie Brown!" I jest, in return. I've always had a liking for him, too. How could I not? There's an above average chance that he actually *is* Santa Claus. "How are ya, bud? How's business?"

"Ah, things are just peachy, my man," he says, in a relaxed manner. "The man ain't gonna hold us down, no way, no how, eh, ol' buddy."

"That's my boy!" I keep the flow of levity going. I enjoy seeing Chuck in this kind of mood. "Viva la resistance!" I say, in my best French accent. It sends Chuck into a giggling fit from which he barely recovers.

"What brings you in, today?" he asks, finally, after gathering himself. There appears a look of genuine concern and interest on his face; truly the mark of an honest, decent man.

"Well, big guy," I begin. "I need a good shovel to dig out a dead tree in my yard and a few of those LED light bulbs. Don't want David Suzuki coming to our fair town with a score to settle, now do we?"

Not surprisingly, Chuck explodes into a fit of laughter, once again. He is the type of guy who just makes you feel great, all the time. Whether it is by laughing at your mediocre jokes, or by some other means, Chuck is always able to fix a damaged self-esteem. He can also fix your plumbing, but that's a different thing all together.

Actually, I rather pity this aspect of Chuck's personality. He doesn't have the ability to discern elegance from simplicity, or brilliance from normalcy, and merely goes, gleefully along, with the pursuits of those around him. For me, that is a weakness. He is certainly a nice man, but I am annoyed that he has never once demonstrated, at least to me, any type of backbone that can stand up to mediocrity. He is surely cursed with a disease that limits him to laughing at everyone's jokes and making everyone feel good. How that sickens me; how his giggle nauseates my belly. Is he destined to spend his entire life as an animate scarecrow, only to resonate happiness and laughter into the lives of the townsfolk? I'll bet, when his wife was stolen from his loving clutch, he hurt in ways a scarecrow could not, and maybe, only for a moment, he experienced what it was like to be a real person. A deserved lesson, if you ask me.

"Not a problem, Bry," Chuck responds, finally. "Terry!" Chuck calls to his eldest son. "Get Bry one of the new shovels that we just got in, and some of those LED light bulbs."

"LED?" Terry questions, loudly, from somewhere in the back of the store.

"Yes, LED!" Chuck answers. "We don't need any trouble from Mr. Suzuki, now do we, Terr?" Chuck giggles at his own joke; well, actually, mine.

"Good one, dad," Terry retorts, sarcastically, displaying a level of cynicism absent in his father's personality. I never spent much time around Chuck's boys, but I can only imagine that the passing of their mother must have hardened them, unlike their father. The loss of a mother is quite a drastic way to produce an appropriate level of scorn, but, then again, the strongest steel is sharpened by the hardest rock.

With his father's appreciation, Terry produces a shovel and box of bulbs. He wipes his right hand on the back of his jeans and extends it forward, over the counter, to invite a handshake.

"How are ya, Mr. Dawson?"

Terry's hand sits extended, and perfectly still, in the air. With his gaze fixed on me, his face exhibits the most definitive conviction. He moves with resolute confidence. I am stunned at how far he separates himself from his father. I am so shocked, in fact, that it takes a moment for me to respond to him. I gather my wits and shake his hand, firmly.

"Fine, thanks," is all I manage to say. A split second longer than normal, I offer, "Yourself?"

"Good," he says, before turning to leave, once again slipping out of sight, somewhere into the back of the store.

There is something "matter-of-factly" in the way he spoke, as if his words didn't matter, one way or another. The way in which his eyes locked upon mine as he said it, indicated that he had already known that I knew the answer. His piercing gaze told me that "good" meant "as-good-as-is-to-be-expected for a boy who grew up without a mother." As the oldest child, he was thrown, reluctantly and prematurely, into a leading role within his family, charged with taking care of both his younger brothers and his grieving father, while mourning the loss of his mother in his own right. He has my admiration and respect even though I can see, in him, a subtle rage filling the void in which his mother's love once dwelt.

Chuck acknowledges Terry's departure and turns his attention, once again, toward me. His eyes are kind, but I see what I have been looking for all along. Just for a moment, his joyful expression gives way to one of troubled confusion, as though there existed a need to scream out in a loud voice, "Why is she no longer!?" His heart, full of ache, along with his soul, full of pain and disbelief for his lost bride, are exposed in his countenance, and for a brief instant, yell to me for the answer. It is enough to confirm my theory. Charlie is filled with a desperate conflict. His wife's love has been replaced, with pain and a hopeless desire to understand her useless passing, a journey that will always end in futility. Terry, on the other hand, shows signs of agony, yes, but not of confusion. Instead, his void is filled with a passive rage, focused inward, so as to fight fire with fire.

"He has her eyes," Chuck sighs. "And he is sweet, like she was."

His smile returns to his face, and he begins to giggle as if warmed by the very thought of her. I, however, am not filled with such tenderness. My feelings are more akin to those of Terry's. An unadulterated rage brews inside. I care not to understand her passing, or the passing of any person, but only to rebel against whatever forces will, so whimsically, pluck life from our very hands at its choosing. Anxiety comes over me, as I imagine myself storming the castles of the gods in armed protest.

"Is this everything?" Chuck interrupts, holding up the two items I asked for.

"Yes, Chucky. That'll do fine," I pay, and as I am about to leave,

I suddenly remember the man across the lake, so I question Chuck about him. "Hey, Chuck?" I say, sheepishly.

"Yes, my man?"

"There is something I want to ask you. You got a sec?"

"Of course, buddy. What's the matter?" He notices the look of concern on my face.

"Well, it's a little strange, I must admit. It's actually gonna sound a little bizarre and I hesitate to mention it. The other night, it just sort of happened and I can't really wrap my head around it. It's a little off-putting. I wish I had more details to tell you, but I really don't underst---."

"Out with it, Bry!" Charlie cuts in.

Clearly, he becomes impatient with my uneasiness and nervous banter, but to my surprise, I am finding it difficult to gather my thoughts concerning the man across the lake. To this moment, I had every intention of asking Chuck, and anyone else who might know something about the feral man on the Hawkins' property, but just as the words should venture to the tip of my tongue, I am filled with anxiety and second thoughts, which cuts them short. If something sinister is really at play, as my feelings suggest, it may not be best to spread knowledge of the man around town. I quickly conclude, however, that, at this point, information about the man outweighs any possible repercussions that might follow. Plus, jolly old Saint Nick behind the counter won't likely cause me any problems.

"I saw a man," I manage to get out, ever so meekly. "I saw a strange man on the Hawkins' property yesterday, and he scared me quite a bit."

"What? You mean across the lake from your place?"

"Yes, on the island just a ways off from my shoreline, and he was quite a sight. He had a wild appearance and did some pretty peculiar things. I was just wondering if you knew anything about who might be on the place."

Chuck pauses for a minute. His eyes sink to the floor, and his eyebrows come closer together. He brings his index finger up to his lips, and grabs his chin with his thumb, completing the "thinking man pose." I almost laugh at how clichéd he looks, like a Greco-Roman bust of a man pondering for, what seems like, an eternity.

"Well," he begins, "there shouldn't be anyone on that property. Old Bo Hawkins died a while back, you know, leaving that island to his only son, Clayton. Old Bo and I go way back. We were friends long before Dotty died. I remember Clayton, running around when he was just a little guy."

"So, maybe, the man I saw was Clayton, then?" I ask. I had never met, or seen, Clayton, before.

"Well, I'm afraid not, Bry. Clayton joined the army straight out of high school and never made it back from Afghanistan. That was quite some time ago, too. Ain't no way you saw Clayton Hawkins yesterday, unless he's back from the great beyond."

Chuck giggles to himself, but I don't let him have his moment. I cut in with a serious tone.

"No, sir. Definitely wasn't a ghost that I saw. He was a savage man, wildly spearing fish in the lake. He wore a barbarian's clothing and stood with a crazed, emotionless look on his face. I saw the man go into Hawkins' old hut. I think he might be living there. Chuck, I'm actually concerned here. The island isn't all that far from my house. This could be something serious."

"Well, I do know one thing," Chuck begins. "Mr. Hammerstein was by the store a little while ago, and he mentioned the Hawkins' property."

Mr. Hammerstein is the local realtor. He is pretty easy to spot in our parochial town. After all, he is the only one usually wearing a suit. To be honest, I never really trusted Hammerstein, but I suppose, on this occasion, he has no reason for blurring the truth.

"He said that after Clayton died, the property belonged to the bank. He also said that the site was off limits and that no one was to be there, for legal reasons. There should be a 'no trespassing' sign facing the road." Chuck's expression changes, and he looks a little more seriously into my eyes. "So, Bry, if you did see someone on that lot," he pauses for effect. "He, definitely, isn't supposed to be there."

An unsettling feeling grips both of us. We stand in worrisome silence for a moment or two, each considering the worst possible outcome of this whole thing.

"Ah, it's probably nothing," Chuck eases the tension in the air, finally, more to convince himself than anything else. He continues, "Probably just some hobo taking shelter in the old hut for a night."

"Yea, that makes sense, I guess."

"Yea, Bry. I wouldn't worry. He probably got hungry and decided to catch some fish for dinner. It's not entirely uncommon up here in cottage country."

"What's not?" I ask.

"For the homeless to take refuge in abandoned shacks and to fish for food. There's only so much the police can do to limit these trespassers."

"Yea, you're probably right," I offer, really only half-believing my own words but beginning to feel better about the whole situation.

"See, nothing to worry about," Chuck says, as a warm smile returns to his face.

Chuck is so eager to make me feel better about this that, when he reaches his conclusion, one can see the pride of achievement radiate from his smile, as genuine as the man, himself. In a rudimental sense, Chuck is a simple man, and his primary concern is to eradicate my worries; figuring out what is going on is a minor second. Nevertheless, his theory is relatively sound, for the moment, but I can't let go of an agonizing concern about the man on the island.

"I know, Chuck. It's just... if you had seen him. It was like... like...like something evil, something sinister. I just can't shake the feeling. If you had seen him, you would definitely feel diff---."

Chuck interrupts me again. "You're just a little spooked, son. That's all. Seeing something like that might spook any of us, but you should try not to let it worry you. In all likelihood, it's nothing. Just a one-time thing, not to mention that whoever it was, probably, won't bother you anyway, even if he puts himself up in the hut sometimes."

"You're probably right," I say, putting on a smile that is not fake, but isn't real either.

I look to the floor, and for the first time since I came into the store, I see Alaska. She hasn't made a sound or left my side this entire time, which is quite unusual for a fun-loving dog, like Alaska, in a store full of potential toys. What a beautiful girl! She sat there obediently, just three inches from my right leg, wagging her tail, her chest puffed out, protective, like a noble knight guarding his king. I think that she can tell, by my atypical manner and tone of voice, that I have been concerned about something all morning. I give her a few pats on the head as reward. She moves in even closer. I would rather have no other dog by my side at this moment. I dare anyone to find me a more loyal dog anywhere in the world. Inasmuch as she loves me, I love her in return. I lift my head to say goodbye to Charlie. We shake hands.

"Thanks, Chuck. You and the boys should come by for dinner one of these days. We can watch a football game, or something, while I fire up the barbeque. It'd be fun."

"Oh, absolutely, as long as that beautiful wife of yours doesn't mind having four more men in the house for a while. We can be a bit of a handful sometimes," Chuck snickers, under his breath.

"Oh, don't worry," I say. "Miranda is tougher than any of us."

Chuck roars with laughter. "I don't doubt it," he replies, in jest. "The sweet ones always are. I don't think, in my entire marriage, I'd ever won a single argument with Dotty. Sweet as could be, but when she wanted something done her way,…look out! Only one way it was gettin' done and that's *her* way. No doubt about it."

Both Chuck and I laugh for a good while. It feels nice to talk about Dotty with this kind of levity. From my experience with her, it's the way she would have wanted us to talk about her, and from what Chuck says about her, we'd be better off giving her what she wanted.

Just as I am about to leave, Chuck offers one last bit of help regarding the man across the lake.

"Bry," he starts. "If anything goes down, you know you can call me, right? 'Cause I'll be there, guns a-blazing, in a New York minute. The boys will be there, too. You can count on that."

"Oh, I don't doubt it. You're a good man, Charlie Brown," I say, just as I go out the door. Alaska follows closely, in a more playful manner. The levity at the end of the conversation puts her more at ease. I am not sure if Chuck is joking when he offers his help, "guns a-blazing", but I don't really think that it matters either way. I am sure it won't come to that.

As Alaska and I get into the truck, an idea fires into my brain. I will pay a quick visit to Mr. Hammerstein to see if he has any more information on the Hawkins' property, or if he can shed any light on the man who is staying there. What a brilliant detour!

CHAPTER 5

SILAS

M R. HAMMERSTEIN WORKS IN A real estate office situated right in the heart of our little town; he is pretty much the only realtor there. He has a law degree from some fancy big city university. I must admit, he isn't a complete sleaze ball, but I will never find favour in the idea of putting too much trust in him. There is just something about the way he looks and the way he moves that reveals a hint of corruption, lying somewhere underneath his perfectly tailored suit, that gives life to my skepticism. Nevertheless, he is the next sensible lead in my pursuit of knowledge concerning the town's unknown visitor. I am not sure how much Hammerstein will know about the Hawkins' place, or the man, or if he even knows more than Chuck does, but one thing that everyone knows about Silas Hammerstein, is that, somehow, he knows things about people, a lot of things. I'm sure that more than one person in our town has entertained the idea that Silas is a gentleman spy, using a low-key career in real estate as a front for his covert intelligence organization, operating at the highest degree of discretion. So, if anyone knows anything about a strange man in our town, it's Silas. Getting the truth from him is a different story all together, but I see no reason why he would keep me in the dark about this.

Hammerstein usually closes his office at 4:00 pm. Providing

that he is not otherwise engaged, I'll catch him before he locks up. I won't take much of his time anyway, because I have to go home and get ready for dinner tonight with the monsters-in-law. I am still planning on asking Jim about the unknown man.

Alaska and I pull up to the realty unit of the strip mall, adjacent to the main intersection of the town, an area that can get relatively busy at certain times of the summer. Today, there are few cars on the roads and even fewer parked in the lot. There is an eerie quietness, of sorts, blanketing the town, and for the first time today, I feel lonely. Even with Alaska there, a desolate solitude clenches the pit of my stomach and twists it into knots. Immediately, I feel an urge to go home; an assault of the conscience, perhaps? I take a deep breath and the feeling weakens. I have every intention of finding out all I can about the savage being who is haunting my thoughts. Ally and I get out of the car. I tie her up outside the unit to a parking meter, where I can keep an eye on her. Although Hammerstein allows it, he doesn't love pets in his office. I look through the storefront window separating Silas' office from the outside winds and see him sitting, underneath dim lights, at his desk. I open the door. The usual ringing of bells, this time, does not announce my presence. The world gets quieter as the door closes behind me, and the gusts of wind outside melt away into a soft hum. There is a serenity about the room, hardly any noise at all, and nothing bright to engage the eyes. I feel like a ghost.

"Mr. Dawson," Hammerstein says, without looking up or removing his pen from the paper. "What brings you here, today?"

He must have seen me get out of my truck because he hasn't laid eyes on me at all, yet. As soon as the thought crosses my mind, his eyes flash in my direction, attracting mine. He waits for an answer while I realize that he has, intentionally, avoided any pleasantries.

"Oh, I just have a few questions about the Hawkins' property. I was wond---."

"Take a seat," he interrupts. "A fine piece of land that would serve as a wonderful extension to yours, if you wanted to build a boathouse or a cabana. You could probably put in a walking bridge to connect them, if you wanted, and we could make sure it was safe for children, in case you and the Mrs. decide to have a kid or two one day. Or we could..."

I stop listening. Silas is the prototypical salesman. He hardly ever lets you get a word into the dialogue, and his jaw, rarely ever, seems to need a rest. I hope that he has this much to say when I ask him about the strange man. Luckily, as I check back in on the conversation, he finishes his sales pitch.

"So, if you're interested, I can shave off a percentage point from my commission, just 'cause I like ya'. What do you say?"

I laugh hard, on the inside. In his office for thirteen seconds and this guy already has my future all planned out with a new piece of property, two kids, and a boathouse. Oh, and he's giving me a discount on his commission, "just 'cause I like ya'." Funny, considering this is the first time we've had a face-to-face.

"Uh, no thanks, that's not why I'm here."

"Oh, well, I do have another property I think you and Miranda might be interested in. That yard of yours is probably feeling a little too small, especially with young ones running around, oh, and Alaska, too. Ya' never know when ya' might need someth---"

I expect him to remember a lot about me, but this is uncanny. He knows exactly where I live, the size of my yard, the Hawkins' property, my wife's name, and even the name of my dog. Although I have to hand it to the guy, it's my turn to interrupt.

"Uh, Hammerstein? That's not why I'm here."

"Oh," his jaw finally slows down. "What do you need, then?"

"Well, I saw something strange on the Hawkins' property and was wondering if you had any knowledge of what goes on there."

"What do you mean, something strange?"

"Well, I saw a man there. He seemed to be living there. There was something sinister about him, something frightening. I don't know what to make of it."

I am having trouble organizing my thoughts. I know the

information that I am giving is in no way enough to go on, nor is it delivered with any degree of efficacy. I have so much to say about the man I saw that I don't know where to begin. I can only muster up fragments of obscured facts.

"And he was stabbing fish," I continue. "I mean, he was spearing fish, probably for food. If you could see him…I'm finding it difficult to explain what I saw. He looked homeless, I guess, and he was very…," I pause to think of the proper word, "…violent."

"Violent?" Silas asks. "What do you mean?"

"Well, not violent, I guess, but he looked like a barbarian, or a caveman. He was viciously stabbing at the lake, all the while, maintaining an incredibly stoic look on his face. Scared me quite a bit, to be honest."

I admit my fear to Silas, in hopes that he will return my honesty with some of his own. I cannot imagine what he is thinking, after hearing the nervous description of what I saw. All I can hope is that he will notice the worried sincerity in my voice and with an utmost regard to its pressing concern, want to resolve the situation. At this moment, I am afraid, afraid that this businessman will not lower himself to deal with what may be the childish worries of a scared man. I am afraid that he will, merely, disregard my fear, like a merciless tyrant who casts a worthless servant to the dungeons. I am afraid that this educated man will meet my distress with mockery and laughter. I begin to convince myself that the presence of the unknown is obviously innocuous, and my juvenile pursuit is simply a waste of time. How idiotic can I be? My mind is, clearly, exaggerating any cause for concern into a hyperbolic frenzy. I am a child, falsely dwelling in an adult body. Reason and maturity escapes me. I feel like leaving, immediately. Am I, foolishly, wasting this man's time? Perhaps, I can blame this on my moderate education. If I were smarter or more prominently schooled, I might avoid this embarrassment altogether. My struggle through this anxiety sparks my brain to tell my body to give up and go, but then, unexpectedly, Silas responds.

"Well, that is quite frightening," Silas says.

My thoughts exactly! An unknown, barbaric wild-man, ferociously stabbing for fish on a deserted property so close to mine is clearly a cause for fret. My concern is not exaggerated whatsoever! In fact, my desire to procure the identity of the unknown man is absolutely justified. This is a serious issue that involves the entire town and Silas and I are on the case. I feel confident that we are the right men for the job. *My* passion, and *his* knowledge; there is not a better combination anywhere!

"In fact, I do have quite a few facts regarding the Hawkins' property," Silas offers. "It's quite the interesting little island."

"Well, let's hear 'em!" I say, vigorously, as I lean in with a boyish grin on my face.

"Alright, well, first of all, the bank owns that property, now. When Bo's son died, his will wasn't in order, so the property was left to his next of kin, who sold it to the bank."

"Yea, Chuck told me that already. He said he talked to you about it."

"Yes, I was in the store, a few weeks back. Anyway, since the bank owns the property, it's off limits to any person. There are a total of five "no trespassing" signs on the island, four scattered, incrementally, around the perimeter, and one, just outside the old abandoned hut. So, if there is someone frequenting the area, they should definitely know it's off limits."

"Well, maybe he's illiterate," I interject.

"Doubtful. It doesn't matter anyway. It's still technically illegal for him to be there, so the police could arrest him if they find him there. That reminds me, if you do see him there again, you should call the police. Everyone in town knows Sergeant Fox. He would be more than willing to help."

"Yea, I've met him a few times. He seems like a nice guy."

"Indeed he is, Brian. He's protected our fair town for years. Now…," Silas pauses. "What I want you to look for is a boat. Remember, the Hawkins' property is an island. The man may be swimming there, but if he has a boat, he'll be able to come and go more quickly. Might be something the police will want to know."

"Yea, good idea," I say, excitedly.

"Also, Clayton's next of kin was a woman who lives on the other side of the country. It's doubtful that the man you saw has any relation to her. He might be a homeless man, or he might be something more menacing. It's too early to tell. On occasion, at the request of the bank, I go down to the Hawkins' property. In fact, I was there just a few days ago and didn't see anything out of the ordinary. I even checked out the hut. Looked like it hadn't been touched in a long time; nevertheless, if you see anyone there, you should call the police. You can't go there yourself to check things out, obviously, but I can try to swing by in a few days or something. I'll let you know what I find. I wouldn't worry too much until then, and remember to keep an eye out for a boat."

"Ok," I reply, hurriedly. "Is there anything else?"

"No, just head home. If he's still there, Miranda might see him and get spooked, especially after the sun sets."

Up to this point, I agreed with everything that Silas said, but why did he bring my wife into the conversation? Is he trying to say I am not fulfilling my duties as a husband, or, that Miranda isn't responsible enough to be left at home, alone, at night? I take offense to his insinuations, and my mood shifts drastically, but I try not to let him notice. I become anxious in my seat. For the first time since I arrived, I look outside and notice the barrenness on the streets of town. That familiar, old, lonely feeling begins to creep up my spine like a slithering snake, injecting its venom into the very core of my being. Alaska is still sitting on the sidewalk, her chest out, like a valiant warrior prepared to come to my defence at a moment's notice, but even the sight of her cannot calm my anxiety. I begin to panic. Is it not strange that he mentions Miranda? Oh, how the viper moves through the grass with such subtlety and stealth, before striking viciously and with such grandeur. Has Silas been covertly mocking me this entire time? Am I merely a gazelle, frolicking naively through the open plains, only to be attacked by a lion lurking in the shadows? Suddenly, I feel trapped. My vision begins to blur. I can no longer hold still in the chair. I feel a rage brewing inside of me. I am now certain of Silas' deceit. I was lured into his office to give away my position, a novice chess player who all too easily reveals his strategy. I grow increasingly angry at the trickery. My wrath, however, is outmatched by my weakness, and I lose consciousness. As my eyes flutter, I see Silas' face, and then, nothing.

CHAPTER 6

TRUST

WHEN I REGAIN CONSCIOUSNESS, I am in the truck, driving out of the parking lot. I give my head a good, hard shake and open my eyes widely, hoping to eliminate the groggy feeling that has come over me. Alaska is strapped into the seat and she is as composed as ever. I must have blacked out or had a panic attack and Silas probably helped me into the truck. I remind myself to give him a call, soon, to thank him for the information and to apologize for fainting on him. I will also ask him about his visit to the Hawkins' place, hoping he actually does as he says he will. At any rate, the sun is, now, descending into the horizon and blistering my view through the windshield. I put on a pair of sunglasses that I keep in the truck and head for home.

During the drive back, I try to recall everything that Silas told me. He didn't give me much information at all, but at least I can be fairly sure that whoever the unknown man is, he is not permitted to be on the island. Also, Silas is the authority in this area, so, if he doesn't know who the man is, I can't imagine anyone else knowing his identity, either. I will bring it up to Jim tonight and then, lay my case to rest, unless Jim gives me something more to go on and the issue warrants further investigation. I feel a little more at ease, thinking that this might soon come to an end. I, actually, don't have the stomach for this type of detective work. I have never been the type of guy to pride himself in leading a double life. The only thing that bothers me is deciding whether or not I can trust Silas. He seemed genuine, but my concerns lay not with trusting *him* in particular, but with trusting, in general. I suppose if Silas has anything to gain by concealing the truth, then he would do so. I don't necessarily see Silas as a villain, but I do view him as I view the rest of humanity, as, undoubtedly, or even eagerly, possessing the ability to sacrifice ethical conduct for personal gain. I can't yet surmise any possible scenario wherein Silas would gain by allowing a crazed wild-man to inhabit the Hawkins' property, but any motive can easily escape my desperate imagination.

I find no solace in Silas' words, as I have no way of proving their validity. His words are either true or false, yet, my trust in them will not sway Madame Justice to affirm their legitimacy. This is trust's great hamartia. In no way will trust in Silas's words cleanse them of poisonous deceit, if they possessed it. Therefore, trust is as empty as the false promises it is often given to. Trust exists only in its pragmatic form, in its concrete form, as it is applied to something. For instance, when two people get married, they are putting their trust in one another, for the act of trust is an intrinsic characteristic of marriage. However, by no means, does marriage signify or necessitate a belief in the truthfulness of either spouse, nor does marriage, axiomatically, provide peace of mind concerning spousal faithfulness. Therefore, trust is only as tangible or useful as the action that precedes it. To explain, I put my trust in Miranda when I chose to marry her, but, in no way does that mean that I think it impossible for her to be unfaithful or dishonest. Miranda used to ask me, whenever I became jealous over her, for any reason, if I trusted her. My response was invariable. I would tell her that I gave her my trust on our wedding day, but those vows I solemnly accepted did not eradicate her ability to cheat or lie. Therefore, trust, as it is viewed by most of my contemporaries, is an illusion. How many men and women claim to have complete trust in their spouses, only to come home, early from work one day, to find their 'soulmate' fucking the neighbour? It wouldn't make a difference if the answer to that question was one or one million. The question, rhetorically, substantiates my claim. The idea that trust, between friends or lovers, can put at ease the concerns regarding unfaithfulness is a hollow notion that should be removed from the modern psyche. Thus, trust should not and cannot provide the peace of mind for which it was designed. The great irony is, of course, that trust was destined to fail at the moment of its conception. Trust cannot procure truthfulness. Trust can only exist when given to that which holds truthfulness and faithfulness as impassable intrinsic properties. People, basically, do not fit this description. It is tragic, I admit. Life would be much easier, safer, and lived all the more to the fullest, if people could be trusted. Alas, not Miranda, or Chuck, Silas, or anyone else is worthy of trust. Simply put, the concept of true trust is absent among humankind.

So, how, then, am I to hold sincere the words of Silas Hammerstein, the local realtor? Between he and Chuck, there are a few things I accept as fact. First of all, no one is allowed onto the Hawkins' island property without proper authorization from the bank. Secondly, and this is due, in part, to my own intuition, I assume that the unknown man is not a relative of Bo or Clayton Hawkins or of anyone else from town, for he is surely not cut from similar cloth to anyone I know. Lastly, I am willing to accept the notion that my next course of action, if I see the man again, is to contact Sergeant Fox. The police are certainly better at handling situations, as this one, than I am, and they have the means to do so, where I do not. I suppose I will keep my eye out for a boat and report such a finding. Outside of that, I am to remain skeptical about anything I hear, or heard, from Silas Hammerstein.

The sight of the cottage gives me a feeling of comfort once more, after such a tumultuous day of investigation. As I unbuckle Alaska's seatbelt, she jumps out playfully, and proceeds to run around the side of the house to the backyard, out of sight. I gather the things

I bought at Chuck's and go into the house. I can hear Miranda, in the shower, so I guess I'll get started on the work. I am hoping to finish before our guests arrive. It doesn't take long to change the light bulbs. Then, I head outside to dig up the tree, which is toward the back edge of the property, near the water. I set down my tools and take a long gaze out toward the Hawkins' island. Waves of lake water are slapping the shore with a hypnotizing rhythm. The gentle sound of splashing they make is the only sound I hear. There is a brisk chill in the air, and the setting sun is about to disappear behind the treetops. The protective lenses of my sunglasses subdue the brilliant shimmer of colour reflecting off the water. Alaska has reclaimed her place at my side. She seems mesmerized by nature's beautiful stage, as well.

The land across the lake is deserted; it sits absolutely still in the watery expanse. No sound or movement emanates from the distant island. For a moment, I consider the possibility that nothing more will ever come of the saga of the unknown man, which, perhaps, is not meant to proceed beyond the first act. Perhaps, the promise of yesterday's feral setting was broken before it was ever truly made. As this thought traverses the boudoir of my brain, I am not filled with comfort or relief, as one might expect. Instead, I am made uneasy by the idea of missing out on the excitement that my personal reconnaissance mission could bring. The exhilaration from last night's occurrence titillated my senses in ways that have been absent in years passed. I now yearn for the type of stimulation that will thrust me out of the clichéd suburbanite rut that brings only a dull sense of mediocrity and routine. Today, for the first time in a while, I feel like I am living a life that is more harmonious with man's true nature than the prosaic apathy I have adopted as a masquerade of a proper life. The chore of having to uproot a dying tree creates a painful irony, when, if not for the intrigue of the unknown man, would be the highlight of my day. I finish the job as quickly as I can. Alaska amuses herself running back and forth across the yard the whole time. Her happiness is matched only by her majesty. She continues to lift my spirits even as the tiresome day comes to its conclusion. I am dirty, tired, and looking forward to a hot shower. I put my tools away in the garage and go into the house via the back door. I find Miranda sitting at the table with her parents. They are early. Great.

CHAPTER 7

JIM

I STARE AT OUR GUESTS LIKE a deer, trapped in the brilliant headlights of an oncoming car. I was not expecting to see them for a few more hours and, as you might guess, that would have been a few hours too soon. They, too, look surprised to see me, as I catch them with their drinks, paused in mid-air. Even Miranda is at a loss for words. An awkward silence, slow and agonizing, envelops the scene. It seems, if only for a moment, that all the world's oration is pinned down against its will, muted by an overpowering muzzle. I find it funny how this simple, sudden surprise can, seemingly, freeze time dead in its tracks and render our party of four, without words. I want the moment to linger, but after the toilsome day I had, I wish for its swift conclusion, and for my head to be surrounded with nothing but the mesmerizing softness of my pillow. Out of sheer morbid curiosity of a possibly ridiculous outcome, I speak up.

"Hey, guys," I say. "Excuse the mess."

Miranda gets up to greet me.

"Oh, that's okay," they both speak in unison. Helen continues speaking. "Sorry that we're a bit early. We had some errands to run in town this afternoon and finished early."

Then Jim offers some words. "Brian, it was my fault. I hope we're not interrupting, but I was anxious to get here to see you guys and all the hard work you've put into the landscaping, before it got dark. The yard looks great! You've done an excellent job."

"No. No. Of course it's okay," I say, as Jim's eyes watch me intensely. Lurking like a hungry lion, he waits to pounce at the first slip of my tongue. I am to remain vigilant in my politeness. Miranda approaches and, with one arm around my neck, she kisses my lips with a softness that delights my groin. Her silky hair frames her face, perfectly, as her stunning green eyes shine like emeralds. For me, her face is never anything less than an exquisite oasis in a desert of anguish. Her beauty never feels routine. As she draws near, my arms wrap around her waist, apparently, without my permission, underneath the radar of consciousness, and I can't be happier about it. Her slender, tight body, firmly within my grasp, feels marvellous. Her scent is intoxicating, and I rest my nose on her neck and take in the full effect. It is a perfume I encountered many times, and, each time, the purpose of the fragrance seduces the far reaches of my brain. I am paralyzed in the most heavenly way. A smile finds its way to my lips, as Miranda ends the kiss, ever so sweetly. Had I the talent, I would paint nature's skies, trees, and sunsets in all their majestic beauty, but each painting would pale in comparison to the portrait of the girl who stands, lovingly-close, within my grasp. I am so entranced that I forgot about Jim and Helen. "If you'll excuse me," I announce. "I have to grab a shower. I'll be with you guys in a minute."

With my quick, self-imposed exile, I think I've escaped the judgemental tyranny of Jim's ever-present watch, but his army of jeers strikes at the final hour. "Hey, Brian, why are you still wearing your sunglasses? Surely, you don't need them inside the house."

What the actual fuck?!

"Okay," I say, as I turn to leave, my sunglasses firmly in position, untouched by the remark.

Why does he have to say that to me? Does the donning of my sunglasses so bother him that he has to speak up, to insinuate the preposterousness of their placement? Surely not! Does he not think that I am capable of assessing the need for sunglasses, or the removal thereof, on my own? In his eyes, I must be an incompetent child, helplessly navigating the streets of life, homeless, hungry, and without pertinent ability to decide the appropriateness of sunglasses.

A gloom creeps into my being. I struggle to shed the hatred and disgust for Jim's words. I can't figure out why he said them, or what he truly meant. I climb the stairs to the bedroom with heavy steps. At the doorway, I lean on the wall and hang my head in brooding defeat. Once again, like a true ninja, Jim Cranston rises from the shadows in flawless concealment, with blade in hand, slashing at my very core. Only he and I, his victim, are aware of the attack, and like a treacherous spectre, the villain returns to his resting place, unscathed. The venom, with which I am stung, slowly infuses my body tissues, crippling me until my thoughts are consumed with his words. "Why are you still wearing your sunglasses? Surely, you don't need them." "Surely, you don't need them." "Surely, you don't need them." "Surely, you don't need them." I can't stop the recording in my head, over and over, and over, until an explosion of revulsion ignites in the back of my mind. How dare he hit me with such virulence?!

My blood boils with thoughts of revenge. I become like a seasoned assassin, stoic, and meticulous. Despite my aggression, I am able to defuse my anger with the pledge that his assault will not go without retaliation. I shower with the most unspoiled precision, timely, and efficient. I disregard the pleasing decadence of the water cascading upon me, as my heart and senses harden with vengeance. I intend to strike back and make an example of Jim, by slashing at his core being and teaching him the potential repercussions of his action. It must be a show of some brilliance and grandeur, in the name of intimidation and humiliation. I imagine a cinematic production, ripe with sensationalism and vigour, ending with a lesson, well-learned, for Jim.

I quickly dress and reconnect with the family. I see my target, playing happily with Alaska. A smile on his face, he pets *my* dog, completely unaware of the torpedo in the water. Oblivious to my intentions, he laughs, frolics, and has fun with Alaska, chasing her 'round and 'round. I only hope that Miranda forgives me for the subtle insults, soon to be thrown Jim's way, like arrows slung from the bows of the Trojan army. I am confident that I can cloak them in such mysterious pretence that, neither Miranda, nor Helen, sees the assassin hiding beneath my skin. In fact, I am sure that even Jim will fail to notice the bombs that I will, so strategically, place in his mind, only to detonate, days later.

As Alaska plays with Jim, I begin to hate the happiness in her eyes. She seems pleased as their fun continues. By no fault of her own, Alaska shares a relationship with my father-in-law that painfully gnaws at my gut. I feel bad for putting an end to their fun, but it's time to tear her away from him.

"Jimbo!" I exclaim. "Why don't you come and share a drink with me?" Do you see how well I hide my attack behind a veil of kindness? Such is to be my strategy for the rest of the evening; sly and slick.

"Sure thing, Brian, I'd love to."

I uncork a nice bottle of cabernet franc and fill two wine glasses, half-full. Very methodically, and without expression, I hand Jim his glass.

"So, Jim, how's work going?" I ask, casually, knowing that it has been struggling in recent months.

"Well, we're kinda' slow right now, but we should pick up in the next quarter," Jim answers, attempting to shift focus from the company's current state. I am not willing to let him succeed.

"Oh, but you're slow right now, huh? Well, if you and Helen need a little something to get through it, Miranda and I would be more than happy to help." I say this with an overt air of pretentiousness, well aware that the Cranstons have millions of dollars put away. Jim owned a successful business for more than 20 years. His company fabricated and sold chemical resistant plastic piping, and became quite renowned in the industry over the past two decades.

"Oh, no, that won't be necessary, but thanks for the offer. It's very kind of you," Jim replies, humbly.

I am shocked that he can muster up enough humility to take the high road, but this only deepens my thirst for pay-back.

"Good, good. So, why are you guys doing so poorly right now?" I dig deeper.

"Well, with the recession and everything, our buyers aren't willing to spend as much. Unfortunately, we are destined to rise and fall with the markets, I'm afraid."

I decide to let him get away with this one, for the moment. "Well, a good product always prevails. I'm sure you guys will be back to normal in no time," I offer, with a fake smile.

"It sure does. Thanks for the kind words, Bry. We could use a guy like you down at the office. I like having people I can trust, around to watch over things when I'm away."

"I'll keep that in mind, Jimbo," I say, fighting back the laughter. There isn't a chance in hell that I would work for him, and he knows it. This tug-of-war we are having, although cloaked in flimsy niceties, is obvious to the both of us. Jim knows of the disdain I hold for him, but, like me, he employs an elaborate façade to mask the exhibition from Miranda, who is yet to learn the truth. In any case, I missed my first opportunity to cast an indignant shadow on Jim's light. Perhaps, I am not being aggressive enough. I will have a better chance of completing my goal over dinner, where I'll have a tactical advantage, and an audience.

CHAPTER 8

DINNER

MIRANDA AND HELEN GIVE US the sign that they are just about to serve the meal. Jim and I take our drinks to the dinner table and sit down. I am conflicted between asking him if he knows anything about the strange man I saw, and continuing my attack, in hopes of getting glorious revenge. On the one hand, I can put off my vendetta to a later date, but, on the other hand, I don't think that Jim will necessarily give me any new information to consider. Chuck and Silas already told me everything that a bystander can know. So, the decision stands; it's revenge, then. I plan for a further assault. Miranda forces me in the other direction.

"Hey, honey, why don't you tell dad about that man you saw yesterday?"

"A man?" Jim exclaims, sarcastically. "What man?"

He'll pay for that tone. Everyone freezes in silence and casts their gaze upon me. I begin to speak.

"Well, I saw a strange man who seemed to be living on the Hawkins' property. He was quite barbaric and aggressive, so I'm a little worried about his presence."

"Barbaric?" Jim asks, aggressively. "What do you mean, barbaric?"

"Well...," I go on. "He was half-dressed, in ragged shorts,

running around the island like a wild man. His stoic expression and the look in his eyes was something fierce, and unchanging. His hair was crazy, spouting from his head in every direction. He looked like something from a horror movie."

"Oh, wow!" Helen says, as she and Jim lock eyes.

"Yea," I continue. "And he was spearing for fish, but not in a normal way. He, literally, snapped his spear into smithereens and used one of the broken shards to stab a fish and bring it out of the lake. Then he ran back into the hut, still holding the shard with the dead fish on it. I saw the entire, beastly scene with my own eyes."

Everyone at the table looks mortified. Miranda tries to speak but the shock isn't letting her brain properly communicate with her lips. Helen's eyes are wider than before and Jim is breathing more heavily than usual. He speaks up.

"He sounds like a…like a… madman!"

A madman. Yes, he certainly is a madman. A madman. A madman. A madman. The echoing in my head is unstoppable. It is confirmed, then. I saw a madman. There is no questioning it. I really saw him. It is astonishing. Billions of people can go their entire lives without seeing what I saw, the truly untamed nature of a madman; a man devoid of any and all domestication, simply living by the purest of mankind's animalistic nature. In his eyes, I saw no righteousness. In his movements, I saw no system of ethics. It is like he was transplanted from the primordial world into the scenic landscapes of our fair town, and now stands like a deadly lion in a swarm of simple gazelles, bereft of love, remorse, or fear.

"Yes, Jim, he is definitely a madman." For once, we agree.

I let the words sink in for a few seconds. Helen is completely speechless.

"Well, what should we do?" Miranda asks, as she finishes serving.

I sort of ignore her question.

"So, Jim," I begin. "Anything you can tell me about the Hawkins' property?"

"Yea, sure I can. It belonged to Bo Hawkins. He and I were good friends before he died. Helen was good friends with his wife, too. We would often go over to their place for dinner or drinks or just to hang out. Bo had a pretty good set of speakers and an old turntable that we used to listen to music on. He had a thing for Elvis Presley and Patsy Cline. Man, we used to listen to those records for hours. Helen and Mary Anne would chat away over tea while we spun the vinyls. Isn't that right honey?"

"Yes, dear. She was the sweetest friend I ever had, and a wonderful mother to Clayton."

"What was Clayton like?" I inquire.

"Uh, well," Helen begins. "I found him sort of charming and that he was of a kind heart. Miranda never took to him, though. She would refuse to come with us when we went over there. Sometimes, he was a bit of a strange boy."

"Yea, mom, well, he was a really weird kid. Everyone in school was afraid of him. He hardly ever spoke to anyone and always wore strange clothes. I never knew what to make of him."

"Anyways," Miranda's father usurps control of the conversation, once again. "We weren't surprised when Clayton went off and joined the army. Frankly, neither were his parents. We didn't hear about him again until we found out he had been killed in Afghanistan. What a shame, but at least his parents weren't alive to hear the sad news. Actually, we only found out because Si Hammerstein came around telling everyone that the property was off limits and belonged to the bank."

"So, is there any reason you can think of that would make sense for a madman to be living there now?" I ask, assertively.

"Well, not unless Clayton never really died and is back to claim his land," Jim says, with a chuckle. He is joking, but I am interested in this theory. After all, if Silas is in cahoots with Clayton, they can easily concoct a scheme like this, especially if Clayton is a deserter and needs a place to hide out. The hypothesis sparks my next query.

"So, was Silas involved at all with the Hawkins' or with Clayton?"

"Not that I know of," Jim answers. "I don't even think Silas was a realtor when they bought the island. In fact, Clayton may not have even been born."

That doesn't support my budding theory, but it doesn't oppose it either. Clayton and Silas may have got in touch after Mr. and Mrs. Hawkins died. After all, Silas is the only man in town with connections in various big cities and, perhaps, internationally. I let the idea that Clayton is the madman sink in for a bit. Honestly, I feel comforted by the idea. I doubt that Clayton wants to bring harm to anyone in the town, especially if he has to keep a low profile. Also, service in the army might explain his freakish strength and his primal hunting methods. I am concerned with the madman's crazed expression and movements, but I suppose that a vicious bout post-war trauma might explain these attributes. I am beginning to like this theory more and more, as I iron it out in my head.

"Did you ever hear anything else about Clayton's death?" I ask, after a brief silence.

"Actually, yes," answers Helen, only to have Jim usurp her place in the conversation.

"We spoke to Sergeant Fox a little while after it happened. He said that he was contacted by some army guy who had the details of Clayton's death. Apparently, Clayton wished to have his obituary printed in our local newspaper. Something that Mary Anne, his mom, asked of him before he went overseas. Fox has all the details if you're interested, but it doesn't help us identify your man."

"Not unless there was a mix-up of some sort, or if something sinister is at play."

I am not willing to let my new theory die so easily.

"The army doesn't usually make those kinds of mistakes, Bry."

I suppose that Jim is right. I will check in with Sergeant Fox, at some point tomorrow, but, barring a miracle, I figure the Clayton theory is probably a dead end.

"Why are you so interested in this man you saw, Bry? What makes you think that you're even going to see him again?" Jim asks me.

"Well, for starters, he looked pretty aggressive. The last thing this town of sheep needs is a wolf running around scaring people. I don't know why he was there, whether it was with evil intentions or not, but his presence is quite off-putting, to say the least. Now, I'm not sure if we will see him again, or if he is, in fact, living on the Hawkins' property, but if he is going to be hanging around, on the island, or somewhere else, the residents of this town should know about it, for their own protection."

"Is that not a little premature, Bry? This man has done nothing wrong, other than trespass onto the Hawkins' property, which may have been a simple mistake. He has rights just like everyone else; rights to privacy, the right to hunt or fish, and a right to live in this town, if he wants. Certainly, we should not persecute him for that, should we?"

Oh, how the wretched venom so smoothly spits from his mouth! I stand for justice and security, and Jim undermines my position with poisonous words of corrosion, aimed at imploding the very pillars on which safety and harmony stand. It's a grotesque display, made by a vile, old man, whose reasoning slips from him with each passing day. The propaganda that spills from his lips is predicated on a bed of lies! It is merely an act of dirty politics, aimed at discrediting my noble efforts. Oh, how the cunning in-law nips, ever so weakly, at my heels! Surely, anyone of proper mind can see his true intentions behind the feeble veil of smoke he so insipidly suspends. Surely, anyone of proper mind is able to see that the madman is a threat to our safety and that my ideals are the only maxim to be trusted!

Miranda appears to share my thoughts.

"Come on, Dad. The man is occupying a property in town, illegally, not to mention that he is acting in an alarming manner. Don't you think we should at least find out who he is and what he is doing here? That way, we can make sure everyone is safe, including him. Maybe he needs help, or medicine. If we handle this as Brian suggests, then we can take the proper course of action, and do the right thing."

"Well, I suppose that, since he is trespassing, we should find out what we can do about him, or for him, if he ever comes back."

Oh, how his words sting me like a spear through the abdomen. A politician's politician is Jim. He only half-agrees with my superior ideas and then sneaks in a jab at my credibility, just as the polls close, all the while agreeing with Miranda's comments, only to parade her dominance above mine. Such is the very nature of my relationship with Jim. He, invariably, makes all attempts to demonstrate his daughter's superiority at my expense. It sickens me. I am glad, however, that Miranda has taken note of his delusional reasoning. I do not have the slightest idea what Helen is thinking. In any case, it doesn't seem like Jim has the information to intrigue me, and since I am not after his approval, I feel it is time to change the subject. Apparently, Jim feels that way as well.

"So, when are you gonna get around to repainting those garage doors of yours? If you need any help, I could be so persuaded," Jim says, with a chuckle.

Another attack.

"Probably around the same time you finish restoring that Caddie you got sleeping in your garage." I fire back, forcing a chuckle to disguise the assault.

The whole table joins in the laughter.

"He ain't never gonna finish that dreadful thing," Helen chimes. "It's been sitting in our garage for six years, just collecting dust. I swear I'd sell the bloody thing if it wouldn't put Jim into a conniption."

"I'll get around to it, Helen. Stop your griping. As soon as work gets back to normal, I'll have more free time to finish 'er up."

"Oh, please. You've been saying that for six years."

"Now, just leave me be woman; it ain't bothering you any."

Their jovial banter is beginning to lighten the mood. Frankly, I take comfort in this new found levity. I had such a long day and I am ready to abandon my campaign of vengeance in favor of more relaxed pursuits. I long to be in my warm, cozy bed, next to Miranda, waiting for the sweet touch of slumber to carry me off to a world beyond this one. I glance over at Miranda to catch her covering up a yawn. Evidently, her body shares my yen for rest. I quickly scan our plates to find most of them empty. The meal is coming to a close. I need to accelerate the day's conclusion.

"Wonderful meal, dear. Thanks so much."

Everyone at the table echoes my gratitude and assists in the cleaning up. When the kitchen is clean, to the point where you can't tell that a dinner just took place, we all go into the living room for what I hope will be a quick sit down chat. Although I put to rest my desire to respond to Jim's earlier slight, I can still feel the daunting power he holds over me. Every time he looks at me, I see contempt in his eyes, as they yearn for the moment when Miranda's golden stature stands high above the rubble that was, once, me. Helen too, although benign, so far tonight, is ever vigilant in her anticipation of the right moment to strike me down and fly her daughter's banner above my grave. I look at Helen's chubby cheeks, and soft, curly, white hair, and wonder how so much calculated deceit can come from something so harmless-looking. Jim too, with his regal, white beard, and affectionate smile, has a face that can typically put one's mind at ease with waves of softened friendliness. The wrinkles on both their faces were carved by the goddess of wisdom, which is now used solely for sinister deceit, aimed at the pillars upon which I stand.

In the living room, the Cranstons and the Dawsons speak in an affable manner. Despite the pleasant tones and genial attitudes, I am not very interested in the conversation. I remain imprisoned by anticipation and fear that, at any moment, one of my two mild-mannered in-laws will let loose a purposeful arrow, dripping with disguised disdain, in my direction. I spend most of my thoughts nervously considering what counter measures I will use to avoid or neutralize such a weapon. Unfortunately, most of my time with the Cranstons is spent in similar moods, my radar at its highest level of readiness, fearing an imminent onslaught. I am afraid to be exposed as a fool, or to have Miranda think me one. Her parents, like vultures, circle my every move, ready to persecute, but Miranda, proves to possess an immutable faith in her husband. Her faith inspires me in so many ways and gives me the courage to enjoy being who I am, and to feel comfortable in my own skin. Adversely, I am sure that Miranda's faith in me is like a heated branding iron, searing the skin of her parents. Her undying belief in my abilities and competence must be driving the two seniors mad, as their evil crusade goes begging, time and time again. However, despite Miranda's confidence in me, the Cranstons still manage to cripple me with anxiety, sometimes, by their presence, alone. Each time Jim or Helen engages me in conversation, I can barely hear their voices above the words resounding in my head. "I'm so afraid." "I'm so afraid." "I'm so afraid." The anticipation of an oncoming attack strips me of any and all civility needed to sustain a typical life in this modern world. My breathing halts and my eyes widen with horror, as I wait for an opening where, with only partial consciousness, I rage against my oppressors, without remorse or regret. The untamed barbarism within, explodes with monumental fervour. When a counter attack such as this occurs, the recipient, either Helen or Jim, is neither surprised, nor upset. They too, protecting their only offspring, tap into the essence of primordial man. Thus, my reaction is a seamless response, if not an anticipated one. Sometimes, Miranda notes the severity in my voice and offers calming words of arbitration, but she never faults me for expressing myself in that way. She is simply the honeyed song of tranquility, sweetening the air after the siege.

On this particular evening, very little savagery is expressed, and the conversation remains in good humour. Jim spends most of the time playing happily with Alaska who always seems to brighten his mood quite a bit. Eventually, the conversation dies down, and it is time for them to leave. We all move into the lobby to say our goodbyes.

"Well, thanks for everything. We had a lovely time," Helen says, before giving me and Miranda hugs. Then, she hits me with a wrecking ball. "Why don't we come back on Friday? I'll bake a peach pie, Jim and Brian can watch the hockey game, and hopefully, by then, we can put this madman nonsense behind us."

My whole world flips upside down! How rude for Helen to invite herself over to my house, *my* home. Another dinner date in five days is the Everest of mountains that I do not have the energy or desire to climb. My brain hurts thinking about it. Furthermore, Helen's choice of words describing my experience as "madman nonsense" burns deeply and warrants retaliation.

"That would be great," Miranda says, with a bright smile. "I'll bake some lasagna and put together a salad."

Miranda, unknowingly, agrees to my demise with such haste that I really think I'll love her slightly less going forward.

"Bry, man," Jim says, jovially. "See you soon, buddy." He shakes my hand firmly.

I am in a daze, frozen by the thought of being thrown to the wolves one more time before the end of the week. A question: is the anticipation of death actually worse than death itself? If yes, then, the days leading up to Thursday will be even darker and more painful than tonight was. The true answer to this question can only be found after death is experienced and who can give account of that experience? Therefore, there is no comparison possible. Nevertheless, the musing of it keeps my mouth from properly connecting with my brain.

"Yup," is all I can muster.

As the two old people are about to leave, Jim puts Helen's coat around her shoulders and opens the door. As she holds the door in return, Jim gives Alaska a friendly pat, and verbalizes his love for her. Never before this moment did I feel like Jim owns me. Before the door closes behind them, he flashes me a look that bores into my soul. It is the evilest of stares that tells me everything is happening in accordance with his sinister plan. My torment and his imminent return are important steps in a grand scheme, aimed at my ultimate downfall. The thud of the door, now shut and secured, parallels the sealing of my coffin.

CHAPTER 9

TWILIGHT

OUTSIDE, THEIR CAR STARTS, AND I hear the Cranstons drive away. I stand, demoralized and defeated, staring at the door, until Miranda throws her arms around my shoulders and pulls me out of my fog.

"Honey," she says, softly. "Come to bed. I have to wake up early tomorrow. I'm going into town to run some errands."

"Alright, babe. I just need to let Alaska out, and I'll be right there."

"Okay, sweetie, hurry. I miss your arms around me," she whispers, seductively, as she pulls the hair at the back of my head and presses her lips against mine. Then, she turns and floats up the stairs, her eyes sending me hints of what's to come. I watch her slender body move smoothly, as her hair bounces playfully, and I am eager to feel her warmth, but duty calls. "Alaska!"

I put Alaska on her leash and lead her outside. She is in a playful mood, as usual, but I am tired. When I look at her, I am reminded of how much joy she brings to Jim, my nemesis, who has so infiltrated my life that even the sight of my beautiful dog is denigrating. Outside, we can feel the brisk, night air and hear the crickets, chirping with pounding incessancy. The dazzling moonlight glistens brilliantly off the lake, as the trees around the property are concealed in darkness. I unhook Alaska from her leash and let her run circles around me until she tires herself out. I crouch down on the grass and she sits beside me, panting. Her chest rises and falls, rapidly. I, reluctantly, offer a platonic stroke of her head, and she nestles herself into my arms. I fall in love with her all over again. I cuddle her with intense affection. As our display of adoration ends, we walk toward the doghouse. As soon as she gets inside, she puts her head down and immediately closes her eyes. It has been a long day for her, too, and it's obvious she is as tired as I am

The moon is full and its silver rays shine on me like spotlights, singling me out of all of nature, making me feel, somehow, unique. Standing in the heart of that twilight, a strange feeling of mysticism enters the air, and an eerie chill ripples up my spine with such ferocity. The crickets are relentless in their song: chirp, chirp, chirp, chirp, chirp, chirp, chirp. The pounding rhythm with which they sing is weirdly hypnotic. I can hear the wind blowing through the leaves, as it sends waves crashing into the dock. Each surf hits just seconds after its predecessor, creating a mellifluous beat that is as consistent as the crickets' chirping. The moonlight waltzes with the cadence of the waves. Nature truly seems to be alive, bustling about in a flurry of movements, undoubtedly, acting out the will of Mother Nature. I am the protagonist in a fairy tale, completely entranced by the dreamy beauty of the living world. But all too quickly, my living dream halts.

The wind dies out abruptly, and the lake becomes strangely still. The crickets stop chirping and the moonlight stops swaying atop the pristine liquid, now as smooth as ice. I stand in the rays of the moon, my gaze spanning most of the lake. For a moment, I let the dark majesty of the twilight soak into my being, into my depths, as if my soul were a sponge. Then, suddenly, across the lake, there is a stirring in the shadows. I walk to the edge of the sandy shore, and peer intently across the lake. I can't make out exactly what I am seeing, but there is something definitely in motion on the opposing side; an animal, perhaps. "It's just a deer," I whisper. "It's just a deer."

"It's just a deer." "It's just a deer." I mutter the phrase, again and again, out of a fearful and futile attempt to convince myself of the banality of the ruckus. In truth, I consider only one possible cause of the disturbance. The cabin on the Hawkins' property is partially illuminated by the moonlight, making it is fairly easy to see. Then, the source of the commotion steps into the spotlight. With two slow, weighty steps, a man's figure appears. He turns to face me and I can see one side of his face and the outline of his full figure. Well over six feet tall, in all his feral glory, the madman takes the stage. His long hair falls lazily over his shoulders, filthy with grease and sweat. Seemingly unaffected by the cold, he dons nothing but a pair of tattered shorts. He stands upright, with his chest out; his legs, shoulder width apart; his arms, hanging down at his sides, each hand holding opposite ends of a long stick. He looks like a Roman gladiator prepared for battle, perched like a sentry on the edge of the island, as still as the night.

I, too, remain poised, motionless, not making a sound. I dare not take my eyes off the barbarian. With an incredibly strange guise, his face is impeccably consistent, and so is mine. I cannot tell who or what he is looking at, and although it appears that he is looking in my direction, I will not fully assume that he is. As I gaze at the madman, I realize that I am not quite as crippled by fear as I had been the first time I saw him. I am, by no means, pleased by his presence, but I am experiencing a strikingly less anxious feeling. I begin to scan the statuesque figure for purpose and possible intention. I decipher none, but feel, perhaps, there is a cosmic reason behind his presence. He appears to have no fear at all; he is as confident as he is grotesque, and I feel as if all the stars in the night sky are his to command. A wave of envy comes over me. Living out or beyond any definable sort of civility, the madman is, indisputably, king of his own realm. He has no one to answer to, other than himself; he has no in-laws to tolerate, no light bulbs to change, no trees to plant, and no reason to fear anything. He acts only to fulfill his primal needs and desires. For all I know, this man could simply be on a short vacation. Maybe he has a nagging wife, three bratty children, a boring nine to five job, and a cheap lawnmower that he puts to use every Sunday afternoon, while wearing the same boring golf shirt and generic pair of pleated trousers.

As I stare, uninterrupted, at the madman, I begin to feel a nascent respect for him. There is no anxiousness or angst on his face, whatsoever, and his posture indicates that he knows that his place in this world is outside of it, a place where he, and only he, is emperor. To my own surprise, I actually feel inspired by the man who has chosen not to live as a replica of most others, of course, but who has adopted a certain uninhibited, primal lifestyle, free from the constraints of civilized life. I even consider the possibility that the madman can make a positive contribution to *my* life. His being here is so ridiculous and surreal that I begin to doubt his capacity to bring any form of pragmatic harm to the community. I still feel as though I should address his presence as a concern and report it to Sergeant Fox in the morning, but, for the first time, I feel like there is something to be learned. I take a step back for a wider view of the setting, a scene I am sure I won't ever forget.

Just then, as my holistic interpretation of the scene resonates with a nostalgic feel, the madman takes action. His chest starts to rise and fall more quickly, and with each inhalation, it expands considerably, catching more of the celestial rays. His breathing intensifies so greatly that it now echoes across the lake. The wooden rod he has been clenching begins to vibrate in unison with his breathing. He bends slowly at the waist, dipping his chest over his knees, now locked in attack stance. The moonlight intensifies on the upper portion of his body, as if to spotlight his well-defined, muscular torso. Dreading the thought of what his next move might be, I am gripped by fear and anticipation.

My eyes locked on the madman, I await an imminent strike. My breathing begins to emulate his, my eyes widen, my chest rises and falls rapidly, and my muscles tense, involuntarily. The veins in my arms bulge through the layers of skin that blanket them. My senses are heightened and alert. My vision becomes clearer, and the sounds of the night are more potent in my ears. My core temperature rises quickly, and heat radiates from every pore. The droplets of perspiration, that have made a home on the surface of my skin, feel like tiny ice pellets, as they are activated by the chilled, night air. My tactile sense races off the charts. I am aware of the webbing between my fingers. I stretch them apart to mask the eerie feeling. My feet identify the fabric that encases them. The hair on the back of my neck stands up and I feel the twilight breeze fondle it, ever so softly. The overload of sensory stimuli is mind-blowing and for the first time, I am remarkably perceptive of my physical and neurological responses. Even my movements are more mechanical; my stance widens, not of my own free will; both elbows bend to ninety degree angles, and I assume a defensive position.

All at once, the madman bursts into motion. He begins to run forward, in my direction, each step, pounding the earth below, and each leg muscle, flexing firmly with every hit to the ground. His hands firmly clutch the wooden rod. His arms swing mightily, to and fro, in concert with his hammering footsteps. His long hair bobs as the wind rummages through it. His austere expression, all the while, unchanged; his glare glued my way. Like a blaze of fire, that would rip through a parched cornfield, he sprints across the hard terrain of the island, toward the water. Beginning about forty meters inland, the distance to the lake falls rapidly with each sprint. Thirty meters. Then, twenty. Then, ten. Five.

I can hardly believe what I am seeing. I find it hard to breathe, as if my lungs have stopped working altogether. I would only realize later, that my hands were clenched, so tightly, the flow of blood to my fingers was restricted. My white-knuckled fists begin to burn and ache from the compression. My heart is racing, pumping blood wildly throughout my body to keep up with my excited breathing. I watch with unbridled anticipation as the madman nears the edge of the island.

With about two meters remaining, the madman abruptly digs

one foot solidly into the dirt before him, recoils his left arm back, as far as it can go, and propels the pole forward, high and far into the night air, akin to an Olympic javelin toss. My eyes follow the spear. The wood rockets in my direction, horizontal throughout its flight. Then, it dips, and pierces the water, provoking only a subtle splash. As it submerges out of sight, I glance back to the island. The madman takes gladiator posture once more, arms at his side, and both hands on the stick, which has reappeared, in whole. He squeezes the timber tighter and tighter, raises it high over his head, and brings it down quickly, breaking it in two, over his right knee. As loose shards of wood spray wildly about him in the air, his eyes do not move to catch sight of a single splinter. His grimace returns, and his gaze revisits his target. With his teeth clenched, he crams the two remaining weapons into the ground with one plunge, each. He rises with fluid haste, turns, and quickly escapes back into the darkness and out of sight.

I am mortified, and physically, in shock. My lower jaw hangs like an empty playground swing. My extremities are numb. I struggle to move, still dazed by the experience. Somehow, I stumble back into the house, manage to locate the couch, and spill my body onto it. My head is spinning. I close my eyes, and my nightmare ends.

CHAPTER 10

FOX

I WAKE UP IN AN UNCOMFORTABLE position. My neck is bent in a way that I don't think necks should bend. My hips ache, telling me how unhappy they are with my position. My feet are bare and cold, and my lower back hurts something fierce. My right arm is a twisted mess under the weight of my chest, and my left arm droops idly to the floor; despite the terrible numbness, I can feel the hardwood floor with my fingertips. As consciousness returns, I choose to lay motionless, sure that any ill chosen movement would break at least three bones in my body. So, I just, sort of, roll to my left, off the front edge of the couch, until my back hits the floor, with a thud. The meeting with the hardwood knocks the breath out of me. I lay still, trying to reclaim lung functioning. My head throbs and my eyes hurt from extreme fatigue. My mouth is dry and has a bad taste. My battered body tries to get up, but even the most subtle movement kills, and I can't shake the grimace from my face.

I stagger to the kitchen to grab a glass of water. On the counter there is a note from Miranda. It reads, *"Went into town to run my errands. Missed you last night. Boop <3."* I totally forgot that she was waiting for me in bed last night. I guess the second appearance of the madman rendered my mind useless for any concerns other than him. I take a quick look outside. The sun is rising and glistening off the morning dew. A moderate fog has taken hold of the fields and hills outside and I can feel the chilled air coming in through an open window. I cannot break free of last night's scene and images of the madman. I remember everything clearly. The one-man play unfolds seamlessly in my mind, with each act perfectly intact. It has left quite the mark, and I, the sole member of his audience, did not achieve a proper catharsis upon its climax. In fact, I woke up this morning, confused. I do not know what to make of what I witnessed, nor do I know what to make of the madman and his actions. However, in my current, enfeebled, mental state, I figure that the best course of action is to try to put it out of my mind and talk to Sergeant Fox as soon as possible. I quickly eat breakfast, down some pain medication, and get ready to head into town.

I think that Alaska might enjoy the ride into town. On my way out the back door, I glance at Alaska's dog house. It is empty. I check both the front and back yards, but she is nowhere to be found. I return inside, thinking she may be sleeping. Nothing. After a thorough sweep of the cottage, I suppose that Miranda took Alaska with her; not an entirely unusual thing for her to do. Before I go outside again, I peer through the kitchen window and look at the Hawkins' property one last time. The island looks so peaceful, so undisturbed. Its tranquility and normalcy infer the idea that the scene from last night never actually happened. Even the broken spear that the madman pounded into the ground is gone, and no trace of him can be seen anywhere. If not for my vivid memories, I may believe this to be true.

I get into the truck, and head to the police station. Our town is a quiet one, virtually devoid of crime. Most of the time, Sergeant Fox is at his desk while his constables patrol the town. I can't remember the last time someone broke the law. Even the teenagers here are quite well-behaved; very little mischief happens. There is a bar in the heart of town, called *5th & Main*. It's named after the intersection on which it stands. It gets fairly rowdy a few nights of the year, but nothing antagonistic ever happens. The bar owner,

Clint Wellby, doesn't tolerate any violence or ruckus of any kind and has a really good relationship with the townspeople and police. He is a gentleman, and people feel safe when they go to his bar. In all odds, the police in this town will sooner die of boredom than from an actual violent threat. This definitely contributes to my concern over the madman. I am not used to seeing anything of the like in this town. I suppose that if I spent more time in more urban centers, the madman would seem run-of-the-mill, and I'd ignore his presence. Nevertheless, the thought of finally bringing the madman to the attention of the proper authorities gives me a feeling of comfort, not just because police awareness is the first logical step to actually defusing the situation and creating a safer environment, but because I feel like, for the first time, I am unloading some of the weight from my shoulders. Since I first saw the madman, I have felt alone in my efforts to resolve the issue. Jim, Chuck, Silas, and even Miranda have not truly engaged the issue as I have. I am hoping that the police will take some of the concern away from me. I suppose that because I have been the only one to bear witness to the grotesque presentations by the madman, I am the only one who can truly know of the potential danger.

With the radio off, the cabin is quiet, and I sit, with my thoughts. I realize I am depressed; last night's occurrence killed any happy-go-lucky feelings I possessed up to that point. I pull into the police station parking lot and quickly get out of the car. The sun is shining brightly, and the air is hot and muggy. I begin to sweat, immediately after exiting the air-conditioned truck. The heat hits me with such force that I find it hard to breathe. I hurry into the police station where I am again greeted by cooler air and cover from the hot sun.

The scene, inside the station, is unlike what one would imagine. It is not busy. Officers are not rushing around, frantically trying to solve cases. There are no criminals being taken into custody. In fact, there is hardly anyone here at all, and in place of the clichéd crime-fighting frenzy, is a remarkable calmness. I can see only one person, a female officer behind what appears to be the front desk. She is writing something and her head is buried in the paper. Her hair is tied in a tight ponytail that hangs out the opening at the back of her police cap. She is a slender lady, with well-defined bone structure, not far along in her years. She is in a blue police shirt that has been neatly ironed. Her name tag is aligned perfectly with the right angles of her shirt pockets. It reads, *"Higgins"*. She does not even look up to acknowledge my presence. I watch her for a moment. She continues to write and file papers at a steady pace. I approach the desk, timidly, distracted by all the visual data. On every wall, there are clocks that tick loudly at each passing second. Most of the walls are generally colourless, giving the station a hospital-like feel. It isn't until I am up against the desk that the officer finally lifts her head to greet me.

"Hello, sir," she says, very matter-of-factly. "What can I do for you?"

"Yeah, hi there, my name is Brian Dawson. I live over on Piper's Creek Road. I'd like to speak to Sergeant Fox, if possible."

"Sure. What seems to be the problem?"

I pause for a moment find the easiest, most benign way I can think of to describe the madman.

"Well, I keep seeing someone trespassing on the Hawkins' property. It's just across the lake from my house."

"Ok, well, typically, you would fill out a police report for that kind of thing, but I'll just get Fox and he can decide on your next steps."

She turns and walks away. Her toned legs are hugged tightly by the standard issue, black dress pants. Her ponytail bounces playfully as she walks towards Fox's office.

"Thanks very much," I call out, for politeness sake. She doesn't respond.

The Sergeant's office is located at the back left end of the precinct. His door has a glass panel with the words "Sergeant Fox" in bold black letters. Higgins knocks just above those letters. Through the half-closed horizontal blinds from the 1980's, I can see Fox pull an ear bud out of his ear. Higgins enters the office and leans against the open door. They exchange words that I can't make out. Then, Higgins waves me into Fox's office. She holds the door open as I enter. I thank her, but again she gives no response. She has not shown any expression the entire time, acting, most likely, out of nothing but efficiency. I ask myself, "When did the police force start accepting applications from robots?" I watch her; she turns to leave, goes back to the front desk and, without excitement or despair, returns to her administrative duties, as if she is completely desensitized to the work and world around her. I try to imagine what her life is like. I think that her career as a police officer is, perhaps, far more monotonous than she anticipated it would be, as a youngster coming up through the academy. Maybe, she was once full of zeal and enthusiasm, only to have that part of her personality sucked from her by the endless stack of paperwork that hits her desk every morning. I would wager that she never once had to remove her gun from its holster, in this small, quiet community. I doubt that when she was young, this is where she envisioned her future would be. Perhaps, she turned down a modeling gig under the bright lights of New York City in favor of attending the academy, only to regret that decision years later. Her blasé attitude suggests that I am on to something.

"Come on in, Brian," Fox's words dissipate my thoughts on Higgins.

"Hello, sir," I say, as we shake hands.

"Please, call me Vince. So, what can I do for you? Higgins tells me that you've been seeing someone on the Hawkins' property?"

I am pleased by his friendliness but I feel it inappropriate to call him by his first name. After all, he holds a position of authority and respect, and we aren't close enough, yet, to allow for it. All of my life, I wanted to be a humble man and I feel that true humility is the culmination of many little humble moments.

"Yes, and, from what I found out, there shouldn't be anyone there. So he's definitely trespassing."

"And you don't recognize this man?"

"No, not at all."

I go into detail about everything I saw. I describe the madman's actions, appearance, stoicism, and over-frightening and grotesque presence. Fox sits and listens quietly, asking questions only when prompted. He has a look of genuine excitement on his face. I am not surprised by his intrigue. This must be the first interesting case he has had in months. His eyes widen at certain points in my story, and by the end of it, he is bubbling with child-like enthusiasm.

"Ok, let's go!" Fox says, without hesitation, like it isn't a big deal.

"What?"

"Let's go," he says, this time pointing at the door.

"What are you talking about?"

"Well, you're coming with me, aren't you?"

"What? Where?"

"To the Hawkins' property."

We both stand in silence for a moment as his words sink in and the shock wears off. I am falling in love with his uninhibited enthusiasm. He is several years my junior; I place his age somewhere in the late twenties, and he possesses a candid impulse that I've seen fade in most men my age. He does not seem afraid or concerned about going to the property, much like a child who wants to do something dangerous, without fully understanding or recognizing the potential hazards involved.

"Is that okay? Are we allowed?" I ask.

"Allowed? Brian, I make the rules in this town," he says, with a sly smile. "And even if we're not allowed, what's gonna happen? Are we gonna get arrested?"

"Yea, but what about the bank? They own the property, don't they?"

"True, but I'm doing them a favor. They may have a trespasser on their property, and, as an officer of the law, I feel the need to rectify the situation as immediately as possible." I can almost see the subtle sarcasm dripping from his lips.

"Plus," he continues, "I won't tell, if you don't," he adds, with a devilish grin. "Actually, there's some paperwork we would normally fill out before we did this kind of thing, but we can do that retroactively, if we find anything. No use doing more work than we have to. Just hop in your truck and follow me to the marina. We'll leave our cars there and take the police boat to the island."

I haven't felt this kind of excitement in a long time. I am actually giddy. My heart is racing, and my mind begins to forecast all the possible, crazy things we may find. I am betting that the hut is filled with a bunch of barbaric nonsense, recognizable only to the madman himself. I may finally get to see his living quarters, undoubtedly a wretched place, unlivable for the modern man. Then, I realize that there is a chance that we will, actually, see the madman, himself. I delight at my optimism. It's like getting a chance to meet a rock star for the first time. In my mind, the madman now holds a certain celebrity status that I rather envy. Although he has *me* to thank for promoting his fame, I am sure that more than one person in this town would jump at the chance to see him, up close. Fox just heard of him and is already breaking regulations to secure the opportunity. I am sure that the story of the madman visiting our fair town will be told and retold, for many years to come.

Fox and I leave the police station in haste. I can feel his excitement emanate from his body with each move he makes towards the door. On the way out, he yells back at his associate. "Hold down the fort, Higgins. We're gonna check up on the Hawkins' property."

"Sure thing, boss," she replies, without looking up. Her face of indifference speaks louder than her words. Her writing continues, without pause, and she pays me no heed, as I pass by her desk.

CHAPTER 11

THE LAKE

S ERGEANT FOX AND I JUMP into our cars and speed off towards the lake. I am having trouble keeping the accelerator from hitting the floor. I feel like a young child on Christmas Eve, excitedly anticipating all the presents that would appear on Christmas morning. At the moment, I am frantic about the barbaric artefacts that we'll find on the island to prove that our fair town is being terrorized by a sanguinary madman; knives, swords, bows, arrows, slaughtered animals, tattered clothing, or maybe even a hog's head stuck on the end of a spear, attracting airborne vermin. The possibilities are endless and my mind seems to want to land on every single one of them. I can barely keep my truck in the proper road lane, as we hurry towards the marina.

I feel as though Fox is as excited as I am. Judging from his reactions during our conversation, he seems to have a primal lust for this kind of adventure. His young mind is eager to investigate a savage mystery, as this one. I am, however, slightly concerned about the way in which Fox wants to deal with the madman, should we find him. I am willing to solve the issue, magnanimously, offering help to the man, if he's willing to accept it. I can't imagine that arresting the man and throwing him in jail, only to release him a few days later, will have any positive impact on the situation, or guarantee that he will leave our town. I hope that Fox is in agreement, but he and I left the station in such a hurry that we didn't get the chance to talk about possible remedial actions.

As we near the marina, my body stiffens, naturally, in preparation for a potentially-threatening engagement. I am so excited about this ever so significant step in the investigation that I completely neglected the fact that we are about to venture into dangerous waters. My skin tightens, and my body runs cold. My jaws clench tightly and my eyes grow dim. A despair possesses me, in the same way that a cold night sky engulfs a once warm and sunny day. My skin's typical reddish hue is replaced with a paler white frost, and from it, radiates an icy chill that sends shivers down my spine. I become conscious of a heightened perception, and, like a deadly assassin, I am fixated only on the madman and the task ahead. Any innate sympathy or pity is destroyed by a numbing coldness, as I distance myself from typical humanistic elements.

Fox's car pulls into the marina. I am close behind. We park side by side, and I feel like a member of a posse, riding into a helpless town to serve up some justice. My chest swells with pride. I swear that, in the rear view mirror, I see a black Stetson on my head, but at second glance, it's gone. We both hop out of our cars, making crunching sounds as our boots hit the coarse gravel that makes up most of the roads in the area. My eye is on Fox as we move toward the entrance to the marina. I notice the pistol at his side and draw a breath of confidence. I don't think there will be a need to use it, but at least Fox has a consideration for preparedness, as I do.

"Wait here. I'll be back in a sec," Fox says, as he enters the marina.

It's a simple building, the exterior, entirely, white stucco. A glorified hut, it stands at the end of a short dock surrounded by my neighbours' boats. I recognize most of them. Miranda and I are planning to get one as soon as our finances allow it. Jim and Helen have a boat, and they let us use it whenever we want, so there is no ruse on our procuring one. I scan the boats until I come upon the one that belongs to my in-laws. It is probably the nicest boat of the entire lot, but that means nothing to me. Next to it is the police speed boat. It has a fresh paint job and a huge motor, bolted to the back. The decal "POLICE" is pasted, boldly, on each side of the boat. It's a beauty, with white leather seats and chrome accessories. I am titillated at the prospect of flying across the lake in this beast of a machine.

Suddenly, Fox explodes from inside the building, hasty determination in every step. A set of keys rattles, aggressively, in his grasp.

"Let's go," he says, without looking at me.

He walks with militant purpose along the dock, his eyes focused on the police boat. He unties the ropes that secure the boat to the dock. I follow closely behind and join him in loosening the knots. Fox jumps in, without hesitation, and quickly starts the motor. A thunderous roar comes from the engine. I can feel the vibration in my chest. The dock trembles as the engine continues to rev with animalistic ferocity. Then, it dies to a purr, and reverberates through the air. I push the front end of the boat away from the dock before I jump in. Fox turns back to look at me.

"You might want to sit down," he warns. "And hold onto something."

A derisive smile rips across his face as he delivers the line. Every one of his straight, white teeth shows his excitement in commanding the massive mechanical achievement, fifteen feet behind him. I sit down immediately. Fox remains standing behind the steering wheel and the protection of the windshield.

With a celebratory yell, he hits the gas, hard, and the sound of the engine erupts like a volcano, spewing liquid lava behind the boat, like the proud peacock displays his exquisite tail. The forward propulsion pins me back in my seat, and I grip the handle bar, now with both hands, as strongly as I can. I try to pull my head away from the headrest but I am beaten back by the sheer accelerative force of the engine. Only after we reach a moderate speed, am I able to move more freely in my seat. Fox is still standing in a power stance at the helm. I look over my shoulder to see that the marina has become a distant landmark.

We speed along the water toward our destination, leaving a huge wake behind us as we go. The wind is ripping through my hair, and I take a moment to enjoy the ride, before crawling back inside my hardened shell. Fox savours the pleasure of the entire ride; his smile indicates a state of complete euphoria. My heart is warmed slightly at the idea that, sometimes, the simple pleasures in life can fan the remaining embers of childlike innocence into bright flames of fun. We continue to split the waters ahead, for a short while.

"Brian. Brian!" Fox strains to be heard over the sound of the engine. He waves me to join him at the front of the cruiser, so I quickly move into the seat directly to his left.

"What, Fox?"

"I wanted to tell you that, when I was inside the marina, I spoke with the owner. I asked him about your man and if he noticed anything weird around the lake or around the Hawkins' property."

"What did he say?"

"Jeff said he didn't notice anything out of the ordinary, but he wasn't watching the Hawkins' property, in particular, of course. He did say that there are wild animals living on both sides of the lake, but he hasn't seen any, lately. He was thinking that one may have found its way onto the island. I didn't tell him about the madman. Didn't want to scare him for no reason, ya' know?"

I met Jeff a few times, but don't know him, personally. From what Miranda tells me, he is good friends with her father and gives him a deal on his docking fees. Everyone in town knows Jeff, at least a little, especially if you are in need of marina services.

"Yea, of course. Did he say what kind of animals?"

"Just various ones, I guess, different ones at different times of the year. I do know that we have hyenas, bears, skunks, ya' know, things like that. But that doesn't really help us, does it?"

I don't answer his rhetoric. He doesn't seem discouraged by the words of the marina owner, and neither do I. Why would we be? I'm sure Fox doesn't doubt my testimony in any way. I have seen the madman, twice, and I trust my own eyes. No question about it. Jeff's words say more about his personality than they do about my account of the madman. The man owns a small waterfront business, whose revenue relies on the lake, alone, and he isn't even aware of a potentially-threatening trespasser. His words speak of his negligence as a businessman, but they surely do not put my version of the madman sighting in doubt. Jeff is either blind or stupid. There are no alternatives, unless he is in cahoots with the madman. I feel no need to defend my position to Fox, Jeff, or anyone else. It is of no matter. After all, pretty soon, Fox and I will be upon countless pieces of evidence proving that the madman is, in fact, trespassing on the Hawkins' property.

"Hey, Fox."

"Yea, Bry?"

"Don't you think it's strange that Jeff hasn't seen anything? I mean, he has a business to protect. He holds cash there overnight, doesn't he? You'd think that he would be more vigilant and aware of what goes on around the lake."

"Yea, well, that's why I asked him. I figured he would know this lake better than anyone, but if your man is staying out on the island, Jeff might have trouble seeing him. It's quite a distance from the marina."

"Yea, maybe that's it," I say, only half-believing that theory. "You don't think that Jeff is involved, do you?"

"Nah, It wouldn't make any sense. This guy probably comes to the island once in a while, at night, to take shelter in the abandoned hut. You're just lucky that you've gotten to see him, twice. We'll definitely find some remnants of those nights when we get there."

Knowing Fox takes me at my word relaxes me. He has a good head on his shoulders and a good sense of things. I am starting to understand how he got promoted to Sergeant at such a young age. His impeccable sense, along with his uninhibited zeal to enforce just policy, undoubtedly, ensured his quick rise up the ranks. I sit back in my seat and put any concerns over Jeff's words behind me. We approach the island and Fox slows the engine in preparation for docking. Fox spins the boat parallel to the shore with a skill that tells me he has done this move before. Fox promptly hops out of the boat, hammers a spike into the sand, and ties up the boat with a makeshift knot in the rope. The hut stands on the opposite side of the island.

"Want me to tie up the other rope?" I ask, as I, too, get out of the boat.

"Nah, one should be enough."

"You sure that's gonna hold?"

"Oh, yea. We won't be here very long. It'll be fine."

Fox's cavalier attitude is beginning to be a cause for concern. He doesn't seem worried about the madman, nor is he concerned about proper procedure, and now he has parked the boat too hastily for my liking. Earlier, I enjoyed his free spirit, but now, I am worried that one of his short cuts is going to backfire. This is the first time that I have ever set foot on the Hawkins' island and an eerie feeling grips me, knowing that the madman was here, as few as twelve hours ago. I don't know why, but I feel like I am trespassing on sacred ground. The irony is staring me right in the face, but I pay no attention to it. It's like, at any second, the madman will jump out at us from behind the bushes and tell us to get off his property, and in my current state of anxiety, I will, probably, comply, speedily.

The landscape of the island is quite peculiar. The beach, about 80 feet in width, faces the marina, to the south. It is the only sand on the island. The remaining shoreline is comprised of rock that fades gradually into the lake, and bushes, that hug a bit of the shore on the east side of the property. There is no dock, which is why we are using the beach as a parking spot. The rickety, old dock that served the Hawkins family for many years is gone, taken, either by the bank, or by the lake. I am not sure. The interior of the island is flat and covered with long, wild grasses and weeds. There are no trees on the island. When the Hawkins family lived here, however, the grass was very well kept. Everyone in the town knows that Bo Hawkins' lawn was as plush and green as the golf courses nearby. He was very meticulous in the way that he mowed and treated his lawn. For a retiree, his attitude wasn't all that unique. I'm sure he would turn in his grave if he knew the present state of his beloved grass; as wild and unsightly as the madman, himself.

I follow Fox towards the hut, and he points out each of the "*No Trespassing*" signs that the bank posted, after assuming ownership of the island. Just as Silas had said, there are four signposts, equally-spaced around the perimeter of the island and one right beside the front entrance of the hut. They are impossible to miss. The hut is located approximately 20 feet from the nearest shoreline and is the only remaining structure on the property. When the previous owners were alive, a quaint house stood in the middle of the island, but it was condemned and demolished, when taken over by the bank. I can't help but sense something missing on the ground upon which it once stood. It feels almost as if its absence reflects an erased piece of the Hawkins' legacy. From what I understand, their humble abode stood for multiple generations, spanning a hundred years. It's sad to think that the once vibrant bloodline, named Hawkins, is now invisible to the generations of people that would exist in its wake.

Fox and I, mere steps from the abandoned hut, exchange a look that tells me to prepare myself for the possibility of something important. He clutches the pistol by his right side in readiness, and we both come to the wooden front door, broken in more places than it is fixed. Standard yellow "caution" tape barricades the door. With his left hand extended, Fox twists the doorknob. It is locked.

"That's strange," he mutters.

He drives himself closer to the door, using his shoulder to barge his way into the hut. Abruptly, the bolt breaks free and the door flies open. A cloud of dust and smell of stale fabric blossom out from the opening. Fox and I both step back waiting for the smoky air to clear. I peer inside the shack. The air is so filled with dust and smoky residue that it is difficult to see anything within the barn-board walls. The hut is a simple structure, box-shaped, with a flat, shingled roof. The shingles, of course, are as dilapidated as the wooden walls. Clinging to its last breath of life, the cottage is fighting off fatal decay. The wood is rotting and discoloured. It looks as though a strong wind would be able to blow it apart like a pile of leaves, but here it stands, the only remaining edifice of the Hawkins' splendored past.

A beam of light that shines through the lone window illuminates the air, teeming with dust particles, so that it clouds my lungs at the mere sight of it. The light shines to the ground, illuminating a few of the wooden planks that comprise the floor. They are old, decaying, and slathered in dark grime. There is a stale dampness in the air of the hut and suggests that neither the door nor the window had been opened in quite some time. Fox holds his breath, squints, and pokes his head into the hut, while the remainder of his body rests outside of it.

"Nothing," he says, as he quickly jolts his head out of the murky fog.

He pushes the door wide open to allow an influx of air. It creaks eerily. As the cabin air begins to clear, I poke my head in, and his words are confirmed. There is absolutely nothing inside the cottage; no convicting artefacts, no Christmas presents. The grungy floor and wooden walls house nothing but musty air and a sour odour. I walk in, open the window, and scan the entire place one more time. There is nothing on any of the walls, or even the ceiling. Ruling out the possibility of stumbling upon a secret passageway, this has been an endeavour of complete futility. Without waiting for my reaction, Fox walks around to the other side of the hut, scanning the outside walls for the slightest of clues.

"Anything?" I ask. He shakes his head, without taking his eyes off the hut.

After we take a few more minutes to survey the hut and the surrounding grasses, our zeal hits rock bottom. We look at each other, scratch our heads, and just, sort of, shrug our shoulders in bewilderment. There is not a single shred of evidence inside the hut or anywhere on the island to point toward inhabitation; yet, I saw the madman here, mere hours ago.

"Well," Fox says, as we stand around, aimlessly. "Ain't this a conundrum?"

I am at a loss for words.

"Why would your man come here, but not seek shelter in the hut?" he continues, rhetorically.

Silently, we both mull over the question. I don't have a good answer.

"Listen, Brian," Fox says, after a while. "I'm gonna head back to the station to see if I can get some answers. This is really strange. Maybe he just comes here to fish. It's just really strange."

Perplexed by the situation, Fox can only speak in monotonous fragments.

"Good idea," I offer. "I'll head home and ask Miranda if she's noticed anything."

We jump in the boat and fly back to the marina. The return boat ride is in stark contrast to our earlier one. The sound of the engine is more annoying, the seats are more uncomfortable, and Fox does not captain the boat out of sheer pleasure as he did before. A sombre mood has gripped us both. No words are spoken and smiles are the furthest thing from our faces. The silence reeks of disappointment. A short while ago, success seemed so resolutely imminent. Coming up empty is tough to swallow. What bothers me most is the fact that I am, now, completely out of leads. I was counting on the evidence we were supposed to have found at the hut, evidence that would have provided several budding theories of who the madman is. I suppose that Fox is deliberating the same realization. The moment he saw the hut was empty, his mood shifted to discontent, faster than mine, and his childish impetuousness was replaced with a disciplined focus. It gave me hope, but also made me feel like I let him down in some way. It's no wonder the trip back to the marina was quick and mute.

Fox secures the boat to the dock, and promises me that he will do everything in his power to figure out the situation and identify the madman. He apologizes for wasting my time, but I reassure him that we are just unlucky. It is a peculiar exchange. Fox is upset with himself for today's failure. I take some of the responsibility, but he stubbornly refuses. Our parting is a solemn occasion; we simply say our *goodbyes* and go in separate directions. I hop into my truck and drive off, spinning the tires, and spraying gravel everywhere. I carry a feeling of hopelessness, all the way home.

When I arrive, the scene I come upon is considerably worse than the one I left behind. Miranda is sitting on the front porch steps, weeping, her face buried in her hands. Her sobs erupt with such ferocity that her head bounces up and down, her hair flopping in every direction. An explosion of concern and worry sets off inside, and I run short of breath. I park the truck as swiftly as I can. As I run to Miranda's side, I notice there are people in the backyard. I can't make sense of what I am seeing. My brain is having trouble processing the influx of sights and feelings.

"Miranda!" I yell. "What's wrong?"

There is no change in her position and no words offered in response. I sit down beside her and tightly wrap my arms around her shoulders. I, lovingly, echo my concern.

"Miranda, what's wrong? What happened?"

She finally pulls her hands away from her face, revealing her tear-soaked palms. Her crimson cheeks are iced with liquid lament, and droplets of sadness cling to her chin. She stares into my eyes and puts her trembling hands into mine. She labours to calm her breathing, in an attempt to resolve my distress, but all she can muster is a whisper.

"Alaska's dead."

CHAPTER 12

THE DOCK

THERE ARE QUITE A FEW people standing around Alaska's dead body. One of them is a police officer, who covered Alaska with a white sheet. He introduces himself as Mark Pratt, and tells me that he was the first to arrive on the scene, about thirty minutes ago. Miranda called the police when she found Alaska, twenty feet from the edge of the lake, apparently, drowned. Constable Pratt isn't saying much, just hanging his head in morbid silence.

The others include our veterinarian, Pamela Chun, who confirmed the death. She is a nice lady, and Alaska took very warmly to her. Miranda and I get along with her well. It is evident that she shed a few tears before my arrival. Jim and Helen are here, too. They attempt to console Miranda, their arms wrapping her firmly, as she sobs.

Clouds are rolling in overhead, and the sun is beginning to set. The air chills as the temperature drops, noticeably, telling tales of a coming storm. The lake is peaceful; in fact, an eerie calmness has floated into the entire area. I can't totally describe the feeling but there is a stillness, a stillness that reflects Alaska's lifeless spirit. I find it difficult to fight back the tears. Alaska is dead. She will never again draw breath in this world. As I look at her corpse, sadness sinks in.

The deepest roots of the tree of sorrow entangle my soul with the fact that Alaska's body is no longer Alaska. The substances have not changed; her legs, paws, eyes, skin, fur, and blood, all remain, but now, these things are merely casings that no longer house a living spirit. She is as a chair, or a desk, or a hat, or a puddle. That which was once my beautiful Alaska has become the mere shell of a dog. From this point on, Alaska will exist, only, in memory; a part of this world, no longer. I stand, considering the sheet-covered mound. I entertain the hope that a magician comes by, and pulls off the linen shroud to reveal Alaska, resurrected, dancing with delight, as she had done so many times before. Alas! A dream. It is not to be so.

Dr. Chun and Constable Pratt approach me in a cautious manner. I offer a smile to ease the tension. Pamela speaks first.

"Brian, I am very sorry to have to ask you this, but the constable and I need to speak with you in private. It's important."

"Sure, that's fine. I'll just get Miranda and---"

"No!" Pam interrupts, in a loud whisper. She collects herself and starts again. "I'm sorry, it's just…we don't want Miranda to know this just yet. Please, let's speak in private, only the three of us."

"Okay," I say, but it is more of a question than an answer.

I have a terribly-suspicious look on my face, one that reveals my thoughts, perfectly. I cannot imagine, for the life of me, why they want to talk to me in private, without Miranda's knowledge. I suggest to her parents to take Miranda inside. I tell them I will handle everything else. They oblige, without any hesitation or rebuttal; an unusually-pleasant exchange with the monster-in-laws. I signal to Pam and Mark to head down to the dock, where there are chairs for us to sit on. I take the remaining seat and gaze over at the island. My mind is completely blank. Any idea or inkling of the conversation to come is non-existent, as is the life of my loving pet. I stare blankly at my two guests. No one says anything for a long moment. I can feel their fear and trepidation.

"Guys, come on. Someone has to say something. This is ridiculous."

"Okay, okay," Pam is finally about to get something out. She continues, "We found something that is sort of alarming."

"Go on."

"Well, when Miranda pulled Alaska from the lake, she called me immediately, and I called the police immediately thereafter. Constable Pratt and I arrived at the same time. Miranda was huddling over Alaska's body, and she was crying pretty hard. As soon as I could, I gave the body a thorough check. Alaska was dead, and had been for some time. But, then I noticed something else, something... concerning, to say the least."

I feel an agonizing tension grip my stomach. My eyes widen and I am unable to speak. In fact, I am unable to move, frozen to the edge of my seat. My teeth clench together involuntarily in preparation for imminent devastation.

"I found Alaska to have bruising around her throat and neck, suggesting that she had been strangled prior to her drowning."

The madman! Her words ring through the air like an air raid siren. In mere milliseconds, I convict the madman of the crime and sentence him to execution. A dark fury rages inside of me, a fury that will not rest until the madman is served an excruciating vengeance. Justice, itself, will not satiate my hunger for retaliation. Only revenge will cool my fiery wrath.

Pam continues to speak but I can barely make out the words over the screams, resonating from the mania within my heart, soul, and mind.

"Without the proper equipment, I won't be able to confirm the details, but if I had to guess, I would say that the strangling had more to do with Alaska's death than the drowning did. I know this is hard to hear, but it's really important that you understand these words."

Constable Pratt tries to get my attention. "I'm really sorry about everything, Mr. Dawson. This is truly a tragedy."

I can barely produce a thankful nod, as the constable glances my way before he continues.

"We were thinking about what may have caused this. It is

possible, although unlikely, that the bruising was caused by another animal; maybe a bear, or a buck, or a bigger dog, perhaps. It could have been a snake, maybe, or something from the lake. I realize that these are unlikely scenarios, but the one that makes the most sense to me is that she may have gotten tangled up in the reeds and was pulled deeper into the lake by an undercurrent."

"There's a problem with that theory, though," Pam interrupts. "The bruising on Alaska's neck is pretty severe."

A tear streams down my face.

"I highly doubt that that type of bruising could be caused by the reeds. Even if an undercurrent took a hold of her, the reeds would have broken easily or been pulled from their rooting, especially considering Alaska's size and weight. I strongly question the validity of this theory."

I shoot a look over at Pratt. He shrugs his shoulders, apologetically.

"Now," Pam carries on, in a serious tone, "we have to consider the possibility of something else. We have to consider the possibility that this was done intentionally, by a person. Maybe, she scared someone and they reacted out of self-defense. Maybe, it was a teenager, playing a prank, until things got out of hand. I don't have the answer, Brian, and I don't want to think about the possibility of it being deliberate. I know it's unreliable, but it is possible."

Maybe Pam doesn't want to think about it, but I lust after that sinister idea. It fuels my rage and I drink it deeply, as I listen to her speak. Pratt picks up where Pam leaves off.

"Because of the curious nature of the death, we will perform an investigation. Quietly, of course, so we don't bring more drama to you and your family. I know the sergeant will want to be pretty thorough, but to be honest with you, Brian, I doubt we'll find anything. What evidence could we possibly procure that would lead to a conviction? No fingerprints or witnesses, anywhere around here. Now, I've already called Sergeant Fox and he's on his way down here. He might have some ideas but I wouldn't expect much. It was probably just an accident, anyway."

I want to mention that I saw the Sergeant earlier, but neither Mark nor Pam know about the madman, and mentioning him may just add more confusion to the discussion. Fox will be here soon and I feel more comfortable letting him go over the details. I look at Mark with a sharp glare and he, sheepishly, returns a glance that offers his condolences.

"So then, why are you telling me all of this, if there's nothing you can do, anyway?"

Mark opens his mouth to answer but Pam jumps in. Mark's jaw hangs down, in mid-air, his mouth open.

"We wanted you to know the truth, Brian. And we wanted to give you the chance to tell Miranda, yourself. Or, perhaps, you might choose to keep this from her. She seems pretty upset. You may not want to further upset her, at least, not right away. As of now, Miranda thinks it's an accident. Accidentally drowning, for dogs, is not entirely a rare occurrence, and I'm sure she will accept this theory as the ultimate explanation. After all, it may very well have been an accident, and, even if it wasn't, we may never know what really happened. When I first noticed the bruises, I wanted to tell Miranda, but she was too upset. I believe I did the right thing. You can tell her when she's ready, or not at all. It's up to you. I can take Alaska and prepare her for a funeral, if you'd like. Whatever you need, we're here to help."

"Absolutely, whatever you need," Pratt echoes Dr. Chun's generosity.

There are so many different thoughts racing through my mind that I can't think straight, not even for one second. There is much I want to say, but my emotions are running in a million different directions, and I am not able to slow them down. I do the only thing I can; I thank them for their support, tuck my chin inside the collar of my jacket, and bow my head.

A moment goes by and I hear heavy footsteps behind me, pounding the floorboards, and sending vibrations across the entire dock. I don't look to see who it is; I don't have to. Sergeant Fox rests his hand on my shoulder. Mark stands up to greet his boss. The sun is now almost fully tucked away for the night and the mosquitoes are beginning to nibble at us. The moon is out but the light from the sun is nullifying its impact. I just sit there, motionless. I am tired and my heart is broken. As we sit in silence, for a moment, I finally have a chance to grieve. My dear, sweet, beautiful Alaska is gone. I will never again play with her or drive her to town in my truck. Sadness has torn a hole in my heart that is filling up with hate. My heart aches so much that I think it may burst from my chest, but instead, tears burst from my eyes. Crying, for the first time as a grown man, I weep tears of pure sorrow.

Seeing my tears, Pam takes my hands, hoping to comfort me, but it only makes me yearn for Miranda's touch. Fox tells Pratt to go home, realizing that the night will end sooner, rather than later. The young constable says a few kind words, and leaves without making a big display. Fox, then, asks Pam to leave us to a private conversation. She obliges, but speaks quickly, just before her departure.

"I'd better take care of Alaska, don't you think, Brian?"

"Yea, I guess so," I whisper, only lifting my eyes to meet hers for a brief moment.

She leaves the dock, as Fox takes the seat next to me. Fox does not speak right away; he simply gazes out over the lake and deeply breathes in the sweet night air. I make neither motion nor speech. We sit in silence. Every so often, a loon calls, piercing the night, and the silence. The gentle waves of the lake slowly caress the shore with a cadence that lulls my anger to sleep. At this moment, I feel nothing. My rage falls dormant and sounds of my sadness echo softly against the walls of my empty heart. I feel hollow. I am hollow. In my chair, no longer sits Brian Dawson. Instead, in my chair sits an imposter, a shell of a man once known by that name, a shell that houses nothing of significance. With every tide that rolls in gently against the welcoming arms of the sands, little bits of my spirit go out, bits that I will never reclaim.

"Brian," Fox finally speaks. "I know what you're thinking."

I don't doubt his statement for a second.

"You're thinking that the man you've been seeing had something to do with Alaska's death. Constable Pratt told me about the bruises. Hell. That was the first thing that came to my mind, too, Brian, I don't blame you one bit for how you feel. Now, I can't imagine the sadness that you're going through, but I do know a thing or two about anger. You simply cannot take matters into your own hands, Brian. Just let me handle this. I will do everything in my power to solve this case, but the last thing I need is you putting a bullet hole through some homeless guy who's probably suffering from schizophrenia or something."

"I'm to bottle my rage, then?"

"No, Brian. I want you to let your rage go. To do otherwise would equate you with the madman himself. But, what are you gonna do? Hunt the man down in a manic campaign of vengeance? Find your humanity, Brian. Don't allow the beast to take control."

"My wife is inside the house, balling her eyes out," I said, beginning to let the rage out. "Where is the humanity in that?" My voice growls, as the words escape my mouth.

"I know, Brian, but you can't fight evil with evil. Focus on Miranda, and comforting her. Focus on Alaska's funeral and grieving in a healthy way. Fight back against the rage. Don't just bottle it up but turn it into something else, something good. Don't let evil consume you, okay, young Skywalker?"

I offer no reply. From a comedic standpoint, his joke is genius, I have to admit, but I am in no mood for humour. His attempt at levity fails to cheer me up in any way, and I offer no fake smile in reciprocation. Making light of my desire for revenge only fuels my anger, as I think about cutting off the madman's head with a light sabre. In all seriousness, I do understand his point, but my rage continues to grow, nonetheless.

Fox tries again, after his joke failed its task.

"And I'll keep you updated about the case. You should take a break. This is not your responsibility, it's mine, and you have my word that I will be as diligent as humanly possible. I will get to the bottom of this, Brian. Believe me. Now, go inside. I'm sure your wife needs you."

He is right. Miranda needs me, and I don't want those blood-sucking parasites that she calls "mom" and "dad" to fill her head with lies and fabrications about me, as they probably are. Fox and I shake hands, he offers his sympathies, and leaves.

CHAPTER 13

THE KITCHEN TABLE

I MAKE SURE TO LOCK THE door behind me. When I look up, I see Miranda sitting at the kitchen table, between her mom and dad. Her face is dry, she has stopped crying, but her eyes are red. Miranda's torso rests on the table, and my in-laws hang their heads in sorrow. I walk in, and all eyes lock onto me. Miranda immediately fixes her posture, but her face remains gripped by sadness. There are three coffee cups on the table, each filled to a different level. I notice a pot has been brewed and is sitting on the counter. There are cookies on the table, as well, but they are untouched; they are more for display than anything else, I suppose. The heavy silence seems to resonate that of a desolate grave. No one has the energy or inclination to animate themselves in any way. Here we are, like zombies, petrified by our anguish, motionless, speechless, and hoping to wake from a nightmare we all share.

I am well aware that my consoling skills will be put to the test over the next few days. There are a few things in life that I excel at, but, in this area, I am a novice. I never know what to do or what to say to someone who is grieving, let alone my own wife, who is experiencing the same pain that I am. They say "death is a part of life", and "life goes on." I am sure whoever invented those clichés did so with the noblest of intentions. The expressions are genuine attempts to lessen the impact that death has on those that remain living. They are meant to convince us that life is a circular entity, encompassing birth, death, and everything in between. I, respectfully, disagree. While death both marks and ends a span of life, death and life are, certainly, two very different things. When we are born, we begin, simultaneously, living and dying. The two opposing forces wage war across the battleground of our existence and our birth venerates the day in which we are forcibly thrown into the chaos called "life." Existence is not an intrinsic quality of human nature; therefore, birth and death mark the beginning and the end of a life span that is but a mere fraction of human history and even a smaller fraction of the universal timeline. Clearly, dogs are cursed with the same cruel misfortune. Death, then, is the force that puts an irrevocable end to life. Life, then, is but a brief moment between birth and death. Humans are like trees; we are born a product of our parents, we grow, strengthen, and produce fruit. Our roots cling desperately to life, as if we would live forever, if not for the reaper that invariably strolls by, at the chosen hour, and cuts us down. Death, then, is only as much a part of life as the reaper is a part of the tree he destroys. Alaska has fallen to the reapers blade; she would never again possess life in this world.

Death, however, does not necessarily put an end to existence. While it, undeniably, trumps human life, it has yet proven to conquer the state of being. What happens to us after we die? I can tell you that I, Brian Dawson, haven't the slightest clue. I am positive only of my uncertainty. I cannot soften Miranda's hurt by telling her that Alaska is in a "better place." That claim is no more substantial than the claim that Alaska will spend eternity in painful torment. How, then, am I to console Miranda? Her love for her dog does not end with Alaska's departure from this world. Love has the ability to transcend this world, as it seeks out those who are no longer a part of it, but, to the people who grieve death, it is but a mere messenger that returns empty-handed; an unfortunate truth. Undoubtedly, Miranda yearns for something that can never again return to her, and so do I. Although humans possess knowledge of the absolution of death, regrettably, we maintain desires that are fulfilled only by death's revocation. This is the great lament of those who grieve.

I walk slowly and heavily toward the table. I pull out the chair at the head of the table, closest to the back door. I slump down in my seat and hang my head. Miranda gets up quickly and comes to sit on my lap. No one says anything, but tears begin to course down her face, once again. I hold her tightly and she buries her head in my chest. I look at my in-laws and force a sheepish smile. I propose dismissal.

"You guys can be heading home now. It's getting pretty late."

They shoot a glance at each other before returning their eyes to mine.

"Thanks for staying with Miranda, too. I really appreciate it, but I don't want to inconvenience you guys too much."

"It's no trouble," Helen says. "We could even spend the night, if you want."

"No, no, that's not necessary. I think we're gonna head up to bed anyway. It's been such a long day."

We all get up and head to the front door. Miranda walks close to me, never lifting her head from my chest. She wraps her arms around my neck as I feel her tears stain my shirt. Not surprisingly, the mood is sombre and not many words are spoken. Jim goes into the closet to fish out his wife's jacket. He wraps it around her shoulders, as he has always done. I notice a particular sadness in his eyes that he has never revealed before. Helen notices it too. She puts her hand on his face, ever so tenderly, just before kissing his cheek. He smiles with appreciation. Jim is usually too proud to show his appreciation for his wife's tenderness, but on this night, I doubt he has any defense against it. I am not the only one to notice that Jim has always had a special kinship with Alaska. He loved her deeply and is greatly saddened by her death. She always held a special place in his heart. With Miranda and me failing to extend his lineage, he focused his love on our pet. I think he may have seen her as a grandchild; he definitely treated her like one. I know he is struggling with the pain her absence brings. He no longer possesses a loving muse on which he can place his affection. I decide to invite them to her funeral.

"So, guys, her funeral is tomorrow, probably some time, in the afternoon. Dr. Chun has her now and is going to prepare her for the ceremony. We'd like for you to be there, if at all possible."

"Oh, of course, darling," Helen says, as she kisses the side of my face that Miranda isn't occupying. Jim says nothing. "And if you guys need anything, anytime, please let us know. Jim and I would be happy to help out in any way we can."

Miranda finally leaves my side to hug her mother; it lasts longer than usual.

"Much obliged," I say, as Jim takes my hand and shakes it, firmly. He remains silent, although it feels like there is a dormant eruption of words, waiting to explode, just behind his sealed lips.

As he shakes my hand, he looks into my eyes. A flicker of sadness, of course, remains, but the whites of his eyes tell a different story. He appears angry with me. Perhaps he holds me responsible for Alaska's death. Perhaps he considers my actions negligent and the ultimate cause of the accident. Surely, he will not blame his precious little girl for the accident, even though she is just as responsible as I am. Surely, he did not see the bruising. Dr. Chun had Alaska covered with a blanket by the time the Cranstons arrived. I can't figure out the reason behind the malevolence in his eyes. Perhaps, now, he views me as an expendable part of the family. At least, when Alaska was alive, I held some importance to him, as Alaska was *my* dog. But now, I am completely useless to him. I know he disapproves of me and is aching for the chance to say so. Has he found it? Can the death of my dog really provide him with the opportunity he needs to drive a spike into the heart of my marriage? Perhaps, he will threaten to disown Miranda if she does not comply with his wishes. Perhaps, he will threaten me with physical harm if I do not grant a submissive divorce. The look in his eyes tells foreboding tales of epic proportion, wherein Jim, the protagonist, will rescue his helpless daughter from the evil clutches of her inept husband. I am sure of it. I begin to brace myself, mentally, in preparation for the coming onslaught.

As our handshake comes to an end, my feet plant themselves firmly, expecting the worst. I am prepared for either the verbal, or physical, attack. Suddenly, a large tear streams down Jim's cheek and falls to the floor. His eyelids flicker, he pulls me in close, and throws his arms around me, locking me in a warm embrace.

"We love you, son, and we're here for you," he whispers, as his face presses upon mine.

My arms, floating in the air, take a moment before they close in around him. My confusion is matched only by the tightness of his grasp. A ploy? I question his actions in my head. His words and his arms feel so sincere that I can only imagine genuine thoughts inhabiting Jim's heart and mind. Can this actually be "love" in its authentic form? His lingering embrace suggests that it is so.

As he pulls away, he grabs my shoulders with both hands, not quite ready to let me go. I feel awkward. His eyes are full of tears. I wonder how it is possible for a grown man to cry this much over a pet that was not even his. As I look upon Jim's soaked face and watery eyes, I feel awkward, knowing that, in front of him, stands a man, normally in charge of his emotions. My eyes have dried since the talk on the dock, and my face shows few signs of sadness. With my sleeve, I wipe the tears from his cheeks and take pity on him. How weak he is to display this kind of emotion. Is he not able to keep his reserve in the presence of his sworn enemy? I, on the other hand, am as a Roman general, statuesque, and brave, not allowing the emotions of my heart to consume me. This weak, old man poses no threat to me, and I will be the one to lead this family out of mourning. They turn to leave, and Jim holds the door open for his wife. I grab Miranda by the waist and pull her in close to me. I glare at Jim. I am the new authority in this family. I know it and he knows it, too. Soon, everyone will know it. My throne sits high atop both our households, glistening with gold and silver, made of glory, and is, rightfully, mine.

After the door closes, I kiss Miranda on the lips, a kiss in celebration of my kingship. She feels the strength of my arms as I hold her body close to mine. As I remove my lips, ever so softly, from hers, I can detect a slight shiver running down her spine. Tears still float in her beautiful eyes. I wipe them dry and kiss her again, this time caressing her face with both my hands, sliding my tongue gently into her mouth. The kiss lasts quite a while, until Miranda pulls away to whisper, "I love you, Brian." I tell her to head upstairs to bed and I will meet her shortly. I go to the front door and turn the lock into place.

CHAPTER 14

THE FUNERAL

T HE MORNING STARTS SLOWLY; WE just putter around waiting for Dr. Chun to arrive. Miranda and I haven't spoken much since we woke up, but no tears have been shed and the mood in the household is a definite improvement over that of last night. Miranda tossed and turned through the night, quite a bit but, eventually, found sleep. I woke up, feeling refreshed, after a sound night's sleep.

After my shower, instinctively, I opened the bedroom door to let Alaska in, but, when silence and an empty space greeted me, I was reminded of our loss. The sun is rising on the other side of the lake and shining into the bedroom, causing me to squint as I get dressed. It prophesizes of good weather for the funeral, but I am in no mood to consider the ironic ramifications of sunshine at a burial. I think funerals are stupid. We pay our respects to an empty shell. As much as I want the lifeless mass to be Alaska, the thing we are about to bury is not her. So, why do people feel comforted when the hollow bodies of those we love are in the ground? Is it a comfort derived from knowing the dead have been properly venerated? Perhaps. I wager that most people find solace in that, however, I struggle to confirm that this type of ceremony aids grieving. The dead are surely not affected by the earthly right we offer them. It is likely that Alaska will not benefit from these rituals, and neither will I. Nevertheless, I submit to the empty routine, hoping that Miranda finds peace and serenity, as her heart continues to mend. I finish getting ready and go downstairs.

I can hear Dr. Chun and Miranda in the kitchen. Pamela must have arrived early to make preparations for the funeral. When I come upon the two ladies in conversation, I notice that Miranda has put out a lovely spread of snacks. I am not exactly sure how many people will show up today, but it is good that Miranda has something to keep herself busy with.

"Nice spread, honey," I say, as I give her a kiss on the cheek, trying to keep the mood light.

"Thanks, babe," she replies, with a cute smile.

I am glad that she seems to be in good spirits. I look over at Dr. Chun, sipping a cup of coffee.

"And Pam, thank you so much for everything. You really helped us out a lot."

"No problem, Brian. I know how hard it is to deal with grief and the administrative stuff. Everything is all set up. I finished most of it this morning. It's no trouble at all, really."

"Well, thanks. I don't know what we would've done without you."

As I speak, I glare into her eyes, suggestively, so that she knows exactly what I mean. I am not just thanking her for the funeral preparations, but for concealing Alaska's bruises from Miranda, as well. I think my subtle message is well-received. I have decided not to tell Miranda about the possibly sinister marks on Alaska's neck, at least for the time being. I find that there is no need to upset her, just yet, but if evidence of violence comes to light, involving the madman or otherwise, I will probably want Miranda to have all the facts.

"So, why such a big spread, honey?"

"It's for everyone to enjoy after the funeral. I figure we can have a little reception in here for people who want to stay and chat, and maybe tell stories about Alaska. I think it will be a good thing."

"That's a wonderful idea, babe. How many people can we expect, today?"

"Well, me and you. Pam makes three. My mom and dad are coming of course, and that makes five."

Pam continues the list. "Sergeant Fox is coming too. Actually, he's the one who helped me dig the plot in the backyard. He also helped me carry the rock that I engraved as Alaska's tombstone."

"Yea," Miranda continues. "And dad told Chuck Smith, so he'll be by as well. It's gonna be quite the turn out for our little angel."

Upon hearing Alaska referred to as "an angel", Miranda and Pam both smile and are warmed by the idea of Alaska's progression to a better, more heavenly realm. I, however, am all the more upset by the word. Firstly, there is no way to be sure that Alaska is in a better place, let alone possessing angelic qualities. Secondly, I am shocked at the number of people who feel the need to attend a fucking dog's funeral. Oh my God! Humans are too sentimental for their own good. We waste our time dressing up our dogs in sweaters and putting them in purses and burying them, while we neglect the needs of human beings. What a joke!

"It's nice to have all of their support. Some people are so sweet," Miranda says, finishing her thoughts.

"Absolutely," Pam concurs. "Only during times like these is the goodness of people truly revealed. It fills me with hope for humanity despite all that's wrong in the world."

"Oh, I agree," Miranda says, without hesitation. "And, I am sure, that wherever she is, Alaska appreciates it."

Miranda ends with a smile and a faraway gaze on her face. My eyes are filled with alarm; *"Wherever she is'? Are you kidding? She's in a box, and soon to be in a hole in the ground!"* But before I can deal with the stupidity of the matter, there is a rumbling at the front door. Jim and Helen are here and have let themselves in, without knocking. Jim hangs up his wife's jacket before doing the same with his, like always. How mundane.

"In here!" Miranda yodels excitedly, prompting the old couple to make their way into the kitchen.

Jim and Helen saunter slowly into the kitchen. Helen is buried under a pile of food that fills both her arms. Even Jim holds a basket of muffins that looks awkward in his large hands. Miranda rushes to help her mom and I grab the basket from Jim and shake his hand in greeting and gratitude. Everyone in the room exchanges pleasantries. Miranda and I add Helen's gourmet contributions to the table; cakes, pies, muffins, cookies, and banana bread. There was hardly a baked goodie that she didn't bring.

"Helen," I say, in amazement. "Wow, that's quite a lot of stuff you brought for us. How did you even find the time?"

"Well, I did most of the baking this morning. Actually, did a bit of it last night, too. Plus, I already had some of it in the freezer. I even made that apple crumble you like so much."

"Aw, Helen, that's too kind of you. Thanks so much!"

"No trouble at all, Brian. I am happy to help. Just make sure you have some of that crumble and tell me what you think of it."

"Oh, I'm sure it's great. It always is."

Our banter makes me nauseous. The aromas of all the food doesn't help, either. Although, as much as Helen and I hold a secret hate for each other, I have to admit that her apple crumble is absolutely out of this world. It might just be the most splendid dessert I have ever eaten in my life. Assuming that it isn't glazed with poison, I am definitely going to have some, maybe more than my fair share, despite my moral dilemma regarding enjoying the fruits of your enemy. I am reminded of last night, and the exchange of power from Jim to me. I am certainly adamant about solidifying my new position in this family, and I want to do it quickly to avoid any possible resistance.

"So, Jim," I call out, in the middle of random banter throughout the room. "Why don't you say a few words about Alaska today, during the funeral? We all know that you had a special connection to her. I'm sure she would appreciate that. Okay? Thanks."

I quickly turn my gaze from Jim and dig into Helen's apple crumble, with arrogant authority.

"I would be happy to, Brian."

"Perfect."

As I leave the room, I express no emotion to Jim's response, illustrating that I am not giving him much of a choice. I really have nowhere to go; my exit is simply for effect. Jim is going to learn his place in this family, and it's the small dealings, like this one, that teach the most effective lessons. I can see, through the window, the preparations that Pam and Fox have made. There is an excavation, with the dirt piled to one side. The tombstone that Pam made for Alaska has been placed at the head. The stone is quite lovely. There is a flattering picture of my beautiful blue-eyed pet in the middle, just above some writing that I can't quite make out from this distance. I imagine that it is either the dates of her life span, or a sentimental quote of some kind. There is a large, sealed wooden box resting on the table next to the hole. Surely, it houses Alaska's lifeless corpse. The wood is polished oak, quite lovely as it glistens in the sunlight. Even though Alaska will never know, and even though it will make very little difference in the end, I enjoy the fact that Pam thought to give Alaska a beautiful resting place. Pam is a beautiful person, who really cares about animals. Her talents would be a waste if she were anything other than a veterinarian.

When I return to the gathering, Sergeant Fox and Charlie Smith are mingling and munching. I am happy to see that the mood remains light. It is quite the contrast from the gloomy fog that enveloped the atmosphere in the house last night. I sense that those who are gathered here for the funeral are more interested in celebrating a life than grieving a death, and I share the feeling. I enter with a smile and thank everyone for coming.

Fox offers his condolences and informs me that Constable Pratt expressed an interest in coming today, but unfortunately Fox needed him to complete an assignment. I appreciate Pratt's concern.

"He's a good kid," I tell Fox.

"Yes, he is," Fox replies, as he puts his hand on my shoulder.

Everyone is standing around nervously, as if waiting for me to signal the start of the funeral, so, as head of the household, I will not keep my public waiting. I am first to exit, holding the door open for my guests to go through. I lead the procession across the lawn to the gravesite. I put my hand on Alaska's casket and thank everyone for coming, once again. We all encircle the grave and gaze into the empty hole. The mood begins to darken. A blanket of sorrow descends as we stand in silence, heads bowed.

"I want to say a few words to initiate the proceedings," I begin. "Not a single person in this world was as close to Alaska as I was, and I doubt anyone loved her as deeply. The words that I am to speak come only from the heart. May they fall upon eager ears so that the memory of Alaska rises to the fore and may all those, here today, find comfort in it. We are gathered to bid farewell to a loved one. Death may have stolen our dear companion from us, but Alaska will remain embedded in our hearts because it is love that will keep her memory alive.

What is it to die? I dare say that the answer lies in the hearts of those who yet live. It is our responsibility to ensure that Alaska's death is not greeted by sadness alone but with joyful tears that rejoice in the love she has left behind. It is, perhaps, a god's burden to bear, but it has been entrusted to us and, as we lower her into her grave, we are called to remember her. Close your eyes and remember her. Remember her life and her love, so that she would exist as more than a slave to death. Remember her so passionately as to strike fear into the reaper, himself. Remember her so passionately as to make death tremble, as we reminisce of our dear, Alaska. She belongs in our hearts, our souls, and our minds, forever, so that we may still feel her warmth and find comfort in our memories of her. May love be the dagger with which death is struck down, and as we drive the dagger through the heart of the reaper, may our arms be driven by thoughts of Alaska. Sing songs of triumph in her name, as death falls to its knees, defeated. Love her with a pure hunger that shakes the foundations of life and death. Do not relent in your campaign until the walls that separate the living and the dead are reduced to mere rubble. When the smoke from the wreckage clears, standing proudly will Alaska be, her piercing blue eyes as lively as ever. Heed my words, friends, for if we are successful, Alaska will never die, and we will, forever, stand in loving triumph. Thank you."

I don't believe a single word that I say, but I feel like a fucking god. The crowd looks at me in absolute astonishment, slack-jawed, and silent. I am king, and nary dare a soul challenge my authority. Not a single tear is shed. My words empower these people above sorrow. My intent, perfectly and masterfully, achieved. Attitude reflects leadership, and I, as king of this realm, will have my people possess attitudes of strength and passion, not of sadness and despair. I will provide my people with hope. I will thrust them into battle against darkness, instead of allowing them to wallow in defeat. If it weren't a funeral, my speech would be met with cheers of celebration, chants of my name, praises to my words, and applauds for the aims to which it speaks. As I take my place in the circle, the cloud of awe is not yet dissipated. I have successfully transported my audience into a different world, a world where hope slaughters sadness, and they are mesmerized by the inferno of power that I have, so brazenly, delivered.

I stand, royally, within the group, absent of a throne to sit on. I offer Jim to the crowd.

"Now, I have asked Jim to say a few words. So, Jim, if you wouldn't mind, please continue the proceedings."

"Of course, Brian. Thanks."

Jim staggers slowly to Alaska's side. He puts his hand on the wooden casket, as I did, and takes a moment, with his eyes closed, for a few deep breaths, preparing his emotions for their solemn journey. He removes a piece of paper from his pocket, faces the crowd, and drops his head. His hands tremble, and the paper flaps in the air, like the wings of a bird. Finally, he steadies himself and opens his speech.

"Hello everyone. I want to thank you all for coming today to celebrate the life of our beloved, Alaska. Death is a tragedy that affects everyone differently. I know we are all mourning the loss of our loved one, and, from the bottom of my heart, I pray that your sorrow be lessened as we grieve together. My heart bleeds for Alaska, but it also bleeds for you, who stand before me. My heart, like yours, is broken. There is a pain in my chest that won't go away no matter how much I try to cast it out, but my pain is stronger, knowing that my friends and family share it with me."

A tear streams down his left cheek.

"I always felt that I had a special bond with Alaska. She and I would play together lovingly for hours upon end, enjoying each other's company. And although that will never again happen on this earth, my heart will be eternally warmed by the memory of those times. I implore everyone here to do the same. Reminisce about the times that you and Alaska spent together and allow the memory of the love shared to warm your hearts. Close your eyes and think of Alaska. Do you remember the love that you felt? Do you remember her beauty, her striking blue eyes? Love each day as if it were spent in playful jest with her. Honour the life that Alaska lived by sharing your love with those around you. She would want that for each of you. Alaska loved me dearly, and I loved her in return. When I close my eyes, I can recall her scent and the softness of her fur that caressed my hands and fingers. I fell asleep with her in my arms many times and I still reach for her when sleep blankets my consciousness. I looked into her beautiful eyes as many times as I have seen the sun set and never once did I grow tired of the gaze given in return. In the days to come, I will surely dream of her, magical dreams, like we used to have as children wherein the chains of life are not so tightly bound around our feet. I know that I will dream that Alaska and I exist in a world where every joy and happiness is a possibility, and when I awake, I will rage against the cruel reality. I will cry and I will cry and I will cry as if my tears could be used to purchase her back from the merchants of the great beyond, but in the end, I will possess but the sobs of a sad, old man. My memories will live as Alaska cannot. I will never forget her, and I know that she will never forget me. So, to each of you I say, never forget her, because I am sure that she will never forget us."

I look around me. There isn't a dry eye in the crowd. Jim continues.

"I feel a hollowness in my heart where Alaska's love once dwelt. It cannot be filled. Her love cannot be replaced. Losing loved ones is a part of life. Losing, in general, is a part of life. As we grow older, death takes things away from us, but it will never take away my love or memories of you, Alaska. I love you with all my heart. I love you in ways words can't explain. I loved you for your entire life and continue to love you now."

Tears are streaming down both of Jim's cheeks and his eyes are filled with despair. Miranda and Helen burst out with emphatic sobs that echo across the expanse of the lake. Even the sergeant is ferociously wiping his tears away and fighting to keep his emotions at bay. Only Chuck holds his reserve, his tears confined to his eyes. He and Alaska messed about playfully a few times, and I'm sure that he developed a bond with her in that short time, as most people did.

"I love you, my sweet girl. I never got to say goodbye to you, and that breaks my heart. Wherever you are, I want you to know that, although I now must live in a world in which you do not exist, I consider it a lesser place. And, although we carry on and fill our days with routine and schedule, until the pain subsides, the world will never be the same without you. We may eventually come to terms with your death, but I promise you, we will never replace you. From this day forward, every quantum of happiness we might experience, every victory we may achieve, every relaxing moment we get, every kiss we share, and all the sincere moments we could encounter in our lives, will be corrupted, having a slight taste of poison, and, although we may enjoy them in a bittersweet way, your death will forever mar the pure forms of joy we were meant to experience. I love you, my dear Alaska. I love you, my dear Alaska. Goodbye."

Toward the end of his monologue, Jim's lips are so overwhelmed with salty fluid that his words slur. His eyes, like morbid waterfalls, push out tears as quickly as they can, which journey to, and drip from, his chin. His hands begin to tremble, again, as he lowers his paper. His mouth frowns in ways I'd never seen on a grown man. Jim tries to dry his face with his sleeves, but the non-stop flow of tears overwhelms the saturation capacity of the material. He hangs his head in sadness. He loosens his grip on his paper and it falls to the ground like a dying leaf in autumn, floating back or forth through the air, as it descends. Unaware of what to do with his empty hands, he folds them in front of himself, ever so penitently. His groans become audible, as he weeps. His knees quiver; he supports himself against the table as he loses balance. For fear of collapse, both Miranda and Helen rush to his aid. They throw their arms around him in support, despite their own cries of anguish.

Chuck and Fox put a hand on each of my shoulders, in response. I am furious at the two men for thinking that I require their comfort. I stand, staring at the puddle of tears that constitutes my family. I pity their weakness. I pity Jim and his sappy speech. I pity his tears. I pity his weakness. I recognize that his speech lies in stark contrast to mine, as it revels in its own sadness, possessing no triumph, whatsoever. It pulls, ever so cheaply, at the heart strings of the naive crowd, but I am not fooled. I am not tricked by its lies and deceits. Jim's speech is clearly an attack, directed at me, a feeble attempt to equate *his* relationship with Alaska to mine. He makes a pathetic attempt to win the hearts of the assembly by spewing vulgar lies about his love for my pet. In no possible way can his love for Alaska run as deep as he claims. He hardly had a bond with her at all. His propaganda sickens me and dishonours Alaska's memory, poisoning the very purpose of the funeral. His serpent-like sham has seemingly gone unnoticed by most of the group, but I am privy to his intentions and will not let them go unpunished. I am growing more and more frustrated with the scene before me. My hands clench in anger as I ponder the two men who, mistakenly, came to my aid, and my own wife, who foolishly comforted a serpent of a man who seeks to undermine my kingdom by tainting the memory of my beloved dog. Luckily, Pam interrupts, resuming the proceedings. Perhaps, she, too, sees Jim's malevolence through the smoke screen he has created.

"If Jim and Brian wouldn't mind, could I please have you gentlemen lower the casket into the ground," she says, as she assigns the duties and takes charge of the program.

The miserable "pool of lament" is forced to disperse as Jim makes his way over to the casket. A cold-as-steel intensity grips me. I, sluggishly, pace toward the casket, my eyes fixed, probingly, on Jim. Like a hawk, I stand over him, and accept the wicked conviction that is trying to possess me. My body, instinctively, emulates that of the madman. My chest puffs out and my facial features are seized in a stoic expression. Jim looks up, meets my eyes, and is taken aback at my ominous glare and intimidating stance.

"Ready to lift the casket, son?" Jim cues me for action. He is perplexed by my appearance.

"Yea, sure," I growl, my eyes still fixed on his.

"What's wrong?" Jim asks, as we each get to our respected end of the casket.

"Nothing. Just want to honour her memory, that's all," I retort, rhetorically, sending him the message that I am on to his schemes.

"Oh," Jim mutters. "Well, that's why we're here," he says, with a smile.

As he picks up his end of the casket, he lowers his gaze, but I do not. Jim is such a competent double agent that even now he refuses to reveal his true position, even as I call him out on it. He never feels out of character, but he is aware that I know the truth. I grab and lift my end of the casket, taking note of the weight in my hands. We lift it off the table and carry it toward the grave.

No one says a word until we stop on the cusp of the grave. I finally remove my evil gaze away from his deceitful eyes. We wait for instruction, but when none comes, we lower the casket into the ground, in unison.

"Wait!" Miranda screams.

Everyone pauses in silent amazement. Miranda unhooks herself from Helen's arms and approaches the casket, as Jim and I hold it in mid-air. We are too afraid to move, waiting on Miranda's action. Facing the casket, she rests both hands on the top, and, very softly, kisses the glossy wood. Her lips linger for a warm second. As she pulls away, she lowers her head, and whispers, "I love you, my little girl."

She backs away, folds her hands, and drops her head. Everyone, including Jim and I, has his eyes fixed on Miranda. We rest the casket in its eternal setting and take our places beside Miranda. Chuck and Fox begin shovelling the soil back to its origin. With each heap of dirt that lands on the wooden box, I feel a piercing ache strike my heart. As the coffin falls out of sight, I worry that the memory of Alaska will follow. The two men finish their labour, and, when the hole is filled and the dirt is flattened, Pam bends down and sticks a single rose, upright, into the soil. Its red petals stand out, distinct against the dark soil. The guests smile at its sight, but I see only the blood of my fallen girl, shed at the hands of the madman.

Miranda invites the crowd into the house. Hugs and kisses abound and camaraderie oozes, as the group wipe their collective tears. The dark cloud of sadness that hung over the group during the funeral begins to dissipate, and the overall mood lightens with every step toward the house. I look back at Alaska's grave, and see the single flower perched proudly, its petals buffed brightly by the sun. It stands alone, representing both death and life, a symbol of Alaska's passing, but, also, of her life, our love for her, and of the future. I feel a natural connection to the blossomed beauty, for I, too, stand alone, and although most affected by Alaska's death, only I hold the responsibility of pushing this family past it. I am alone in my experiences with the madman, being the only one to have seen him, and I am the only one who is genuinely concerned with his presence and who recognizes his likely role in Alaska's death. I feel the weight of the world on my shoulders, but I, like the rose, will stand proud, chest out, and full of passionate intent. I will be the sole protector.

CHAPTER 15

THE RECEPTION

O UR HOUSE IS FULL OF lively chatter and hungry bellies, slowly filling up with homemade goodies. The men gravitate toward the living room, where they are enticed by a particular baseball game. The women, sipping on tea and eating biscuits, take refuge in the kitchen. Our living room and kitchen are an open concept design and I find myself somewhere between them.

I feel like an outsider to both cliques. I stand with my back against the wall, assessing the groups' dynamics. Chuck, the most rugged of his group, is most interested in the game. His passion lifts him off the couch during the intense moments. Fox endeavours to gain favour with Chuck by showing an interest, partly fabricated, in the game. He sits next to Chuck, responding eagerly to Chuck's moves. Jim sits, demoralized, on the arm of the couch. He knows a fair amount about sports, but isn't fanatically involved with any. He is docile, for the most part, but makes comments, now and again, between mouthfuls of pistachios from a bowl on the neighbouring coffee table. Fox offers me a seat, but I give a simple wave, indicating that I am content where I am.

The ladies in the kitchen are not totally dissimilar from the men, positionally-speaking. Miranda sits between the other two, leading the conversation and dictating the direction it takes. Pam sits to

Miranda's right, studying Miranda, and responding readily to her words and to her gestures. Helen stands to Miranda's left, her back against the counter. She is minding the steeping tea and is only half participating in the conversation, a skill she learned from Jim, no doubt. Helen appears like a figure out of an impressionist painting, blending into the background so gracefully that her presence can go unnoticed. Her white hair melts into the white wall behind her and her dress blurs with the drapes that hang loosely nearby. My eyes relax as they gaze upon her. She notices my stare, greets it with a warm smirk, and is abruptly redirected, as the kettle whistles for her.

I rest my head against the wall behind me, look upward toward the ceiling, and get lost, for a moment, in the hypnotic blandness of the monotonous white stucco. I wonder if any of this is really happening at all. I wonder if my perceptions of the lines on the walls are accurate or if I have been seeing them wrong my entire life. I wonder if the colours are really the colours as I see them, or if they are something else, entirely. I look around with a more serious filter, only to have the fog of existentialism escape my head and dissipate into the atmosphere. Then, I close my eyes and feel a slight burning behind my eyelids. I am tired. When I open my eyes again, after a minute or two, I notice that the dynamics of each group isn't changed at all. The men are still engaged in the ball game, following Chuck into the depths of America's pastime. The women are still conversing light-heartedly, with Helen standing removed, picturesquely disengaged. I feel as if I am trapped in an alternate universe where I am forced to live the same moment, over and over and over, until Captain Kirk and I solve the dilemma. Everyone looks so robotic. I find that I can predict everyone's movements and even accurately predict many of Miranda's words, as she speaks but ten feet away from me. The world, so it seems, has grinded to a halt. The people around me no longer seem like animate beings of free will, but as obviously-predictable machines. I can't help liken my house, at this moment, to an assembly plant wherein automated, lifeless workers carry out their trite duties. I feel like the only natural man left on the planet. Surely, the world has been invaded by a parasitic alien race, possessing humans, one by one, until all life is drained from each one, and I, somehow, remain immune to the alien toxin and remain the last uncontrollable being, obligated to live out his days with knowledge of what has happened. I shake my head at the people in my sight, at humanity, and go outside, alone.

I glance back at the house and through the windows, I see my guests. Miranda is the only person to recognize my escape, as she sees me walk away. We lock eyes for a moment and she throws me a seductive smile. She doesn't seem surprised or worried by my leaving the house. Pam also sees me outside, eventually, but offers no visual response. The men are completely glued to the television and my absence goes undiscovered. I continue to examine the people in the window. After a few seconds, even Miranda completely reengages in conversation. I feel completely alone, again.

I turn and face the lake. The sun is setting, and its rays reflect off the water in a brilliant display of light. The peaks of the waves sparkle brightly as they dance with the wind. I become hypnotized by the twinkling rhythm, showcased by Mother Nature. I watch and soak in its cathartic cadence. The wind is still and the sky displays trace clouds against a pale blue backdrop.

I am lonely and tired, and I am tired of feeling lonely. It has been days since the first sighting of the madman and since then, I have become increasingly distant from the people around me. I stand out from the rest of society because of my knowledge of the madman. I feel more and more reclusive, as time goes on. I am beginning to hate the passive-aggressive tendencies that are so innately embedded in the civility of humanity. I pity those who muzzle their visceral desires and impulses, in order to fit in more seamlessly with the other subdued members of society. I, however, am in no position to judge. I am acclimatized, albeit meekly, to domesticated life. I feel that I left a very real part of myself in my youth, and that the last time I lived life to the fullest, unrestrained by the structures of the social order, is when I was a child. As a man, I am a mere shell of the boy that once was, and I realize that the characters around me share similar fates. Like them, I am so entranced with the sagacious pursuit of adulthood that I lost my true self. I am as robotic as the cyborgs in my living room, desperately trying to submit to the preferred social norms and roles. Is that the destiny of mankind? Are we fated to subdue ourselves in a mechanical attempt to blend in? Are we not gods? Should the human brain not strive for more than subjugation?

We are all born with an internal ember; this ember burns bright upon birth and holds, within it, our true selves and the autonomy to unleash the natural potential therein. I, like those around me, have covered that glowing coal with refined layers of conventionality, and thereby dimming it. My engagements with the madman, however, seem to peel off the layers, and, although I feel more distant from society than I have in years, I am more in touch with myself and the true nature of days long-gone.

A brief thought is born and I chuckle to myself; the madman is unleashing the passionate and more feral nature I have subdued for so long. However, if he is, in fact, responsible for murdering my beloved Alaska, he will soon experience the fruits of his labour. I will, most assuredly, unleash my full, unhindered wrath upon him, and, ironically, he, like the proverbial Dr. Frankenstein, will have created a monster that embodies his ultimate demise. Hilarious.

I walk slowly and methodically along the grass until my feet touch the dock. I stop. Dare I cross the threshold? I can feel the madman, lurking somewhere in the wilderness, and something inside tells me to turn around and go back to the house, as if he will appear only if I will him to. My senses heighten and I grow cold, inside and out. I swing my head around to gaze back at the cottage and at those inside. Nothing has changed. The assembly line of social norms and subdued civility continues with cybernetic precision. My eyes fall upon Miranda, my beloved wife. She is as lifeless as the rest of them. I see a dim inertness in her eyes; she, too, has fallen under life's cruel spell, fated to live out her days as a subaltern, bowing down, not to her fellow man, but to life itself. Her ember is all but gone. I can't bear to look at her any longer. *I* will not be brought to my knees in subjugation! *I* will live as I am meant to live. I dare step onto the solid wooden floor of the dock. It rattles as I make my way to the edge. With every step I take in defiance, the planks creak and moan, like warnings against my journey, but I will not listen nor will I heed their alerts. I am not a puppet, dancing aimlessly as life pulls at my strings. I am a man. I am a god.

I choose a chair, get comfortable, and peer across the lake. I almost wish for the madman to appear. I stare at the island but see nothing. I scan the entire lake. The golden sun is still shining, illuminating the greens, blues, and whites of natural scenery. I see birds fly across the sky in their flocks, and deer scamper around, playfully, in the bushes on the far side of nature's pool. On my throne I sit, high atop my kingdom, possessing dominion over all that surrounds me. I can't remember a time when I felt more alive and powerful. I am excited but my body is still, my heart is calm, my breathing is slow, and my hands are steady. I grip the ends of both arm rests, like the emperors of old.

I rest my head against the back of the chair, and run my fingers through my hair; it is longer than I thought it was. I relax my shoulders as I take a slow, deep breath. I have no thoughts to think. I expect my mind to return to memories of Alaska, but it does not. I hardly miss her at all. I do not yearn for her warmth or the softness of her fur. She was an animal that I fed, walked, and bathed; she was totally dependent on me for sustenance and maintenance. Perhaps, now, she can survive on the merits of her own wits. Such should be the fate of all living things. I do not think of Miranda either. I care little about what she is doing or who she is doing it with. I pity her grief and I wish her a speedy recovery. I do not desire her touch or the tenderness of her warm smile. I have no care for any one of my other guests. I scorn them for coming to my house to suckle at the nipple of lavishness that I have so generously provided, but frankly, I hardly give them a second thought. Those robotic pawns are beneath me. They are so subordinate to the world, a world that they, themselves, create. That makes them subordinate to, even, themselves. I pity them; simple captives, stuck in Plato's cave. Only *I* have been to the surface, only *I* have been enlightened, and *I* am the only one capable of imparting positive influence.

I return to peering across the lake and put the thought from my mind. I am cleansed of all fear and anxiety. I, simply, am. I am nothing more or less than the being that possesses my body. I am me. Suddenly, I am intrigued by something in the distance, a movement across the lake. Something, a fish or a bird of some sort, is in motion, just to the left of the island. My heart remains calm, and my hands remain steady. I sit up in my chair to get a better look. A man is swimming across the lake toward the island. His splashing makes it difficult to distinguish him, but I can guess who it is. His long, striking hair gives away his identity. It is the madman! His muscles ripple with every powerful stroke as he makes a b-line for the island. Surprisingly, I am relaxed. My breathing does not accelerate, and neither fear nor worry has presented itself. In fact, I am so level-headed that I, wisely, begin calling for Miranda. I want her to see the myth in the flesh. Frankly, I want anyone to bear witness to this grotesque spectacle of a man, so that I can delegate some of the responsibility.

"Miranda! Miranda!"

I scream loudly, but calmly, hoping she can hear me from the dock. She cannot. I run up the dock, onto the grass, and in her view, so that she can perhaps see my commotion through the window. I yell again.

"Miranda! Come outside!"

I have her attention through the glass. I wave frantically for her to come out, and I run back to the dock. When I get to the edge, my eyes find the madman, easily, as he propels himself out of the water and onto the shore of the island. He is wearing a short pair of tattered shorts; the rest of his body is exposed. Then, like a bullet, he sprints across the island platform, his leg muscles flaring with every step. He is fixed on the far end of the island.

I can hear Miranda quickly making her way down from the house, yelling, hysterically, "Brian! What's going on?! Brian?! Brian?!"

I do not answer, but keep my eyes fixed on the incredible force that is bolting across the island.

"Look! Look!" I call out, pointing across the lake.

"At what!?" Miranda yells, as she draws closer.

Miranda reaches the dock as the madman reaches the southern end of the island. He takes a hard step and launches himself through the air, with incredible force, his arms outstretched. He reaches a height that rivals the roof of the hut. He hits the apex of his arc, puts his hands together, and dives into the water, just as Miranda arrives at my side.

"What Brian? What's the matter?"

"Didn't you see it?" I question.

"See what? I didn't see anything."

"Ah, you must have just missed it."

"Missed what?"

"The madman. He was just there, running across the island," I say, calmly.

"What? When? Where is he now?"

"Well, he dove into the water just off the south side of the island. Hopefully, he'll resurface and you'll get to see him, finally."

Miranda's heart is racing and she is panting, struggling to catch her breath. I am totally calm. I find the whole thing rather funny. It is almost as if the madman is intentionally avoiding the sight of other people, showing himself to me, alone.

"Are you ok?" my wife asks. "Did he scare you? Did he do anything weird?"

She wraps her left arm around me, as she asks her questions. Then, she rests her face on my right shoulder. I find her neediness off-putting and my eye twitches involuntarily when she grabs my hand. Her hair smells stale and the sound of her voice annoys me.

"Ok, let's go back inside," I say, callously.

"Wait, wait. Is everything ok? What…what should we do? I mean… about the madman and everything."

"Not much we can do right now. I'll tell Fox tomorrow; no need to disrupt the evening."

I see a concerned look on my wife's face. She is caught up in the craziness of the event and her brain is rejecting its disarray. My next words are offered in hopes of putting her at ease.

"Don't worry, babe. I'll take care of everything. I promise. Let's just go back inside."

She is moderately conflicted by the stoicism in my words, but generally happy about the fact that I will handle the madman situation. She relaxes and her respiratory functions return to normal. She takes my hand again, and smiles, genuinely, as we walk up the lawn together. We step into the vestibule and she gives me a soft kiss on the cheek.

"I'm so proud of you, sweetie. You always make me feel so safe," she says, as she stares lovingly into my eyes. She pulls me close and kisses me on the lips, as warmly as she can. I taste the tea on her lips. It is bitter. I have to take a sip of soda to get rid of the fowl taste. Miranda re-joins the ladies in the kitchen, sending me a sultry smile, as she reclaims her seat. I squint in confusion and turn away.

The men are still in the living room. The ballgame has ended but the guys are still sitting around, talking. Clichéd outbursts of masculinity can be heard. Remarks like "What a game!" or "They really gave 110% out there!" or "That Davidson is gonna be a real player, just you watch," pour out from the group, as a cloud of testosterone consumes my living room. They are so busy with their analysis of the game that they don't notice my presence. I wonder if they noticed my absence.

Jim finishes the entire bowl of nuts. He is on the couch now, fitting in more comfortably with the other men than he did before. It is clear the he has loosened up a bit, as he is engaged in the conversation, speaking in a much more casual way than what is typical for him. His voice is more spirited than usual and his gestures are more animated. The grey-haired wasp has been reduced to a fowl-mouthed hooligan, just to prove himself worthy of the friendship of two younger men. How weak the human identity is, so transient is its persona that it sways in the slightest of breezes. I am disgusted by Jim's crippling weakness. I vow, here and now, to cling to my true identity until my dying breath. Never again will I sacrifice my true nature in favor of conformity. I will stand, unashamed of my primal existence, like the madman did right before my eyes, seeking neither approval nor consolation from the invertebrate cowards that surround me.

I look to the madman for inspiration. His exists, unapologetically, and while his intentions may be evil in nature, he rises and falls by the will of his very heart, alone, and in that, I will find my influence. For the first time in my adult life, I convict myself to living according to my true nature, whatever that may be. In essence, I don't really know who I am. Society has set the expectations for behaviour, according to gender and social norms, and I have simply complied with them. Up to now, I lived in conformance to what is proper, and acceptable, and generally expected. I imagine that most people have done the same. I feel like no one really knows anyone else. Even Miranda and I are complete strangers, both wearing masks, sculpted by society's cruel blades, and with every cut, we fall further away from our true selves. Soon, I will discover the true desires of my heart, and I will not hide them from anyone. I will come to know who I really am, and I will stand steadfast in the hurricane of the consequences, thereof. I will be a man, alone on an island, isolated, not just from the people of this world, but from the conventions of it as well. Essentially, I will be a man, apart. In a world of frauds and cowards, I will be real, I will be brave, and I will be unique.

A few quick glances proves that my parasitic guests are still festering in my house, undoubtedly, seeking to consume their host. I grow disgusted by their presence, which is like that of an unruly mess of cockroaches. It is time for them to leave, and with new-found boldness, I demand that they do so.

"Everyone, can I have your attention please? As the host of this get together, I'd like to thank you all for coming. Miranda and I really appreciate your support, and I know Alaska does too. Unfortunately, the night has come to an end and I must kindly ask you all to leave. It has been a pleasure spending this day with you. Thanks again."

My speech comes as a surprise, and everyone sits in confused silence, speechless. Miranda, with a tense look on her face, dares not question my authority in my own house. However, there is one who thinks himself worthy of such an act.

"Leave? Brian? Why do you want us to leave? The night is still young," Jim speaks out. His mouth moves quicker than his brain. But the inadequate human that he is, doesn't know any better.

Fox, a respectful man, is surprised that Jim risks questioning me in my own house, especially on the day of my pet's funeral. He responds to Jim's query by gazing upon him with amazement. Fortunately for Fox, he has the luxury of not knowing what I know, that Jim is a two-faced bastard, a hyena, thirsting to tear at my very flesh with teeth sharpened by hatred and jealousy. Chuck, on the other hand, reacts to Jim's question by sending me an apologetic glance. He, too, knows Jim's character and is not surprised by his reproach. My response is much more calculated. Jim has fallen for my trap. I lick my lips at the beckoning of my opportunity.

"Well, Jim, did I not give an explanation?"

"No," he responds, with a look of bewilderment.

"Hmm, interesting," I say. "Now, get out."

Surely, everyone in the room takes my side. I'll bet that most people are cheering, internally. I puff out my chest in victory. Finally, the evil, old dictator has been challenged, justly, and beaten. Everyone scrambles to gather his things, and I act as if nothing significant happened. I carry on with a slight smirk on my face and proceed to speak in frivolous banter, as I steer my guests toward the front door. They hurry out.

Pam and Fox are the first to leave. I hug them both and thank them for coming and for all their work on the funeral. As Fox leaves, he turns and asks, "Hey, Brian? Is everything alright?"

"Yeah, buddy. I'm great."

I know he is surprised by my interaction with Jim, but I don't want to get into it. A simple answer and mild smirk is his ticket home. He pauses for a moment and looks as if he is going to follow up with another question but decides against it. He wishes me a simple "goodnight" instead and heads for his car, just as Pam drives away.

Chuck is still inside, speaking to the monster-in-laws. Jim goes into the closet, grabs his wife's jacket, and throws it around her shoulders before putting his own on. Does nothing ever change?! Chuck is ready to go. He hugs Miranda, then me, and wishes us well. He does the same to the Cranstons and leaves. I hear his truck start up as the engine roars, but it sits, idling in the driveway.

Ah, alone with the leftovers; the Cranstons. Immediately, Jim comes to my side and puts his hand on my shoulder.

"Brian, I'm really sorry if I offended you earlier. It was not my intention."

"Don't worry about it," I emit, with the slightest of smiles.

The women stand in total silence, watching Jim and I with great intensity.

"I was just confused as to why you wanted us to leave."

"I know you were, but I don't feel that I have to explain myself in my own house."

"Of course, Brian. I'm very sorry. You're right."

"Like I said, don't worry about it."

He hugs me as I finish speaking, then, goes on to Miranda, before clutching the doorknob. Helen gives me a hug but is not her usual, cheery self. She is upset with me for speaking to her husband in the way that I did, and she wants me to know it. She slings me a dark glance that I mirror in return. She moves on to Miranda and the two of them share an embrace that lasts for more than a moment. Miranda is unreadable at this point; I cannot tell what she is thinking or how she is feeling. Helen takes her husband's hand, and nuzzles in next to him. They turn to face us. Both families face off in a classic gunslinger moment, waiting for the other to draw. Surprisingly, Jim shows the remorse of a sweet, old man. For a moment, I consider the possibility that he is actually sorry for overstepping his bounds. Helen, however, like a protective mother goose, hisses at me with vengeance in her eyes, trying to pierce with her stare. I stand tall and glare right back at the old lady. I will not be bullied in my own home. I lean forward, my eyes locked with hers.

"What's the matter, mom?" I ask, facetiously.

Helen scoffs at me and mumbles, "nothing," as she shakes her head. Immediately, Jim twists the doorknob and swings it open. He waves, as the pair exits the house. I quickly twist the lock in place. I furnish a sinister smile, impossible for Miranda to detect. Once again, my castle is cleared of would-be parasites and my kingdom is in good standing. I am lord of the manor and there is no throne worthy of my placement in it.

CHAPTER 16

THE BASEMENT

I TURN AROUND TO CATCH MIRANDA facing me, her hands on her hips. Her glare is chilled and nothing about her seems welcoming. She taps her foot in anger, as if demon-possessed. Tap. Tap. Tap. Tap. Tap. Tap. Tap. Tap. The hardwood floor echoes throughout the empty house. Her facial expression indicates that her brain is searching for the proper words, which escape her at the moment, to deliver her anger. I am not surprised. I figure that my attack on her father has upset her.

"Brian?! What the hell was that?!" she finally explodes, her fists clenched, beating the air.

"Relax, honey. Just relax. It's all part of my master plan."

"What are you talking about!?" she screams.

"Look, Miranda, we can't have your father constantly questioning my authority in this house. He has done it before, many times, and I want him to know it's not okay with me."

"All he did was ask a simple question. He wasn't questioning your authority. You were so mean to him, and he's my father, Brian. You can't do that. And what do you mean, "part of your master plan"?"

"To finally get your parents to respect me, dear. I know you can't see it, but they have never respected me and I think it's time I changed that."

"What are you saying, Brian? You're sounding like a lunatic, and what was with that crazy speech you gave at Alaska's funeral? Who do you think you are? Napoleon?"

"What do you mean? It was a great speech."

"No, Brian. It was tyrannical. Did you listen to my father's speech? It was so genuine, and from the heart. Yours was pretentious and over-ambitious. It seemed like you were serving your own agenda rather than honouring Alaska's life."

"How dare you?! You're weak, like your father!"

My insult freezes the argument dead in its tracks. A small tear rolls down Miranda's left cheek. Her face pales, as the blood drains from her cheeks. She looks. Her green eyes, filled with an icy stoicism, stand out brilliantly against the backdrop of her whitened complexion. She wipes the tear as she scurries away. I am left standing alone in the foyer. I feel no remorse. I did what had to be done and I am sure Miranda will agree with me, eventually. My logic is impeccable and my intentions are pure. I seek only to rule over what is rightfully mine.

As my wife runs up the stairs, crying, I am unusually merry. It feels good to give in to my natural desires as I begin to escape from society's agonizing prison. Finally, I am becoming the man I am meant to be, and with that, will come great power. I drool at the idea. A great burden has been lifted from my shoulders and I am finally free, free from the shackles of conformity, free from slavery in life's automated factory, and free from the virus that infects us all, as it seeks to subdue our primal instincts. At last, I am in control of my own fate.

Not only am I not upset by today's proceedings, but I am also inspired and energized by them. I hastily run down to the basement. At the bottom of the stairs, I flick on the light and my whole downstairs world welcomes me. Our basement occupies the same square footage as the main floor and is completely finished.

Miranda hardly ever comes down here, where I spend most of my leisure time. On occasion, I bring many of my friends down to watch a game or just throw our masculinity around, childishly. It is, truly, a man cave. A state-of-the-art home entertainment system poses in front of a set of black, leather couches. A huge, flat screen television is flanked by two giant speakers, which are connected to an old turntable, a gift from my father. I have an extensive record collection that no one really appreciates as much as I do. Miranda's father uses it, pretty consistently. The softer sounds of the music of his time take him back to his youth. The turntable offers him the chance to reminisce, and the music makes him smile, warmly, inside and out.

The games room houses a ping pong table, which isn't getting as much use as it did a few years ago, an expensive foosball table that I got from Miranda's father, and a pool table, custom-made by a contractor friend of mine. On the wall, hangs a dartboard and a few framed vinyl album covers from the 1960's and 1970's. My games room is one of the most extensive games rooms I have ever seen. My friends and I have had a lot of fun here, over the years.

The bar area is a beautiful spectacle; dark hardwood floor, matching cabinets, a black marble countertop, black leather stools, and four glass door refrigerators behind the counter that display a cornucopia of beers, wines, and ciders. Above the counter, suspended from the ceiling, is a chrome rack, where the beer steins and wine glasses hang like crystal bats, reflecting the halogen lighting into rainbows of colour upon the walls. The cabinets underneath the bar are filled with the various accessories anyone might need for a good night of drinking. It is truly a visual marvel, distinguished and classy, and dedicated to the veneration of liquid courage

Overall, the bar was costly and Miranda was against spending so much, especially considering I don't drink very much. However, I do love to entertain and this bar is very conducive to this end. In many ways, this bar is one of my pride and joys and has been the focal point of many parties we've hosted for special celebrations. In fact, I am considerably proud of my communal place, dedicated to entertainment and amusement. I find solace in the playfulness of the space, a space where I can escape the world and my demons, for a little while, at least.

Tonight is no different. I intend to enjoy what is left of the night. I pour myself a scotch and soda, plug my headphones into the amplifier and put a record on the turntable. As the music plays, I easily ignore the hisses and pops that the scratches cause. I watch the record spin, 'round and 'round, therapeutically cleansing me of any residual anxiety from tonight's proceedings. There isn't much to cleanse, though, I must admit. I am at ease with everything that transpired today, and, as I sit in comfort, listening to great music, I feel confident, as king of this realm. Sometimes, kings must make difficult decisions that offend some people, but a good king is usually never fully respected in his own time. His people often fail to see the brilliance of his strategies during his reign, only to recognize said brilliance, after the fact. Frankly, I am happy to fall into this category, as I continue to do what is right and consistent with the feral desires of my heart. Unfortunate as it may be, Miranda is simply collateral damage. I prefer it not to be so, but she is sick with civility's vile disease, just as severely as the rest of them. Her weakness must be cured, and I alone hold the key to the remedy. As of this moment, she means little more to me than all the other sickly lab rats going through the motions of mundane living. I sit cross-legged, unconcerned with Miranda, my marriage, or my relationship with the in-laws. No longer will I try to appease the flawed normativity of matrimony. No longer will I cling, pathetically, to matrimonial conventions by masking my true feelings. I am above such feeble-minded practices, and I vow to eradicate them, along with the weaknesses they reflect.

I finish my drink and pour myself another; this time, a double. I sip the cold liquid through the ice in the glass. My fingers are numb from holding the chilled drink, but, eventually, they escape my attention. The final song on the record is coming to an end. I finish my drink and pour another. I start the flipside of the record and gulp my drink. I plop myself back down on the couch as the world in the song blends with the one around me. My senses dim and my perceptions grow hazy. I stand up, my glass, half-full, put on my headphones, and begin to sing along with the music in my ears. I twirl around, getting caught in the cord. I stumble, trying to untangle myself, and laugh at my own stupidity. I finish my drink, chew a piece of ice, and pour another. I spill a little on my shirt. Two songs play in their entirety before I manage to get my shirt off. For the sake of continuity, I decide to take my socks off, as well. As confident as ever, now in only my pants, I dance, if you can call it that, in ridiculous patterns to the songs playing in my ears. I am untamed by etiquette as I bring the glass to my lips once again. I catch my likeness in a mirror and point wildly at the man, reflected therein. He is as uninhibited as I am, and almost as good-looking. I like him, instantly, and feel a miraculous kinship with him. I speak to him.

"You! You are the summit. You are the summit, my friend. Don't ever forget it."

I stumble closer to him and salute him, as he does the same. I lean toward him; our foreheads meet. Suddenly, cool, silky fingers caress my back. I turn to see Miranda. A vision? I didn't hear her come down the stairs. I sober up really quickly. I remove my headphones and stop the music. Her face is gentler than it was before and she humbly lowers her eyes, only looking into mine, periodically. She slides her arms underneath mine and around my waist before pressing her check up against my chest. She pauses there for a moment before speaking.

"I don't want this, Brian."

Tears start to flow down her face. She has always been quite sensitive and quick to cry.

"I was in bed trying to sleep but I just couldn't. I kept reaching for your hand and missing you. I hate that there's a wedge between us right now. I don't want this, even for a second. Can we please discuss this?"

"Ok, sure," I mumble, as I rest my hand lightly on her side.

I am in no mood to apologize and I get the feeling that she feels the same. I figure that we can still come to a middle ground and return to our amicable relationship; a desirable outcome, considering her antagonistic attitude would reduce the efficacy of my designs. I have to have her in my corner if I am to square off against her parents. As much as I want to, I cannot empathize with her. She is beneath me, a simple pawn in a great game of wits. She has not learned what I have learned. She has not yet come to life, as I have. She is diseased. I mock the blasphemy of her emotions, an imitation of life, governed not by her, as she imagines, but by centuries of social regulation. Her feelings are not her own. She has surrendered them to humanity's societal construct, not yet reclaiming them as I have. She is a robot, programmed by a computer called "humanity", and I will counter her mechanical emotions with a cold impeccability of my own. I will fight fire with fire, by pitching machine against machine. I will attack the very source of her feelings, crippling her argument, and bring her stance to ruin. I allow her the first move.

"Brian, I have to say that I still think that what you said to my father was out of line, but I am willing to admit that he may have gone too far in challenging your authority. And, of course, I should support you in that. I just wish you had handled it more politely. He is my father, after all."

"Ok, anything else?"

I bait my hook.

"Well… I'd like to know why on earth you gave that crazy, aggressive speech during the funeral. It was like you were possessed, Brian. I could barely recognize you."

The sadness on her face is easily recognizable.

"Okay," I say. She has taken the bait. "Let me explain something to you. Over the years your eyes have missed things that my eyes have seen. Your kind heart has muzzled your survival instincts, and because of that, you fail to realize what stands right in front of you. Your vigilance lies dormant within you, hidden inside a quiet slumber. You search far and wide and so intently for the good in people that you fail to see the evil, waiting at your door step. Your parents have always been out to get me. Let me say it again, Miranda. Your parents have always been out to get me, and recently, your father has increased the intensity in which he is doing so. He thinks me unaware but I am no fool! My vigilance is strong! I fight back only to defend that which is deservedly mine!"

I thrust my fist in the air to emphasize the anger that I spout from my lips. "Your father seeks to crumble the pillars upon which our love has been built. He would have seen our marriage to ruin if not for my resistance. My rebuttal tonight was a statement, simple and clear, intended not just for his ears, but for the legion of hatred he houses inside. I will no longer be victimized by his sinister schemes! You Miranda, wish for a polite response from me? Ha! Life has turned you into a robot, meeting civility's cruel requirements at every turn. Such is the path that leads to ruin, I'm afraid. Had I acted similarly, your father would have torn out my heart like a hyena, standing victor over my lifeless corpse."

"Brian, what are you talking about? You are seeing things that aren't there!"

"No, Miranda. Your eyes fail where mine succeed. Can't you see? Everything I do, I do for us. I must defend our house against the violent hordes of evil your father sends our way. I will not stand watching while your parents seek to poison our love. I will show you the way, Miranda. You just have to trust me."

"You know I trust you, Brian, but you're acting crazy. You're just paranoid, and scared, so you're acting out. You need to fight against those impulses and remain civilized. The world is not against you!"

Her words cannot possibly hold any less use to me.

"No, Miranda! In this case, civility is as much an enemy as your parents are. We must fight them both. I can no longer reduce myself to the mere peasant that this world would have me be."

"Ok, Brian. Let's cool down for a moment. Let me try to

understand you and where you are coming from. What have they done to make you feel this way? Be specific."

"Miranda, weren't you there when they spoke to me? Your father suggested that I remove my glasses and asked me when I would finish painting the garage."

She stands in silence, expecting more. After a long moment, she speaks.

"And...?"

"You don't see it! You don't see it! My God, why don't you see it?!"

Both fists fly through the air in clenched rage.

"Their attacks are disguised in the mundane and you do not see it," I continue. "But I forgive you. I will show you the way. Everything I do, I do for us. Everything I do, I do for us. I will reach back into my youth and pull out what remains of my unadulterated spirit and keep us both safe from those that would seek to muzzle our power."

"I just don't understand. You're using such intense language, describing such intense feelings, while there is very little actually going on. Brian... you're scaring me."

I decide to take a more subtle, strategic approach to this battle.

"Alright, Miranda, you're just going to have to trust me. You're blind to your parents' menacing intentions toward me, but I forgive you. They cloak them efficiently, in stealthy pretence, I will admit, so, I'm not surprised that their own daughter has difficulty discerning their true intentions. In any case, I will have more tact while defusing their bombs."

A lie.

"Because I want you by my side, Miranda," I continue. "Without you, there is no need for any of this. And I will rescue you from a life of slavery."

"Slavery to what?"

"Slavery to a lesser you, a version of yourself that has been subjugated to what is normal, or expected, in accordance with the civility of social life. I hold that, over the year, we both have become lesser versions of ourselves in order to fit in to society's inhibiting guidelines. I promise to not let that persist any longer."

"Ok, so what was your speech at Alaska's funeral about? It was superfluously aggressive, no?"

"I believe that there is responsibility in death, and that we, the living, are responsible for keeping Alaska alive in our hearts. Sadness, despair, and nostalgic reminiscing are useless in accomplishing this goal. I felt the need to remind our guests of their responsibility. Your father's speech was an incoherent compilation, comprised of the hopeless ramblings of an old man. In no way will his tearful affirmation of love keep Alaska's spirit alive. His speech was a selfish waste of time and I find it offensive that he would use his words to forward his egotistical cause."

"Well, I guess that makes sense. But, Brian, when most people grieve, they take my father's approach, not yours."

"Most people aren't as strong as I am."

I leave it at that. Miranda pauses in thought, for a moment, and then, shakes her head, as if to shake the confusion from her mind. Her facial muscles relax. She runs up and hugs me tenderly. She kisses me on the lips, before sinking her head underneath my arm. We stay in the moment for quite a while, rocking softly back and forth. I pity the young girl. She is in love with the enemy of her family, and oblivious to my cause, and theirs.

"Be still, my Juliet. Be still, my Juliet," I whisper into her ear, receiving no response.

At that moment, I wonder how it is possible for Miranda to love me as much as she does. I don't have an answer. I wonder if it is possible that I will ever love her in the same way, but I doubt that I am truly capable of love.

"Miranda?"

"Yes, Brian?"

"I'd like to tell you something."

She looks up at me with inquisitive eyes.

"Of course," she replies.

"I want to tell you the real reason I wanted everyone to leave early tonight."

She smiles, mischievously.

"Ok, tell me."

"I wanted everyone to leave so we could be alone."

I grab her waist and, with both my hands, pull her toned body up against mine. Not another word is spoken between us for the rest of the night. Her love and my passion both manifest into the same entity and our separate wills become one. She kisses my lips, as her hands caress my chest. I slide her blouse up and off and feel her skin against mine. I pull her in closer and unhook her bra, her tongue still in my mouth. It falls to the floor. She removes my shirt in return, and I can feel her soft breasts against my chest. I grow hard as my hands slide down her firm legs. Her skin is smooth and it titillates my senses. In less than a moment, we are both naked. She pushes me down on the couch and straddles my hips. Gently, she slides me inside her and begins to bounce with a majestic, rhythmic cadence. Her breasts rise and fall with each springing motion. I wrap my hands around her firm buttocks and pull her in close. Her breasts are pushed up against my chest. We both start to sweat, fusing our bodies together as one. I run my fingers through her long brown hair and feel the dampness from perspiration. Her movements begin to quicken. She moans, now, with every thrust, bouncing harder and harder until she climaxes. I quickly flip her over, spread her knees apart, and press my body between her legs. I enter her. She moans with pleasure. Her toned body arches each time I drive myself into her. Her ecstasy grows stronger and louder. I run my hands across her chest and down her muscled legs. Her soft breasts shake loosely with my movements. I grab her tightened thighs just above her knees. I spread her legs further apart as I pull her body close, entering her repeatedly. Her mouth is open and she is screaming with pleasure. Her eyes roll back and I quicken my pace. She screams louder and louder out of pure ecstasy. I hear her audible pleasure and a devious smile rips across my face. Only a beast of a man can pleasure a woman to this degree. My natural instincts are activated as I pump myself into her, harder and faster. Her body shakes violently and she screams a finale, as I come deep inside her. She continues to moan and twitch as I hold her legs up close against my body. She has reached a higher climax than ever before in her life. In this moment, I am more than a mere man. I am an animal.

CHAPTER 17

HIGGINS

I WAKE UP, AND NOTICE I am on the floor next to the couch, completely naked under a small, thin throw. Miranda is just as naked, on the couch, her face pressed into her right arm and her left arm wrapped around a pillow. Her breasts are packed firmly on the leather cushions and her toned back muscles flank the concave structure of her spine. Her seductive torso is half-covered, her naked legs exposed to the cool basement air. She looks like a beautiful mess, harmonizing chaos and creation.

My head aches and I feel dehydrated, probably from the amount of alcohol I drank last night. Miranda is still sleeping, so I carefully avoid waking her, as I get up and go upstairs to get a drink of water. I am dizzy, too, and as the sun shines through the windows, a sharp pain rips through my eyes and brain. I slam my eyes shut and cover them with my hands in resistance. I stumble my way over to the sink and manage to guzzle down a full glass of water. Immediately, I brew a cup of coffee. I plop myself down in front of the television and start up on a crossword puzzle.

Not long after that, Miranda shows up. She leans against the doorframe of the kitchen entrance in nothing but my dress shirt. Her long, brown hair hangs sultrily around her face. She smiles at me as she folds her arms. Her slim, soft legs, one of which is bent at the knee, sparkle in the rays of the sun. Her left foot is resting against her right shin; an absolutely sexy pose. Although she does not say a word, her sleek body calls out to me, aching for my touch. I cannot take my eyes off of her.

"Hey gorgeous,' I say. "You look so sexy I could eat you!"

She says nothing in response but slithers over to me, sits in my lap, crosses her legs, and wraps her left arm around my neck. I put my coffee cup down and squeeze her tightly with both arms. She stares lovingly into my eyes, then, puts her lips close to my ear.

"There is a sanctuary in my heart of which you are the owner, and I have filled that place with love."

She kisses my lips with aggressive purpose, grabs the back of my head, and forces my lips into hers. She gets off my lap, and goes to the fridge to extract the ingredients for a steak and egg breakfast.

After we eat, Miranda remains at the kitchen sink, still washing the dishes left from last night. I creep up behind her, put my arms under hers, massage her naked breasts, and kiss the nape of her neck. Her eyes flutter and she moans with delight as she leans into the kiss. A few seconds go by, I release my grip and give her a well-deserved smack on the ass, to which she chuckles, playfully.

"Wanna go to Clint's bar tonight, honey?" I ask.

"Ooh, yeah, that would be fun."

Clint is the owner of the local watering hole in town. 5th and Main, as it's called, is a quaint place, and there are usually a good number of people there, at any given time, especially at night. For the most part, everyone who goes to the bar is from town. Only very rarely, will passing strangers stop in, but, even then, they quickly become friends with the townies, a welcoming bunch. Clint is quick with a joke, of course, if he needed to boost the excitement in the bar, and can be the life of a party. I don't know much about his past. Frankly, I don't know anyone who does. He is a closed man, in the most open way. He is very social and outgoing, but he never really engages in important conversation, and when outside the bar, he keeps to himself. He is the type of guy that everyone knows, but not well. It doesn't really make a difference to me; I see him as the perfect bar owner. He doesn't pry into your deep, personal life, but will listen, if you want to share something with him. He won't bore you with mundane details about his own life, but will entertain you with tales of grandeur and jokes that you've never heard before. I quite enjoy his company and always have a good time when I go to 5th and Main.

Miranda turns to face me and continues washing the dishes. The morning sun shines at her through the large kitchen window, putting her beautiful face and sexy body on brilliant display. I stand and stare at perfection. My body aches for the feel and closeness of hers. My blood boils with passion, as my natural male instincts fire up in sexual desire. I am just about to pounce on her, like a jungle beast on its prey, when the phone rings, disrupting my intent. I reach for it, reluctantly, and put it to my ear.

"Yea, hello?"

"Brian?"

"Yes."

"Hey, buddy. It's Sergeant Fox."

"Oh. Hey man, what's up?"

"I'll get right to it. It's about the madman. I'd like you to come down to the station today, if you don't mind. There are some things I'd like to talk to you about. Is that okay?"

"Yea, no problem, what time should I come?"

"Well, I'm just finishing up some paperwork, so why don't you come in a few hours. That cool?"

"Yup, perfect. See you in a bit."

"Thanks, bud. See ya'."

The idea of speaking about the madman gets me excited in ways I haven't felt in a long while, and I am completely distracted from my attraction to Miranda. I fly downstairs as excited as a young child on Christmas morning. I put a record on the turntable and lay the needle down gently. The diamond cuts into the vinyl with a smoothness that I find quite charming. The music plays, I walk over to the bar, take a glass from the rack, and pour myself a beer. I watch the crisp, golden drink cascade into the glass. I rarely drink, and almost never drink alone, but in the last few days, I have felt like dulling my senses with some pleasant self-medication. I sip the beer. It is ice cold but I snicker at the taste. I've always found the taste of beer to be repulsive, like poison, and technically, it is. Although desired by many people, beer really *is* poison to the human body, and its effects are the mere degeneration of bodily and brain functions. I am not sure why so many people drink so much alcohol. I don't really fit in with that crowd. I could never justify drinking myself stupid, in my own mind, but for some strange reason, today I feel like it would be a good idea. That is precisely why I mentioned Clint's bar to Miranda. I am looking forward to letting loose tonight.

I finish my beer and think it my last before I drive into town to meet with Fox. I put the empty glass in the sink and go to the couch. The music is lively and I begin to sing along with the tune. I have been in a good mood all morning and it continues as I listen to the music. I start to play imaginary instruments, and wave my arms around wildly in the air. As the song finishes, I get up, pour myself another glass of beer, and slam it back. The next song begins and I continue to sing and perform the assumed movements of each musician in the band. I walk over to the amplifier and turn up the volume to an unhealthy level. The music thunders through the entire basement; the bass seems to shake the very foundations of the house and I am sure that Miranda can hear it on the main floor. I pretend I am conducting an orchestra to the tempo of the music. With every blast of sound that shouts through the speakers, I flick the conductor's baton, aggressively. I actually feel responsible for the symphony of sound that is pounding through the house. The song ends and I take a bow, receiving applause from an illusory audience. The next song takes flight; a very aggressive song. I pause for another beer. With my baton in one hand and glass of beer in the other, I turn to face the orchestra once more. The baton waves violently, punching the air in union with the thunderous bass. The smile on my face is so genuine and unadulterated that it would bring joy to even the surliest of people. Just as the most aggressive part of the symphony arrives, I feel Miranda's hand tap my shoulder. She winks at me, smiles, and walks over to the amplifier to turn the volume down. She laughs.

"Ha, ha! Brian you look like a wild man, waving your arms around like that. Have you gone mad?" she asks, with playful rhetoric.

"Maybe," I joke, as I finish the rest of my beer.

"And, do you really need the volume to be this loud? It's shaking the whole house."

She chuckles. "Anyway, Sergeant Fox just called again. He said that he's ready anytime for you at the station now."

"Oh, okay, thanks."

"So, why are you going to the station?"

"I'm not entirely sure. Fox called me this morning and said he had some news about the madman. I'm anxious to find out what it is," I report, casually, trying to conceal my excitement.

"Really? I wish I had gotten to see him last night. I just missed him I guess, although he hasn't been causing anyone any harm lately."

I struggle to keep the truth about Alaska's bruising hidden, though the news is pushing on my tightly-closed lips and pressuring my mouth like an expanding hot air balloon. I still think that the madman is responsible for Alaska's death, but I am not ready to tell Miranda, yet. It will bring no benefit to our family at this time; it will only upset Miranda. It is difficult to hold my tongue.

Telling a half truth, I respond, "True, but it might just be a matter of time until he does." I try to end the conversation, "Either way, I won't feel safe until we figure out what's going on. There's no use speculating, until then."

"True enough," Miranda replies. "And when you get back, we'll have some dinner and then head out to 5th and Main? Is that still okay with you?"

"Sounds perfect. Anyway, I'd better get going."

"Are you sure that you're okay to drive? How much beer did you have?"

"Nah, I'm fine. I only had one glass."

Another lie, and no remorse.

"Well, I can drive you into town if you need."

"No, I'm fine. Like I said, I only had one."

A third lie, and still no remorse.

"Ok, honey. Dinner will be ready when you get back."

Miranda kisses me on the cheek and runs up the stairs in haste. I pour myself another beer and gulp it down as the song finishes. I stagger over to the sound system and shut it off. I am drunk. My senses are numb and I have little control of my movements. I am in a super-good mood, though, probably because my inhibitions are numbed. As I turn to head upstairs, I am hit with a momentary dizzy spell and lose my balance. My head bobbles involuntarily, for a second, and before I can regain control, I smash my leg against the couch, sending shooting pains up my thigh. Grimacing, I clutch the afflicted limb with both hands and stumble to the top of the stairs, taking heavier and louder steps than usual. I find nothing but humour in this calamity.

I barely remember to grab my wallet and keys, before heading outside to my truck. I am careful to avoid contact with Miranda in fear that she will notice my drunken state and forbid me from driving. I am fine. In fact, I am convinced that I am an even better driver in this state. I turn the engine over. I don't remember hearing the roar of the engine but the radio is on and I've got traction, so I figure the truck is running. I don't think people should drink and drive but I am no ordinary person! I am a god! I am a king! I am ruler of this home, of this town, and of the people who I allow to dwell here. I am not restricted by the rules created to govern ordinary people. I am above them, beyond them. In no way do those rules apply to me. Drunk or not, I will not give up the freedoms that are, rightfully, mine. I am to reclaim them, whenever and wherever I want.

I speed along the road, headed for town. The truck wavers slightly, from side to side, but I pay no attention. The driver's side window is rolled down and the fresh, cool breeze feels delightful on my face. I am not afraid. I repeat that thought, over and over, in my head. I am not afraid. I am not afraid. I am not afraid. I am not afraid. I am not afraid. I am not afraid. The absence of fear feels wonderful for so much of my life has been lived in terror. I used to be afraid that the Cranstons didn't like me, that people judged me for my lack of education, and that Charlie is a better father than I will be. I used to be afraid no one in town actually liked me, and I was even afraid that I would never be good enough for Miranda. I was, generally, afraid to do anything that I truly wanted to. The fear came out of a concerned paranoia that folks around me hated elements of my uniqueness. It was as though every time I expressed myself, my peers despised by opinions and ideas. Even as a child, my true thoughts seemed to diverge from what was normal, so I hid them. Despite my best efforts, I could not contain all of my instincts every moment of the day so they would surface every so often. They were met with hatred and judgement. As I grew up, I learned to suppress those emotions, feelings, and instincts, so as to conform to society more seamlessly. I sacrificed my true self for a more normal, accepted existence, but, at this very moment, as I drive, I am free from those fears. I no longer desire to fit into an ideal, social mould. Right now, I am not denying myself the true pleasures of being me.

Once again, I find my thoughts focused on the madman. He is also a man with no fear and no desire to subdue his natural instincts to worthless human constructs. He is above society, beyond it, and I will seek the same position in this world. I let myself imagine the possible particulars that Fox wants to tell me about the madman. Maybe he has discovered his identity, or maybe he has the madman locked up in a jail cell, waiting for me to identify him. Maybe the madman has confessed to killing Alaska, and Fox wants me to hear his very confession. My mind is flooded with ideas and I enjoy every notion.

Up to this point, the madman has garnered celebrity status around town. He is known by the police, my immediate and extended families, Chuck's family, Jeff, the marina owner, and anyone else who has heard of him. In my mind, however, he holds something more than simple notoriety. He is not necessarily something to aspire to, but, to me, he has definitely become an icon, representative of certain aspects of a desired lifestyle and mentality. He has no fear or inhibition; he is as naturally himself as he can possibly be, and his attitude is not adulterated by an obsessive need to assimilate to society, as that of most people. I want what he has, ardently, and I often feel that achieving that level of autonomy should be the main priority in my life.

I pull up to the police station and park my truck out front, a bit over the markings, but I can't be bothered to correct it. I shut off the engine and an eerie silence overtakes my faculties. In a moment, I collect myself. An intense paranoia sweeps through my mind. I worry that Fox will sense my drunkenness, so I take a few deep breaths and try to get myself together. I swish my mouth out with some water from a bottle in the cup holder, and pop a few pieces of gum into my mouth to mask the odour of alcohol. I sit and chew, until the unpleasant taste that has infected my mouth since my last beer is replaced with that of a more pleasing peppermint. I take a few more deep breaths and venture out of the truck. The ground sneaks up on me, as I exit the driver's side, causing me to stumble, but, immediately, I regain composure and walk tall toward the entrance of the station.

Somewhere between the truck and the front door, I convince myself that I can pull this off without notice. With each step, my confidence grows, and at the moment when my hand pulls the door open, I am composed and poised. I stroll, casually, into the lobby. The first thing I see is Officer Higgins, inhabiting her usual space behind the front counter, head down, writing on a stack of papers.

Typically, as I enter, her head remains down, and her expression, the only one she has ever displayed, remains sterile. Her hair is tied in its usual tight ponytail, hanging out through the opening at the back of her police cap. I marvel at the definition of her facial bone structure. I never noticed it before now, but this time I can't take my eyes off its outline. She glances long enough to recognize me. She is strikingly beautiful. I stare at her breasts as I approach, trying to determine their size through her tight police shirt. Her lips are full and I imagine how they would feel pressed against mine.

As I near the counter, she yells out, over her right shoulder, to Sergeant Fox, alerting him of my arrival. Her voice is strong and youthful, with a subtle, sexy rasp. The sound of it excites me. I draw closer and lean over the counter to engage her attention.

"Higgins, can I ask you something?" She finally raises her head and peers through my sunglasses with a rather annoyed look in her eyes.

"What, Mr. Dawson?"

"Why would anyone on earth quit modelling to become a small town police officer?"

Charm oozes from my tone.

"What are you talking about? How would I know?" she says, rather rudely. I am, however, unaffected by her surly response.

"Well, why don't you tell me why *you* did? Maybe we can start there," I say, with a tempting smile. I am sure no one has ever been so debonair.

"I was never a model," she argues, quite frankly. The softening of her face muscles, nonetheless, indicates she is warming up to me. She hasn't smiled, just yet, but the tightness in her expression is loosening, ever so subtly.

"You sure?" I query, slyly, not letting go of my tempting smile, meant to be flirtatious. "You can admit it, you know? No one will look at you any differently, I promise," I coax, as confidently as I can. I slowly turn my focus elsewhere, making her yearn to have it back.

"And what do you know about models?" she asks me, my back turned away.

I return my attention to her and see her smiling, pleasantly. I have her. I lean one suave arm on the counter and flash a devilish grin that entrances her. I dip my head and peer over the upper rim of my shades, hypnotizing her even more. Her breaths grow more rapid in anticipation of my response, as her chest rises and falls more quickly now. Our eyes lock and she has completely forgotten about her previously-captivating paperwork.

"I know that even the best models in the world aren't as beautiful as you are."

I wink at her and walk around the counter, toward Fox's office, not waiting for a response. Her jaw drops and she stares in awe. I am not sure why I flirted with this young girl, but I did and it went really well, clearly. Habitually, I am not nearly as smooth with women. Without prediction, the madman's effects are displaying benefits. I feel so free, free to be myself, and free to say whatever I want, without worrying about the outcome.

As I walk by Higgins, I check her out, fully and unashamedly. I look over her entire body, from head to toe, with no consideration for subtlety. She is well aware of what I am doing, and she is not offended. In fact, she bites her bottom lip out of sexual excitement, as my gaze caresses her firm body. Our eyes then meet again and she begins to smile, seductively. I return her smile with a sexy grin of my own. My eyes are full of powerful confidence. My glare seems to drive her wild. Her hands begin to pull tightly at her shirt, tucked in at the waist, in a sexually-nervous display of pent-up energy. I turn, and even though my back is now her scene, I can feel her eyes follow me, and her pheromones exploding into sexual frenzy. I smile a sinister smile of victory, as I come to Fox's door, knowing I have left her wanting more.

The blinds of Fox's office are completely shut, so I knock on the door and wait for a response. I stand with my hands on my hips and my chest puffed out. I have the confidence of a champion Roman gladiator, returning home after a brilliant victory, to the delight of everyone in the Colosseum. Finally, Fox comes to the door, opens it slowly, and with a gesture, offers me a seat. There is a quiet nature about him, today, much different than the brazen young man who greeted me the last time I was in the station. He closes the door behind me, locks it, and sits down behind his desk.

The mood in the office is sombre, to say the least. He makes eye contact, only briefly, and it appears his chin has an attraction to his chest. Fox doesn't say a word. He is fidgeting, nervously. I find it strange that, after inviting me to meet with him, he is struggling to engage. I grow impatient.

"So, Sergeant, what's up? Why did you ask me to come down here?"

My words surprise him, as he realizes he can no longer dodge my attention. He settles down, and with a serious expression, he folds his arms on the table, his fingers entwined, and leans forward. I am gripped by intrigue, but am calm and relaxed. I cross my legs casually and lean back in my chair. He begins to speak.

"Something happened," he starts. He pauses, as if to regain his strength, before continuing.

"Something bad has happened, Brian." He trembles as the words leave his lips. He fails to make eye contact and his face becomes deathly pale, as he continues to stammer.

"It's bad, Brian--- and I'm not sure what to do."

I lean forward with interest, uncrossing my legs.

"What happened, Fox? What happened?"

He finally builds up the strength to meet my eyes, but conveys only weakness and sadness. He stares at me for a moment, fights back tears, and steadies his lower jaw. As tears slide down his cheeks, for the first time, I see Fox for the child that he still, actually, is.

"Mark Pratt is dead."

The incredulous news bounces off the walls, leaving a deafening ringing in my ears.

"What!?" I holler, in total surprise.

"Yea, dead," he replies. "But it gets worse."

The crushing weight on my chest makes it difficult to inhale.

"He was murdered," Fox continues. "Murdered, in his own home, just last night. I found him this morning, in a pool of blood."

My heart sinks to the floor. I can't move and can barely get the air I need to breathe.

"What in God's name happened?

"Well, I went to pick him up at his house this morning, like I always do before our shift. I was already somewhat concerned because I wasn't able to get a hold of him all morning. When I walked up to the porch, I noticed the front door was open, slightly. I began to worry at that point, so I rang the doorbell. I waited a minute or two but there was no response. I pulled the gun from my holster and kicked the door open with my foot. It swung open easily and I entered the premises."

Fox is speaking to me with increasingly 'cop-like' jargon. He reverts to such diction when he is worried or scared. He is shaking as he tells his story, his voice, unsteady, and his tears flowing, consistently.

"As soon as I entered the house, I saw clear signs of a struggle. Furniture was knocked over, the television had been smashed, there was a bookcase on its side, and shards of broken wood all over the floor. I didn't see Mark, until I probed around some more. I found him in his bedroom. He was lying face down in a puddle of blood. He had severe bruises on his body and multiple stab wounds. I alerted the proper authorities and they arrived shortly after. There's a CSI team from the city there, right now. I just got a call from the coroner. She told me that Mark had thirty six post-mortem stab wounds. Apparently, he had been beaten violently, with a large piece of wood, and succumbed to the trauma to his face and vital organs. After that, though, the killer stabbed him thirty six times. Thirty six! Thirty six?! Thirty six. Thirty six."

He repeats the number until it becomes a chilling whisper, barely leaving his mouth.

"The coroner said that the killer would have known that Mark was dead long before he stopped stabbing. Evidently, Mark was unable to put up much of a fight. There were no skin cells under his fingernails. In fact, there was no blood outside of the bedroom. The CSI team said that means the killer ransacked Mark's home after he had killed him. Also, it is very likely that Mark was still asleep when he took the first series of beatings."

Fox is giving me information at a torrid pace, like it's poison, and he is desperate to spew it from his body. I don't find it hard to keep up; however, every word he says stings my brain and leaves a mental scar. The description is horrifying and my stomach turns as Fox unfolds the account. My mind is racing to make sense of what I am hearing and my heart aches at the loss of a human being. I wait for Fox to say the name of 'the madman'. That's all I want to hear. I want Fox to stand up and shout it in anger. Vengeance rages in my heart, and it's as if hearing the name of the madman will free my rage from its chains. I feel like I am going to explode, my seams bursting with violent thoughts of revenge. I am about to be consumed by my lust for violence, when Fox continues, so I listen, intently.

"Apparently, Mark was stabbed with one of his own kitchen knives, the only thing missing from the house. Obviously, we are unable to get prints from the missing knife, but that also means that the killer did not enter Mark's house with the intention of robbing him. It seems as though the killer entered the house for only one reason, murder, cold-blooded murder."

I shudder upon hearing the motive.

"Wait, so how did the killer get into the house?"

"I was told that the killer picked the lock to the sliding doors at the back of the house. This means that the killer left through the front door, leaving it open, as he left. I guess he wasn't too concerned with concealing his identity, leaving through the front door like that."

"So when did all this happen?"

"I'm told that it probably happened between 2 and 3 o'clock this morning. It was still dark out and, apparently, there are no strong witnesses to anything peculiar. I haven't even told Higgins yet. I don't know how she's going to take the news."

Then, it dawns on me that I was invited to come down to be told personally.

"So why did you call me down here? You think this has something to do with the madman, don't you?"

"Yes, but not only that. I am officially making the madman a prime suspect in the case. Unfortunately, this also means that, as per prudent protocol, I have to properly submit the report of Alaska's bruises."

"Wow. Okay, yea, that makes sense."

I am surprised at how quickly everything is happening and how serious everything has just gotten.

"And, just so you know, Brian, I will be in contact with Silas Hammerstein. He has banking connections and will most likely be the best chance of identifying the man you've been seeing."

"I've already spoken with him. He gave me some good information, but nothing that you don't already know."

"Be that as it may, he's still our best lead in identifying our man. Plus, he's bound by certain confidentiality restrictions, so he may not have been able to tell you everything. He'll be legally obligated to give me all the information he has on the subject. I'm betting that he knows a thing or two that he hasn't told anyone yet."

"But wait," I interrupted. "I thought you would have contacted Silas days ago, when I first told you about the madman. Why didn't you?"

"No, no, I did. I've been trying to contact him since we found Alaska. No one at the station has been able to get a hold of him. You know as well as I do that his secretary works out of his office in the city. We're still waiting for a response from her, too. As soon as I get in touch with him, I'll let you know what I find out. If I don't hear anything by tomorrow, I'll finally get to use my badge for more than a paperweight."

"What do you mean?"

"Well, I'll procure a warrant, allowing me to search his office for information. It should be easy now that we've had a murder. I mean, he might be on vacation or something. If that's the case, it might take weeks to hear back from him. I'll have to accelerate the process. We don't have time to waste, here. After all, there's a killer on the loose in our town, like a wolf, running wild in a herd of sheep, tearing at the collective heart of our fair citizens."

"It's a scary thought, isn't it Sergeant?" I ask, rhetorically.

"Absolutely, it is, which is why I want your help on this. I could use all the capable minds and able bodies I can get. I would feel a lot better knowing that the town, as a collective unit, was united against this threat. The evening news will announce the murder and imply that the killer is still on the loose. That will make our citizens aware of the situation and allow them to take whatever precautions they see fit."

"Sure, Sergeant, I would be happy to help."

I have the eagerness of a young child.

"But, Brian, there are two things I need you to do for me. I need you not to talk to the press about the madman. The last thing this town needs is a rumor about a killer madman, when we have no evidence linking him to the crime. The fact that we've known about his existence might upset some people, even though we really have no legal reasons to suspect him."

"Okay, sure, and what's the second thing you want me to do for you?"

Fox leans in, with a deadly look on his face, his determined eyes lock onto mine like two missiles.

"I want you to help me catch the son-of-a-bitch!" His thunderous words resonate across the entire room and reverberate in my chest. My eyes widen with excitement and my heart pounds.

"And, I know I'm putting you at an inconvenience by asking you to be honest about Alaska, which probably means that you'll have to tell Miranda the truth about what happened. I apologize for that.

I hope that she's not upset at you for withholding the truth, until now. She seems pretty rational and I'm sure she'll understand that you only did it to spare her feelings. Anyway, I just want to thank you for everything you've done lately. I know it's been a difficult time for you, but I'm guessing that you're as motivated to catch this creep as I am."

He is right about that.

"Alright Fox, when do we start?" I ask, licking my lips at the notion of a hunt.

"For now, I want you to go about your business as usual. I am going to use you strictly for reconnaissance, and I will let you know when it's needed. There is no sense putting you in harm's way, but so far, you're the only one who has seen the madman, so I figure that you're the best man for the job. But, like I said, as of right now, I want you to stick to your plans. Did you have any plans for the rest of the day?"

"Yea, Miranda and I were gonna head over to Clint's tonight. Chuck's usually there and I felt like getting a few pints in me, ya' know, to try and loosen up a bit."

"Perfect. Keep calm and act casual. I'll swing by the bar later on and give you some more instructions. I might need you to do something as early as tonight. Mark's funeral will be in a few days and I'd love to be able to tell his family that the murderer has been caught. He was a brave kid and his death will have been in vain if we can't take this killer down. Are you with me, Brian?"

"Damn right."

We shake hands with fierce intent. Fox has a way of making me feel like a young soldier heading off to war, excited, confident, and ready for battle. I jump out of my chair, stand at attention, signal to Fox that I am leaving, and swing the door open with very real purpose. I feel so alive, that rare feeling when both the brain and body are united by a strong, common goal. This type of readiness is typically reserved for the imagination of children, but here it is, hardening the inner core of my being, as I walk through the office.

I notice that Higgins is not in her usual place at the front counter. I imagine her in the bathroom, playing with herself to erotic thoughts of me. After all, that type of veneration is fit for a king, like me. Outside the station, I proceed proudly to my truck, ignoring the breeze that pushes at my face. I get in, start the engine, and head home. As I speed through town, I notice townsfolk out and about. I take pity on them, for they will never know the true feeling of freedom, like I do.

CHAPTER 18

THE TRUTH

ON THE DRIVE HOME, I begin to sober up. I think about how to tell Miranda the truth about Alaska's death. I try to predict her possible reactions. A woman's mind is often a convoluted arena, and she may very well accept the past decision not to tell her, or she might throw a shoe at my head. It can go either way. Maybe I should get a helmet, just in case. I keep the windows rolled up and leave the radio off to avoid any distraction while I prepare the words for a difficult conversation. I should focus but thoughts of Officer Higgins interrupt with greedy incessancy. I can't get the image of her sexy, tight body off my mind. I want her. I lust after her. Miranda and what I have to tell her don't matter anymore. I think only of Higgins and imagine what I would do if we were alone, together.

I am home. I spring out of the truck, look around for Alaska, and remember that she is tucked away in her grave. I miss her. Inside the house, I notice that the kitchen table is set for a grand feast. I beg the gods to spare me from my in-laws. I don't see or hear Miranda anywhere. As I draw closer to the table, I take note of only two place settings, and breathe a huge sigh of relief. I swear that if Jim and Helen are here, I will run right back into my truck, and drive far, far away.

Miranda strolls into the kitchen, quietly, puts her arms around my neck, and kisses my cheek. She has an innocent smile on her face.

"So, it's just the two of us?" I ask, out of sheer paranoia, even though the table is set for two.

"Yes, honey. It's just you and me." She smiles, kisses me, and pulls out my chair. My heart aches as I sit, knowing what I have to tell her. She went to all this trouble for me, and I have to give her bad news. I debate postponing the details of the bruising on Alaska's neck, but I know it won't be any easier for Miranda if I wait. It's hard to look at her, as she takes her seat across the table.

"So, how was your day, honey? What did Sergeant Fox want to talk to you about?"

No turning back now.

"Not so great, babe. I have some bad news."

I stare at the food to avoid her gaze.

"Bad news? How bad?"

"Pretty bad actually, and it affects us, indirectly."

I am hesitant to get in to the thick of the story. I am more comfortable beating around the bush. Even though I have recently begun to view Miranda as a robotic slave of the social system, I view her as innocent, undeserving of the pain I am about to deliver. Yet, suddenly, a peculiar and entirely different thought comes to me. I think the pain may be good for her. Perhaps, it is pain that emancipates us from a shackled life of conformity. I am certainly no stranger to pain, but I have been freed. Miranda will simply have to endure what I have lived with for so many years. In all likelihood, she will be better off because of it. My heart grows tough and I launch into the story.

"There's been a murder in our fair town," I report, abruptly.

Miranda freezes, her eyes fixed on mine.

"A very gruesome murder, actually, and some of the details are going to upset you, but I want you to be strong."

"Who died? What happened? I...I...." She begins to panic. I interrupt her.

"Just relax, babe. Let me finish. Everything is going to be fine, I promise."

"Okay," she says, submissively, and slouches down in her chair, making herself smaller. She drops the cutlery on her plate, making an unpleasant sound. The food is getting cold, as is the mood. I take her hand, and her eyes re-engage.

"Officer Mark Pratt was murdered in his home early this morning."

Miranda jerks her hand from mine, bringing it up to cover a gasp of shock.

"He was beaten to death with a piece of wood while he slept in his own bed. Sergeant Fox found him in a pool of blood."

Miranda's eyes widen with horror, as I share the gruesome details.

"Not only that, but the killer stabbed him thirty six times after he was already dead. You know what that means, don't you?"

"No, what does it mean?" she drags her words in suspense.

"It means that the killer got pleasure out of it."

I let that sink in for a moment. Miranda's eyes begin to leak sadness and overwhelming surprise.

"He used one of Mark's kitchen knives, too. Didn't leave fingerprints or anything like that, so the police don't have any leads. Fox told me that a CSI team from the city was at the house all day and that the murder will be reported on the evening news."

"Do they…do you…does Fox think this has something to do with that homeless guy you've been seeing on the Hawkins property?"

Clever girl.

"I'm glad you ask. Actually, Fox and I both think that the madman might be involved with the murder, especially when you consider that Mark was savagely killed with a simple block of wood."

"Oh, my goodness. I can't believe this is happening." Miranda trembles in her seat.

"There's more, I'm afraid. Unfortunately, this murder has something to do with us."

"What do you mean? How? What are you talking about?"

I see the fear in her eyes as clearly as I hear it in her voice.

"Now, before I tell you, I want you to know that I don't want you to get upset with me. I think you might, but I don't want that. If you do, it won't be justified. I had to do what I did to protect you. I had only the most noble of intentions, I assure you. I forbid you from getting angry with me. It is not deserved, nor will it be tolerated."

"What are you saying, Brian?"

I take a deep breath.

"Okay, so, we do expect the madman to be involved in Mark's murder, but we also expect him to be involved in Alaska's death. When Dr. Chun examined Alaska's body more closely, she found bruising around her neck. I, immediately, accused the madman but Dr. Chun and the police assured me that it was just as likely that Ally got caught up in the reeds and choked. But now, considering that she never had any problems with the reeds before, we're thinking that something sinister may have been at play. I guess Fox thinks the deaths are linked and may have something to do with the madman. We're doing everything we can to---"

"Why didn't you tell me?" Miranda interrupts, solemnly.

"I was going to, but I wanted to wait until your grieving was over. I was afraid that it would make you feel worse and I didn't want that. Plus, at the time, we didn't really have any reason to suspect foul play."

"Except that you knew she was strangled," Miranda charges, sarcastically.

"Yea, but it was just as likely to be the reeds, or even another animal. Look, Miranda, we still don't know what happened. It may have been an accident. It may---"

I stop, mid-speech, as I see her shake her head in disappointment.

"You should have told me," Miranda says, stoically, a fire raging beneath a calm visage.

"That may be so, Miranda, but remember that I was grieving, too, and I thought I was making the best decision at the time. It broke my heart to see you as sad as you were. I really didn't want to add to your pain. My sole priority was to help you be happy again. It's always a husband's first priority. I'm telling you now because Fox is making the madman a prime suspect in the Pratt murder, and he'll probably try to link the two crimes. I haven't enjoyed keeping this from you, Miranda."

Miranda sighs. After a moment of silence, she lifts her head and shoots me a striking glance.

"I understand, Brian. But I'm sad, and I'm scared. There's a killer on the loose in our town, and he's been on our property! What are we going to do? This is insane!"

"Well, the police are going to handle it, and Fox---"

"Forget the police!" Miranda roars, with rage.

I am frozen by her words and aggression.

"Do you love me, Brian?"

"Yes."

"Then, find this guy and slit his throat!"

Miranda stands up and storms off, tears moistening her face. I am awed by Miranda's hostility. She rarely loses her temper, but this time, she is more savage than ever before. She doesn't promote violence in any way, but it is clear she is afraid, and her rational mindset is replaced with a lust for vengeance.

I sit back in my chair, musing all that has just happened. I think it all quite absurd. A strange madman comes to town, and then, murders start. The facts are inextricably linked, but I find no solace in this theory. The atrocities are adopting pragmatic form, as our town begins to live under a blanket of terror.

Over and over in my head, play my wife's ferocious words. "Then, find this guy and slit his throat." "Then, find this guy and slit his throat." "Then, find this guy and slit his throat." Over and over, again, the recording resounds, aggressively, in my head. I can't forget her words, nor can I forget the look on her face. Her soft spirit was absent from her eyes. An entity, fuelled by pure rage, has taken its place. Initially, the terror in her eyes was easy enough to see, but the conversation ended when that terror turned to hatred, hatred for the killer, hatred for the madman, and hatred for fear, itself. I take her words to heart. "Slit his throat." "Slit his throat." Do I really have to slit his throat? Will justice or vengeance be served through this particular act alone? Surely not. I am, however, under loving orders to execute justice, apparently, by killing, if necessary. Miranda said, "This guy." It plays on loop. "This guy." "This guy." "This guy." I don't know who "this guy" is. Perhaps, it's a woman, or a child. A teenager? Quite clearly, Miranda's quarrel lies not with the killer, but with the idea of the killer. In any case, I have been charged with the responsibility of eliminating the threat altogether, and I will do just that.

I ponder the kind of person it takes to perform such a task. The answer comes to me immediately. I think of a lion that possesses the strength, the intellect, and the courage to protect its pride, and rule the jungle; an ideal figure to emulate. My primal instincts have been unleashed and are eager to prepare me for the assignment ahead. The town is my pride and I am its Alpha male. The town will succeed or fail by the blanket of protection that I provide. Hope is rooted more deeply in me than in anyone else. I am king. I am Alpha. I am protector.

It is a tumultuous time for my pride; a jackal lurks in the shadows. It seldom reveals itself, playing the most sinister of games. It moves to strike us down, one by one, until fear and death have gripped our hearts and minds. It has been successful. The town is beginning to panic and the local media is about to announce the murder. Like a chess master, the jackal has strategically positioned his pieces and is soon to strike, once more, at the sensitive flesh of our fair town. I, like the vicious kings before me, will stand and fight. And I will be victorious!

My thoughts turn to Jim and Helen, who have, incessantly, torn at my underbelly for years, waiting for the right time to launch one final offensive to cripple my spirit, once and for all. Their schemes are remarkably similar to that of the jackal that tears at the underbelly of our sheepish town. I hate them, as I hate Mark's killer. I decide to deal with the jackal in the same way that I will deal with the Cranstons, by unleashing my primal instincts. I plan to eliminate the threat as quickly and efficiently as possible. One thing that I am sure of is that Jim and the jackal have much in common. In fact, as I let my thoughts wander, the distinctions between them begin to blur. Both are vicious schemers, intent on terrorizing me and all those whom I love, most dearly. Helen, too, cannot be forgotten. She is a demon, disguised as a harmless angel, and has a constant desire to infiltrate my defences and destroy me from within. She, too, is a jackal, and would soon feel the wrath of my ferocious nature.

I am not subtle in my assumption that the madman is guilty, although there remains a slight chance that Mark's murderer is not the barbarian that I have seen on the Hawkins' island. In any case, I will be as a beacon of hope, shining brightly, for the whole town to see. I will conquer those who seek to destroy me, and save the town from a vicious killer. I will be an example to all those who are enslaved by their pathetic desires to conform to social norms, all those who sacrifice their true natures for the sake of fitting in.

I begin to eat.

CHAPTER 19

I AM MAN

I T WAS A PEACEFUL MEAL, but now I think the right thing to do is to go upstairs and see where Miranda is hiding out. She lay on the bed, her face buried in the pillows. I sit beside her, gently, softly lay my hand on her back, and stroke her hair, affectionately. She lifts her head, slowly. There's evidence she has been crying; her hair is stuck to her face, but after brushing it away, I see the glitter of dried tears on her cheeks. She makes no movement and offers no words. The unbridled rage she displayed before dinner no longer exists. I snuggle in close, continuing to smooth her hair. So much like a child she is, forever in need of my comfort and guidance. Oh, how I pity her. In this cruel world, I am sure that my doting over her is doing more harm than good. How I wish she were tougher and more mature. My meditation shatters when she finally speaks.

"Sorry about that, Brian. I didn't mean to storm off like that. I'm just so scared, scared of being helpless, and scared of being hopeless. If people are dying, then---"

"It's alright, Miranda," I interrupt. I hold her face with gentle hands. "I don't blame you for being scared. I think a lot of people are scared. This is a terrible situation."

"Yea, I know, but I shouldn't explode like that," she admits, clearly fishing for reprieve.

"True," I say, giving her none.

"And I really shouldn't take my anger and fear out on you. You don't deserve that," she continues, apologetically. "I'm just terrified, Brian. First, there's a madman running wild, just across the lake from us. Then, our dog is murdered, and then, a police officer is killed in cold blood. I feel like we're all getting picked off, one by one. Any sense of security that this town once offered has been completely obliterated. I feel as if it's only a matter of time until death enters our front door, Brian. I don't think I can live like this."

"Well, first of all, we don't know if Alaska was murdered or not," I assert, partially in jest, to lighten the mood.

"Be serious, Brian. No number of reeds in the world would have been able to strangle Ally. She was a big, strong Husky, and she never went into the lake without us. You know that."

"Yea, I know. Okay, I suspect foul play, too. I just don't want to jump to conclusions."

"Jump to conclusions? Brian! Mark Pratt was bludgeoned to death, and then stabbed thirty-six times, for nothing but pleasure, and you're worried about jumping to conclusions? Give me a break, Brian! Conclusions are jumping at *us*, at this point."

"Alright, you're right. There's a madman on the loose, slaughtering people, one by one, in hedonistic cold blood, with his bare hands, a block of wood, a butcher knife, and his indulgent lust for carnage. Let's just put that on the table and take it for granted. Feel better?" I ask, sarcastically.

"Well, at least we're finally calling it like it is. So what are we going to do about it?"

"Fox is doing everything he can, and tonight, at the bar, he's gonna give me some more instructions. We're going to get him, Miranda. I promise. I promise I won't let anything bad happen to you."

"I know that you mean it, but in reality, what chance do you have of protecting us from a crazed killer?"

And just like that, she cuts off my balls.

"I mean, no one around here knows how to fight or anything. Shit, Brian, you've never been in a fight in your life. And the police, obviously, can't protect us. They're the ones getting murdered." Miranda sighs, then, continues. "Maybe, we should just leave for a while, until this whole thing blows over. What do you think?"

"I think we have an obligation to this town and to our loved ones, to help defend them from all threats that may knock at our doors. Isn't that what---"

"Oh, please Brian, don't romanticize it. I don't want to be hunted like fucking deer! I don't want to die, Brian, and I don't want you to get hurt, either. Why don't we just leave and let the police handle everything?"

"Look, Miranda, life rarely gives us responsibilities that we are happy to receive. We need the town to band together. If we left now, we ruin any chance of that. Plus, if everyone leaves, the killer might leave, too. And he might move on to another town, or just wait for us to return. I don't know what's going on, Miranda, but I know leaving isn't the answer to our problems. I can't help but feel integral to this whole thing. It seems the madman has chosen to reveal himself only to me. If he's going to try to kill me, or anyone I care about, he's gonna have to be willing to take on the entire town. That's the highest form of love, Miranda; facing death for the people you care about. I don't think we should leave."

"But this doesn't have to be *our* fight. Why can't you just let it go?"

"Ok, fine. I'll make a deal with you. If we can't solve this by the end of the week, then we'll leave. Until then, keep the doors locked," I demand, with a grin.

"Gaahh! That doesn't make any sense Brian. But, fine, we'll do it your way. Remember, I do have my parents to think about."

"Exactly," I say, proudly.

I realize how much I enjoy the thought of an upcoming battle. Finally, I have reason to put the full array of my newly-found confidence on display. I am reborn, and beyond the sheltered realm of society. I vow that, from this moment on, I will live only according to my natural, unabated instincts. I think that if I, successfully, honour my primal self, I just might have a chance to stop the madman. I feel like it is our only hope.

Miranda turns over and stares up at the ceiling without emotion, her eyes directed straight ahead. I lie beside her and replicate her stare. I think to myself, I am man. It is the only clear thought that I can hold in my head. I am man. I am man. I am man. And man, I truly am. I embody the quintessential spirit of man. I am tapping into something that I have missed my whole adult life. I savour the moment, in sweet anticipation of battle.

I get up and go into the bathroom. The mirror reveals changes; my hair looks longer and coarser, the veins in my arms protrude more distinctly, the hair on my face seems thicker and darker, and my chest flares out more. These physical changes seem to reflect the change in my newly-adopted attitude. I sense a darker aura surrounding my soul. I lean toward the mirror and growl at the reflection.

"What are you doing, Brian?" Miranda scowls.

"Brian growl," I grunt, parodying the speech of cave dwellers. I no longer see need for eloquent speech.

Miranda laughs, hysterically.

"Well, what Brian want do now?" Miranda tries to mimic the low gruff pitch.

"Brian nap now." Another attempt at troglodyte-like tone.

I slip roughly under the bedcovers, turn my back to Miranda, and pass out.

CHAPTER 20

THE NIGHTMARE

M IRANDA IS NO LONGER IN the bedroom and I am alone, once again. I must have napped for more than an hour. I jump in the shower and let the water rain down over me, as I close my tired eyes for a moment. I recall my nightmare, which sends shivers up my spine. It was quite a vivid nightmare, and as I recap the events, an eerie feeling grips me, again. I dreamed of gargantuan spiders, with hideous legs, evil eyes, and black and white fur. They crawled toward me, peering at me with sinister eyes; their intention was evident, and terrifying—kill Brian! They came in droves and eventually broke into my fortress, my home. They attacked from all angles, scurrying around, quickly. Armed with a knife, I began stabbing at them in a wild attempt to save myself. Each time I slashed one, the wound would magically heal, and the spider would double in size! Soon, my fortress was swarming with them and I ran outside. I gored them, ferociously, but they continued to grow larger, more frightening, and more sinister with every slash. They multiplied at such a rate as to completely bury the entire house and grounds. Panic-stricken and riveted with fear, I began to run. I noticed I wasn't wearing any shoes, and the cool dew of the grass on my bare feet made me stop. I saw Miranda in the kitchen window, by the sink, washing her hands, surrounded by a black and white mass of spiders. She seemed protected by an invisible force field; immune to their evil. She looked at me, smiled, and I woke up.

I shudder at the thought of pure evil emanating from the spiders in my dream, an evil that cannot be killed or reasoned with, hell-bent on destroying me. It has such a hold on me, cerebrally, that I check the floor of the shower, fearful that I might see a furry, black and white invasion at my feet. I have never been into dream interpretation, or kismet, or anything like that. To me, that stuff is childish voodoo, or outright scams, but I must admit, I am fighting the urge to interpret the message of *this* dream. I make a conscious effort to reject the nightmare, and focus on the warm, cascading shower stream.

I get out of the shower and start getting dressed. I am not sure what to wear. It was really warm earlier, but the night might bring in some colder weather. I can hear Miranda shuffling through the kitchen drawers, downstairs.

"Marrrr!" I yell out the bedroom door, making sure my voice carries all the way downstairs.

"Yea, hun?" she yells back.

"Is it warm outside, still?"

"Yea, it's still really warm," she confirms, knowing the reason for my question, intimately. "Just wear that nice, blue dress shirt that you have, with those new tan golf shorts. Roll up your sleeves and you should be fine."

"Are you sure I'll be warm enough? Like… what are you wearing?"

"I'm wearing shorts, Brian. Just look."

She runs up the stairs quickly, and slides into the room, putting her outfit on display. She is wearing a white blouse, tied at her waist, exposing her toned, bronzed midsection. Below that, a sexy pair of cut-off jean shorts, that expose quite a bit of thigh. It is quite the lascivious ensemble. Her hair is tied in one long braid that falls seductively to one side of her face. Her green eyes sparkle beautifully against the flawlessness of her sun-tanned face. She is donning a pair of white-laced, wedge-heeled shoes that accentuate the length and shapeliness of her legs. She presents herself as a supermodel. Miranda looks as sexy as ever and I lust after her. My heart races as heavy waves of erogeneity excite me, almost knocking me off my feet. I am stimulated by every curve of her body. She is a monument to beauty and sexuality.

"You're not wearing that."

"What?"

"You're not wearing that," I repeat, just as dryly and matter-of-factly as the first time.

"I'm not?"

"Nope, you're not," I say, and pay no more attention to her.

"What do you mean, I'm not wearing this?"

What is it with this girl? I think my words are self-explanatory.

"The clothes that you have on," I state, slowly, with a ridiculous emphasis on the proper pronunciation, "you will not be wearing to the bar tonight. Get it now?" I shake my head, in sarcasm.

"Excuse me!?" Miranda exclaims, raising her voice a notch.

"Come on, Miranda. Stop. That outfit is way too revealing. There are going to be plenty of other men at the bar tonight and no wife of mine is going to dress like that."

"Brian!" she is yelling now. "I wore this for you! I wanted to look sexy for you!"

"Yup, I understand that, and I appreciate it, and you look fabulous, but it's just not gonna happen, okay? Thanks." A very facetious distain drips from my lips with every word.

"You can't tell me what to wear, Brian."

"Nope, you're right. But if you still wanna be married to me in the morning, you won't wear that. It's up to you, kiddo."

She hates when I call her "kiddo."

"You're insane, Brian. What the hell is the matter with you?"

"Well, how would you feel if I dressed in a way that would attract attention from other women? Huh? You probably wouldn't like it either. Please, Miranda, don't make this difficult. I don't want to fight with you. Please, put on something less revealing. You can wear that for me when we get back home tonight," I snicker, jokingly. Miranda is having none of it.

"What do you think of me?" she asks. "Do you think I am some sort of slut that wants attention from other men?"

"Well, since *I* don't want you to wear that, I'm not actually sure *who* you are wearing it for. In any case, it's disrespectful to dress like that, especially if it bothers *me*."

"Are you nuts, Brian? We're going to the bar tonight to dance and have fun. I want to wear something fun!"

"Okay, wear something fun, but not revealing. I'm sure you can throw something together. Lord knows you have enough clothes in that closet of yours. I have to say, if you can't find something fun and respectful in the plethora of clothing you have back there, you've been wasting your money."

Miranda begins to get extremely frustrated. Her face is turning red and she is on the verge of tears. I decide to go with a softer approach.

"Look, sweetie. I just get jealous sometimes, that's all. I mean, you're the hottest girl in the entire town. I don't want guys getting the wrong impression and I don't want people to think my wife is a floozy. I know *you* may not care what other people think, but *I* do. Please, just consider my feelings."

"Brian, I don't want you telling me what I can and can't do," she states, calmly.

"I don't want that either, but I also don't want a wife who dresses like that with other men around. So, you make the choice. Fair?"

She doesn't answer me. She just goes into her closet, slamming the door behind her. It seems my softer, alternative strategy worked, but frankly, I am angry that she even has the audacity to resist me. Do I not sacrifice many things to appease her feelings? Surely, she can sacrifice an outfit for me. My logic is immaculate, and it looks like my demands have been met with little resistance or consequence.

"A piece of me dies every time you do this," Miranda says, as she comes out of her closet, wearing a new, more conservative outfit. I decide not to respond. She doesn't appear angry or sad, just defeated. Her movements are slow and methodical. She sits down beside me, on the bed, her gaze glued to the floor. She folds her hands in her lap, and freezes like a statue. I stare at her for a moment but she does not engage me. Tears do not drip from her eyes, but I can feel her self-worth being sucked from her body, as if she is split open and all that comprises her self-esteem pours out. I really think that people are better at denying their true selves because they have been doing it for years, pathetically trying to conform to fit the molds of a monotonous society. The powers that be need not use violence or fear tactics to keep us lowly peasants in line. They merely need to suggest a proper social order and the pitiful human would desperately try to fit in. Generally, people work mindlessly for the better part of their days, their weeks, even their years, all so they can be functioning members of a structured society. Most people give the better part of their lives to secure a place in social normativity yet, Miranda struggles to sacrifice an outfit, to satisfy the desires of the man she loves. Perhaps, as people are constantly subordinated by society, they feel the need to recapture their autonomy when apart from it. They act out, in spectacular ways, to convince themselves that they are free, despite failing to recognize the flawed logic behind their endeavour. Miranda is certainly not an exception to this category of people.

Her outfit is quite different from the other. She is now wearing a basic pair of flats, undoubtedly designed to be as boring as possible, a pair of blue jeans, that in no way accentuate any curvature, and a short-sleeved, plain white T-shirt, long enough to cover her stomach and buttocks. Her hair is no longer in a pretty braid but tied tightly in a commonplace ponytail. She looks prepared for a dull day of puttering around the house. She so lacks charm and any form of charismatic spark, that I find it difficult to see her as an attractive woman. My jealousy is put to rest. For me, it is the perfect outfit for a night at the bar. More than content, I stand up to leave.

"I don't even think I wanna go anymore, Brian."

"Nonsense!" I exclaim, grabbing Miranda's hand and pulling her up and out the bedroom door.

We run playfully through the hall, down the stairs, and out the door. Night is falling, but the air is warm and humid. I put Miranda in the passenger seat, like a gentleman. I settle myself behind the wheel and fire up the engine. Miranda looks at me as if to say something, but merely sighs and turns away. Backing out of the driveway, I spin the tires in the loose gravel, like a teenager showing off with his dad's new truck. As soon as we hit asphalt, the radio gets switched on. A few minutes of the cold shoulder routine go by, as Miranda leans away from me, her elbow against the door, and her head in her hand. She rubs her forehead in a way that suggests she has a headache. I glance at her, feeling neither pity nor remorse, but the thought occurs that I may have to deal with her childish antics later tonight. I tend to that probability in a proactive manner.

"Miranda, please, I don't want it to be like this all night."

"Well, you should have thought of that before you ordered me to change my outfit."

"I didn't order you to do anything, but if you want to dress like that, when we go out, then I want to re-evaluate my position in this marriage, that's all. No one was ordering anyone to do anything. If you want, I can take you back home, and you can put the old outfit on. You won't have a husband in the morning, but maybe it'll be worth it for you."

"Come on, Brian. Don't you see how insane that sounds?"

"No I don't!" I say, adamantly. "We're both free to do what we want. I was simply explaining the consequences of your actions, had you not known them already."

"I should be allowed to wear whatever I want, Brian."

"Absolutely, and indeed you are, but, am I not, then, allowed to react as I see fit? Or are you the only one with freedom in this relationship? I don't want a wife who dresses like that. If you simply have to dress like that, then this relationship isn't going to work out."

"Oh, fuck off, Brian! You're impossible!"

"Excuse me?!" I scowl, as the inside rage begins to grow, exponentially.

She doesn't respond.

"Did you just swear at me?" I prod, bringing the truck to a dead stop at the side of the road.

"Leave me alone, you idiot," she retorts.

"Okay. Get out," I tell her, cloaking my intense anger in a calm pretence.

"What?"

"Get, out."

"What are you talking about?"

"Get out of the truck, Miranda! What is so difficult to understand?"

The colour of her face pales as fear takes hold.

"I'm not getting out. That's crazy. We're---"

"Get out! Get out! Get out! Get out!" I scream, ferociously, stomping the floor of the cab like a crazed lunatic.

"Stop Brian, Stop!" Miranda shrieks, in complete horror, tears running down her face, and her back pressed up against the door.

"Get the fuck out!" I yell so loudly that I taste blood in the back of my throat. I smash the steering wheel with my fists in a wild frenzy. "Get out! Get out! Get out!"

Miranda, terrified, opens the door and slides quickly out of the truck. I hammer the accelerator. The engine roars and gravel spews dangerously out from behind the tires. I reclaim control of the swaying truck when I hit asphalt, and the passenger door slams shut. Miranda remains on the shoulder, tears pouring down her face. She collapses to the ground in a puddle of sobbing and unbelief. The rear view mirror keeps her in my sight, but it takes just a few moments to lose sight of her in the darkness of the night. I smile a smile of victory, as Miranda's pathetic face becomes a distant memory. I continue onward into town, the radio still blaring.

CHAPTER 21

5TH & MAIN

I AM SO HOT THAT THE windshield is fogging up, so I roll down the window and rejoice in the cool wind licking my face and neck. Visibility improves. I turn the radio up and sing along, joyfully, with each song that echoes over the airwaves. I cool off to normal, both temperature and mood-wise, and have only a fleeting thought of Miranda. I wonder who will be at the bar, tonight. I hope Chuck is there; he is always good for a laugh. Quite assuredly, Clint, the owner, will be there, too. It has been a while since I last saw him, and I look forward to seeing him again. I know that, at some point, Sergeant Fox will arrive. It is the first time in a long time that I am out without my wife, and this altered dynamic feels good; maybe better, if Fox brings Higgins with him. I drool over the chance to ogle her perfect figure, and I imagine myself caressing her trim and tight body.

The truck approaches the lights of town. A few turns, and I am on Main Street. I roll up my window as I enter the parking lot of the bar. There are other vehicles in the parking lot. I think I'm in store for a wild night. Mark's murder comes to mind. Channel 6 News stated earlier that there was a suspicious death within the town limits, and that more details would be provided as the story unfolds.

I doubt the obscurity of the story keeps many people away from the bar. It certainly isn't cause for panic.

A few steps through the entrance, I survey the atmosphere. The focal point is the long, wooden drinking counter, in the far right corner of the room. Clint is behind the counter, talking to Chuck and his son, Terry. There are two pool tables, presently in use by people I don't recognize. To my left, against the side wall, are a number of cozy booths. Shit! Jim and Helen occupy one of them. They are ordering their dinner, and haven't seen me yet, so I put my head down and walk in Chuck's direction. A few other people dot the pub, but I don't recognize many of them. There is a quiet vibe tonight; the music is playing softly, and voices are at a reasonable volume. I guess it's going to be a quiet night, after all.

When I get to the counter, I throw my arm around Chuck and shake Terry's hand. We exchange words of welcome before I engage Clint. He is happy to see me and I feel the same. We all settle into a nice, social rhythm, as if we don't see each other every day. Clint smacks four shot glasses down onto the bar and fills them with whisky.

"They're on the house, boys!" he announces, with a cocky smile.

We perform the ritual clinking of the glasses, and, in unison, slam the liquid fire back, without hesitation. The alcohol burns on the road to my stomach, leaving an absolutely foul taste. If I didn't know better, I'd think it was poison. I wince at the aftertaste, as my face folds in on itself. It takes a bit of time before I can talk with the guys, again.

"What the hell was that, Clint?"

"Ha, ha," he laughs at my inability to handle the liquor. "Whisky, straight up."

With a chuckle, I shake my head, and my finger, at him.

"Aw, poor Brian. Is a little bit of alcohol too strong for ya'? Don't forget to change your diaper before you leave tonight." Clint takes a stab at me.

The group roars in laughter.

"Oh, please. That stuff is poison. Doesn't take a real man to drink poison and enjoy it," I contest, in defence.

Chuck chimes into the discussion.

"You see, Brian, that's something that a real man would never say. That stuff will put hair on your chest. Have some more. We'll make a real man out of you, yet!"

Clint fills our glasses to their brims once more. I finally realize that, outside of Terry, I am the youngest person in this group. Both Clint and Chuck are advanced in years, and I am still a youngster in their eyes. As the four shot glasses wait, full of poison, my three onlookers are cocked, ready to judge my next move. I take my venom, hammer it back in one fell swoop, and slam the empty shot glass on the counter. After congratulatory cheers, the three men follow suit. They roar with merriment, as they down their own shots of poison, and I join in on the laughter.

"Atta boy, Brian!" shouts Clint. "We'll make a man out of you. Just you wait."

A beautiful young waitress comes by and drops off a huge plate of nachos.

"Here ya' go, boys. Enjoy!" she says. I like her seductive tone.

I know her. She is Jeff's daughter, the marina owner's little girl. I haven't seen her yet this summer, but she has really blossomed into a beautiful woman. She was off at university, as far as my memory serves me. One time, I spoke to Jeff about her schooling. He joked about how devastating the cost was to his bank account, but I have always thought that he was actually just bragging. The girl scurries off quickly to tend to other customers.

"Boys, I ordered some nachos for us," Chuck says, having already sampled a few. "Dig in Brian. It's my treat!"

Charlie, Terry, and I sit for about twenty to thirty minutes, eating nachos and consuming beers. When I, finally, look up from my gluttony, I notice that Jim and Helen are about finished with their meals. They probably observed my presence, so I excuse myself, and head toward their booth. I know that if I don't say "hi", they will, most likely, tell Miranda that I was rude to them, in their age-old effort to sully my reputation and drive Miranda and me apart.

When I get to their table, Jim smiles and greets me warmly, but Helen is as cold as ice. We speak, vacuously, for a little while, until they realize the glaring absence of their daughter.

"So, where's Miranda tonight?" Helen asks, with a cruel look on her face. Jim's ears perk up, attentive to my response.

"Oh, she didn't feel like coming," I tell them, not wanting to elaborate.

"Well, that's too bad," Jim says. "Maybe, we can give her a call, in a little while, and see what she's up to."

"Sure, she's just hanging around at home. I think she was going to try to get to bed early tonight."

"Is she feeling alright?" Helen inquires, like an interrogator.

"Yeah, she's fine. We had a wonderful day together. Just spent it at the house, being lazy," I say, laughing, and trying to lighten the mood.

Helen opens her mouth, no doubt to ask me another question, but a call from the bar interrupts her. I search for the source of the saving voice.

"Yo, Bry. Get your butt back here. We're doing more shots!" Chuck demands, becoming increasingly boisterous.

I turn back to my in-laws. "Sorry guys," I laugh. "I've been summoned. Enjoy the rest of your night."

As I make my way back to the bar, an epic feeling of relief comes over me because I can finally turn my back to Miranda's parents. I hurry to reclaim my seat. Another shot glass awaits. I hesitate. Clint detects my hesitation.

"Don't worry," he says. "I'll make sure you and your truck get home safe and sound."

I grin in appreciation and pound back the whisky shot, just as Chuck and his son finish theirs. I am starting to feel woozy and having difficulty holding my head up. For the next little while, Chuck, Terry, Clint, and I are the life of the bar. We tell stories and jokes, loudly enough to capture the attention of the patrons. I notice Jim and Helen take their leave, and I watch them fade into the abyss of the night. My cares seem to fade away as my senses dim more and more. My eyelids grow heavier and my head wants to lean to one side. I feel as if I might fall asleep. Suddenly, Sergeant Fox and Constable Higgins walk through the front door. Miraculously, I sober up and am infused with energy.

Chuck, Clint, and Terry carry on, as loudly as ever. I slouch into my seat, put my head down and fold my arms. I pretend not to notice the two police officers walking towards us, but I am not surprised when Fox stands beside me. He puts his arm on my shoulder; Higgins, at his side.

"Hey, buddy," Fox opens. "Hope you're not too drunk. I have some work for you to do."

"No, sir, not at all," I reply, lifting my head up to face him. "I was actually waiting for you."

"Yea, sorry I'm a little late. Things were crazy back at the office."

Fox orders two beers. Clint tells them, "They're on the house." The two officers sit down and join in on our boisterous fun. I am surprised at how they begin to let loose, growing louder and louder, as the night goes on. Higgins keeps relatively quiet, but she and I converse, briefly. I notice a certain, devilish look in her eye that is intended only for me. Fox looks uncomfortable in his uniform, while Higgins looks like a sexy stripper, role-playing as a cop for a bachelor party. After some time, Fox pulls me aside.

"We need to talk," he whispers. "It's important."

"Alright. No problem. Let's get a booth."

Fox, Higgins, and I sneak away, unobtrusively, from the group and come together in one of the booths on the other side of the bar. The two of them sit opposite me.

"Brian," Fox starts. "After the CSI team was finished at Pratt's house, they came by the precinct. They just left, about a half hour ago, and they're coming back in the morning. I wanted to get to the island all day today, but they wouldn't let me out of their sight, and

I couldn't tell them about the madman. I'm gonna head over there now and see if I can find any clues linking the madman to Pratt's murder."

"Okay, so you want me to come with you?"

"No, I need you to do something else for me. I need you and Higgins to go back to the station and, retroactively, document all your sightings of the madman. I know it's a little crazy for you to do it now, but if the media finds out, then we'll have "madman mania" on our hands. Also, you might as well document the details of Alaska's death while you're at it. When you're done, Higgins will drive you back here, so you can pick up your truck, or, if you don't want to drive, she can drive you home."

"Okay, sounds good. Anything else?"

"No, the only other thing I can think of is that I still can't get a hold of Silas Hammerstein, so I'll be going to his office after I visit the island. I'll let you know how that goes. Until then, it's vital that you get those documents finished tonight."

"Alright, let's do this."

"Wait," Fox says, with a look of concern. "I'm gonna leave right away. You and Higgins hang around for about ten minutes and then leave. We don't want to arouse any suspicion. Okay, Higgs?"

"No problem, Sarge," Higgins replies, obediently.

We execute Fox's plan to perfection. We go back to the bar and continue to engage with the group. Fox leaves. For the next fifteen minutes, Higgins and I laugh and joke around with the men, as if nothing is amiss. Then, we get up, say our goodbyes, and I tell the guys that Higgins is driving me home, putting to rest any suspicion as to why we are leaving together. Once outside the bar, we jump into Higgins' squad car and head for the station.

I guess the evening didn't turn out to be all that bad after all, but it isn't over yet.

CHAPTER 22

ANIMAL

THE POLICE STATION AND THE bar are so close to each other that Higgins and I could have walked. The fresh air might have done me some good, too, but here we are, in a police cruiser, motoring along the quiet, town roads, like we are running out of time. Higgins drives with determination and I like a woman with a heavy foot. She is non-verbal, her typical stoic facial expression. As she commands the course and speed of the vehicle, the silence is, actually, quite awkward. I am searching for the proper words and timing to initiate conversation. I try to speak, but am crippled by my own fear. Every time I attempt to say something, a voice inside cuts down any rational thinking. Despite the logic, which reassures me that I am superior to Higgins in every way, I am intimidated by the young lady sitting next to me. My mind is filled with anxiety and self-doubt as it reminds me that I'm so scared, I'm so scared, I'm so scared, I'm so scared, I'm so scared, I'm so scared. Over and over, and over again, the voice echoes, until all confidence and logic is obliterated.

I begin to dwell on the madman and how I am failing him, failing to live up to the new mentality I am trying to adopt. A short time ago, I pledged to live without fear, to escape from the tyranny and oppression of social constructs. Now, I am having difficulty maintaining a more instinctual, natural state of mind and being, which my true spirit seeks to reclaim. I hate myself for the pathetic weakness that I have allowed to invade my inner spirit; a weakness that has caused many relapses over the past few days. I feel diseased, like a flawed genetic anomaly, unable to exist in its proper, virile form. I start to panic.

All of a sudden, an untamed courage begins to well inside, like a malignant abscess, seeking to kill the weak Brian Dawson, as fearful and pitiful as he is. It swells, it grows stronger, it attempts to hoist a brave new champion high on its shoulders. It rages against my proclivity to adopt social convention, seeking only, in purest form, to reclaim my feral birthright. My spirit toughens. Pity, self-doubt, and remorse drain from my body like residual waste. I think of Miranda and rejoice at the memory of leaving her at the side of the road. Her weakness sickens me. Why should I allow her inferior logic to inconvenience me? I am king! Her futile desire to oppose me is a thorn in my side, but I need not allow the wound to fester. Miranda has a sick loyalty to social norms that needs to be wiped out, lest she be crushed under the weight of its oppressive bullying. As her husband, I am the one to enlighten her, and tonight's lesson is a simple step toward the light. There are many more to come, although I doubt her ability to complete the learning journey.

I decide to throw my thoughts of Miranda to the wayside. She is mundane and her predictable mentality is of no interest to me. My attentions turn to the woman next to me. Higgins' eyes are locked forward, fixed on the road ahead. Her magnificent bone structure is impossible to ignore. The curvature of her face is delicately beautiful, as if sculpted by the gods. My mouth aches for the touch of her plump lips. With each passing streetlight, the blues and greens of her eyes sparkle, and seem to be the only source of true colour allowed to exist tonight. The moonlight dances off her majestic, blonde hair. Her blue police shirt, wrapped tightly around her torso, cannot hide those sumptuous breasts. Although hidden inside a pair of police-issued black pants, I can follow every inch of her long, slender legs, until they vanish into the darkness beneath the dashboard. She is exquisite, beautiful, and statuesque, and fit for a king, fit for the gods. I want her. Her mysterious silence only makes me want her more. I sense something primal about her that, in and of itself, is driving the lust within me to the level of insanity.

"So, Higgins," I commence, as bare, primal man. "Don't think I ever got your first name."

The look of apathetic arrogance on my face is cold enough to freeze the air between us.

"Vanessa," she responds, without averting her gaze.

"Vanessa?" I repeat, seductively. "A beautiful name, for a beautiful woman."

She flashes me a glance in response. There is allure in her eyes. The raw sexuality between us is electric.

"So, Vanessa, how long is this tedious bullshit going to take? I don't have time for boring crap like this."

"It won't take too long," her answers are very robotic.

I aim to loosen her up.

"That's good. I am anxious to get back to the bar and have more fun. I bet you are too."

"What do you mean?"

"Well, I was just thinking that a pretty, young girl, like you, enjoys that kind of scene. You know, the bar scene. I bet you were excited when Fox had an obligation at a bar, weren't you? I mean, I remember my younger days. I partied like crazy. I bet you went nuts during college, didn't you?"

"Yea, I partied quite a bit."

"I'm sure you did, sweetie, and I bet you really know how to move that body of yours too, don't you?"

"You mean, dancing?"

"Yea."

"Yes, absolutely. My girlfriends and I used to be out of control. My college days were the best days of my life."

"So, why did you come to this lame town? It's not really the proper atmosphere for the popular girl, is it?"

"I guess not, but it's where I was assigned. Hopefully, I can get out of here soon and get to the city. That's where most of my friends are, and they're a lot like me; young and energetic."

"Ooh, energetic. I like the sound of that," I laugh. She laughs, too. Our playful banter is getting pretty thick. I realize that I am overdoing it, but I am not about to stop. My instincts are finally being released to run wild. My inhibitions are dissolving and I can finally be myself, completely, again. It feels good to not be afraid of the outcome.

"So, how long ago was college anyway, sweetie?"

"Um, I graduated about three years ago, but I got my degree first."

"So, that makes you... twenty-five, twenty-six?"

"Twenty-six."

"Oh, just a couple years younger than me then."

We both laugh. She is closer to ten years younger than I am, but I have a feeling that, tonight, it won't matter.

The police station nears, and we pull into the parking lot. Higgins parks the car, shuts off the engine, removes the keys, and gets out with an appealing sexiness. I watch her before I move a muscle; she is mesmerizing and I am hypnotized by lust. I reach for the door handle, missing it a few times, before I can open the door. Higgins is at the front door of the station as I get out of the car. Normally, I would rush ahead to catch up with her, but not tonight. Tonight, I feel an epic calmness, rooted in pure confidence and self-assuredness that causes me to walk slowly, poised, collected, and savvy. Vanessa unlocks the door and holds it open for me.

"Thanks, doll," I say, as I pass her, unconcerned with her response.

I am brimming with confidence. Self-esteem is oozing out of every pore. I strut into the precinct, walk directly to her desk, and sit in her chair. Her eyes never leave me. She flashes a naughty smile in my direction, and proceeds down the corridor to Fox's office.

"In here," she directs, putting my wise-guy boldness to shame.

I follow her into the room. The blinds are shut, and there are papers scattered all over Fox's desk. Higgins takes the seat of authority. I sit opposite her, lean forward, and look up to face her. She takes her hat off, and unleashes her ponytail. Her silky blonde locks cascade around her shoulders, framing her face ever so elegantly. I finally get to see her without her police cap on, and the wait is worth every second. Her beauty entrances me. As her eyes look to the paperwork, mine remain fixed upon her. I can think of nothing else but to have that fine-toned body pressed against me, and my instincts tell me that I will have it, soon. She speaks and wakes me from my trance.

"So, why don't we get started?" she cues. There is mischief in her voice that tickles my senses.

"Of course," I agree. "What's first?"

"Well, we have two things on the agenda. We have to get detailed descriptions of your madman sightings, and we also have to get a statement concerning the state of Alaska's body, as you saw her, after she was pulled from the water. I'm sure Fox will want Dr. Pamela Chun's statement, the autopsy report as well, and he would probably have wanted Mark's too…"

I jump in. "Okay, then. Why don't we start with Alaska, so we can get that out of the way?"

"Sure. Is that going to be difficult for you?"

No.

"Yea, maybe," I moan, milking the sensitive guy routine for all its worth. "I haven't talked much about her since the funeral, and even less about the details surrounding her death."

"Okay," she whispers, as she touches my hand with hers. "We can go as slow as you want."

Her regular robotic exterior that has greeted me in the past has completely defrosted, and she is finally opening up to me. She is amazingly tender, as her soft hand caresses mine. Our eyes lock for a brief before I drop my head in fake sorrow and describe Alaska's death. Vanessa writes, continuing to clutch my hand. I tell the story, uninhibitedly, revealing the details of my experience, unapologetically. Vanessa scribbles, furiously, to keep up with my account. When I cross a sensitive point, she tightens her grip as if to offer an increased level of comfort. I respond with feigned sadness that only seems to draw her in more closely. Frankly, I am not saddened or remorseful by the retelling of the tragedy. What's the use? Tears do not resurrect the dead. Every living thing is subject to the whims of death's cruel tyranny, and Alaska was no different. I am beyond death and the sadness that it causes. I am man, and death cannot touch me.

I go on with my story, pausing, periodically, to fabricate some emotion that endears me to Vanessa. She is falling under my spell. At the account draws to a close, Vanessa is in the chair beside me, her arms wrapped tightly, yet tenderly, around me. My deception is proceeding with pristine flawlessness. A tear, or two, drips from her unfaultable eyes, defining her cheekbones, and outlining the magnificence of her facial structure. I rejoice, internally, in the perfect execution of my scheme.

Vanessa keeps telling me how well I am doing, as the topic transitions from Alaska to the madman. My report, the only one that the police will have, is vital to the investigation. I emphasize how frightening the scenes were, and how I had the courage, strength, and manliness to defend my family. She drools over my virility. I can feel her sexuality rising, as she clings to every word. She begins to drip with desire. I lure Vanessa closer and further in as I emphasize specific words to bring her libido to the fore, words like rippling muscles, savage, strong, naked, feral, intense, dark, and raw. They excite her and I give her all she can handle. She crosses her legs tightly, seemingly, in ecstasy, and begins rubbing her thighs with lust-laden hands. As the description of the madman is completed, Vanessa's arms envelop me, once again, this time, with passion. My heart rate increases and my breathing picks up speed. I grow hot from the heat radiating from her body, as well. I liken the madman to myself, explaining that I share in his raw masculinity. I boast that I will conquer him, destroying him, if need be, in order to protect her and the entire town. I assert that I am more man than he is, and do not hide in the shadows, as he does. She is bewitched by lust and her body aches for mine. She presses up against me to ease the twinges of her desire, but, alas, her futile action has the opposite effect; it makes her want me more. I enclose her firmly in my arms. By this point, she is on my lap, breathing heavily, and her heart pounds against mine, out of control. She licks her lips, out of pure sexual desire. I repeat the words that sparked her arousal, knowing they will strengthen her erotic urges. She squeezes my thighs with raw sexual aggression. I grow hard and, with a violent motion, spread her legs open and pull her in to face me. Her body complies with moans of sheer ecstasy. When I rock her hips back and forth, she drives her pelvis into me, aggressively, and flips her hair back, out of carnal delight. In a frenzy of lust, she continues to sway back and forth, and side to side, rubbing her crotch across my thighs. I caress her thighs, her genitals, and her breasts, and I am as erect as I have ever been in my entire life. She, swiftly, presses her wet lips against mine, hard, forcing her tongue deep into my mouth. At this moment, I have everything I have ever wanted. We are two primal beings, acting out our most quintessential desires, and I do not want it to stop.

She continues to kiss me with blissful stupor, holding the back of my head, and commanding my mouth onto hers. I rejoice with ecstasy when she shoves her chest into my face. I rip her shirt open with savage ferocity, scattering the buttons in all directions. An elegant, lacy white brassiere holds her luscious, picture-perfect breasts, which bounce in playful amusement as she continues to hammer her crotch against mine. I am insanely jealous of the undergarment, and she knows it by my shameless groaning. Still in a state of sexual oblivion, she manages to remove her shirt and throw it to the ground in a crumpled heap. I follow her cue and, with one hand, unhook her bra. Such prowess! She sheds it seductively, displaying her plump items, proudly. She suspends the piece of lingerie above her head for a moment, as if looking for approval, before dropping it to the floor. I squeeze her melons, with dexterity, giving special attention to her nipples. She arches in delight.

I struggle, frantically, to undo her belt, and open the zipper. She stands upright, to facilitate my efforts, and rips her pants in a primal frenzy. She is wearing an incredibly-sexy, white thong matching the bra that lay, helplessly, on the floor. I pause to admire the vision. Her hair is a wild, indecent mess that I liken to the mane of a lion. Her neck and arms are slender and smooth, and her chest is voluptuously perky. Her mid-section is extremely tight and her hips are sensually narrow, giving way to the most incredible legs I have ever seen. They are long and immaculately-toned. Lust rages, uncontrollably, inside me, at the sight of her perfect figure.

She drops her underwear, as my eyes scale her legs and I grunt with an undomesticated sexual desire. She jumps on me and I catch her. With her legs, circling my waist, I sweep the surface of the desk clean with a one arm. Papers, picture frames, reports, and even the computer, crashes to the floor in a spectacular mess. I plop her nakedness down on the edge of Fox's desk, and she undresses me with uncontainable lust.

"Don't worry," I purr. "We can go as slow as you want."

I gently slide myself inside her. She begins to moan with ecstasy, pulling me closer with her legs, still wrapped around me. Arching back, she proudly displays her delicious chest for feasting upon. I drive myself into her with a ferocious barbarism, repeatedly. She screams with pleasure, and it excites me more. In a moment or two, she reaches a climax, as her eyes roll back, and her body relaxes. I allow no time for satisfaction, and no right to protest, so, aggressively, I flip her over, like a lifeless mass. Bent over the desk, her legs are spread, wide and welcoming, so, I enter her once more. She grasps the edge of the desk tightly, as I batter her, again and again, slamming myself into her, harder and harder with each thrust, as if possessed by a lust-crazed sex demon. Her wails of delight quickly turn into piercing screams of orgiastic frenzy. I run my hands along her body, searching to grope her luscious chest. I can feel her body orgasm, over and over, as I grow closer to climaxing, myself. I grab her hips, securely, and pound myself into her one last time. I yell with a primal ecstasy, but my voice is drowned out by her wails that seem to shake the foundations of the station. She rolls onto her back; her eyes still haven't found their way back to their normal position. She sits facing me now, legs crossed, as her body quivers, spasm after spasm.

When she amasses the strength to open her eyes, I am fully-dressed. She comes to me, and throws her arms around me. I slap her ass, hard, leaving a handprint, like I am branding cattle. She sucks air in through her teeth at the sexual sting, and kisses me again, one last time. I don't know if she is aware that I have a wife, but I don't care. I pull away. She stands, naked and cold. With her hands around my waist, she tries to snuggle, in affection, but I toss her aside and leave the room, a god.

Quickly, I exit the station. As my feet hit the pavement of the parking lot, they start to move more quickly. It isn't long before I am running in full stride, not giving the scene behind me even the slightest glance. In truth, I have already, almost, forgotten about it. The only thought in my head is the wish to return to my truck.

After eight minutes of jogging at a quick, but steady pace, I approach 5th & Main. The lights are now off, and my truck is the only vehicle in the parking lot. I unlock the door, remotely, and hop in. My cell phone indicates that I have a voicemail message. I'll check it in the morning. I lie down across the bench seat and close my eyes. Within seconds, I am asleep.

CHAPTER 23

THE NATURE OF EVIL

I WAKE TO THE SOUND OF the news on the television. I'm
confused and groggy and can't yet open my eyes to learn where
I am, but I am not really concerned. I am on something soft,
smooth, cool to the touch, and my body is stuck to it. I expected
to wake up in the front seat of my truck, where I remember falling
asleep last night, but I am surely in a different place, in a familiar
place. The seats of my truck are nowhere near as comfortable as this.
I guess at where I am; the couch in my man cave. I manage to open
my eyes and confirm my presupposition. Still in the same clothes I
had on last night, somehow, I made it back home. I sit up, slowly,
yawn deeply, and balance myself to keep from falling off the couch.
My eyes burn so much so that I have to shut them for brief moments
to ease the pain. I'm exhausted.

I see that the door at the top of the stairs is closed. I can't hear
anything happening upstairs and wonder if Miranda is home. I
check the time on my phone; it's 7:30 am. I remember that I still
need to read my voicemail message. I assume it is from Miranda so
I let it play in speaker mode.

"Brian. It's Fox. I have some news. I went to the island, as I said
I would, but there was nothing there. It was exactly as we last saw
it, like no one had been there in a very long time. This is all getting

pretty weird. Anyway, after that, I went to Silas's office, and, Brian, there's more bad news. I found him dead, stabbed in the neck with a pen, and strangled. It was a gruesome sight. The pen was still lodged in his neck and it looked like he had been there for quite some time, but I'm not an expert in that sort of stuff. The CSI team will arrive in the morning, and I already sent the pen to forensics in the city. If there are fingerprints on it, and there probably will be, we have a chance of identifying the killer, and maybe even the madman. I'm wondering if you have seen him recently, and if you and Higgins finished the reports. I'm gonna head home for now and try to get some rest. Please give me a call in the morning. It's important. Thanks, Brian."

It is quite the shocking news. Silas Hammerstein is dead, murdered in his office. The madman continues his killing spree, this time right in the heart of town. His audacity impresses me. His fearlessness inspires me, and his ruthlessness encourages me. Here he is, the simplest of men, making the greatest impact this town has ever felt. The savage beast will certainly go down in history, albeit for evil reasons, but his legacy will never be forgotten. I'm trying to understand where this level of evil is coming from and how someone could be so vicious. Some philosophers suggest that the ability to commit evil escapes the realm of human reasoning and that secular ethical thought is a fraudulent construct, based merely on the orientation of society. Perhaps, the madman kills for a greater good, one that he has conjured up in his mind, one that only he can fathom. Perhaps, he holds an omniscience of what act would contribute to his greater good, and, if that means murder, then, his faultless conscience frees him to satisfy the requirement, honourably. We cannot know his thoughts or purpose; his rationale transcends society's ethical pragmatism. Perhaps, the madman weeps with every strike of his fists. We are ordinary, feeble people, quick to pass judgement. Do we, who kill each other on a global scale and masters of destruction and ruin, have the right or qualifications to convict? I think not. If we are looking to condemn, we need not look any farther than the nearest mirror. We have failed where the madman has succeeded.

Before I leave the basement to locate Miranda, I call Fox. I hesitate, and it suddenly occurs to me that no one has yet suspected Fox of the crimes; his involvement would make perfect sense. He was close to each of the victims, knows how to commit murder and how to get away with it, and he has been first on the scene, for two out of three. Maybe he planted the madman as a decoy, leaving him with the perfect alibi, should he ever be accused. This theory is weak, in regard to motive, but not to consider it would be as damaging as my failure to spot it. As I reach for the phone, my hand shakes, not out of fear, but out of ominous foreshadowing that I, the protector, am destined to kill Fox. *"Then, find this guy and slit his throat!"* I dial his number.

"Fox? It's me, Bri---"

"Brian! It's about time! Where have you been?"

"What? It's seven thirty in the morning," I respond, condescendingly. "I just woke up."

"Oh, right. Sorry. It's just... I've been up all night. I'm freaking out. I'm in way over my head here, with these murders. Did you finish with Higgins, last night?"

"I certainly did, Vince." Boy did I.

"Okay, good. Listen, I think I'm gonna bring in some help from the city police. I don't think we can do this alone, especially without Mark. I don't know what else to do."

"Yea, sure, that makes sense," I encourage. "But after forensics identifies the fingerprints on the pen, we should have our man, right?"

"Yes, but they would have to match with someone who is already on file. I doubt the madman is on file. Most of the residents are, but if the killer isn't from this town, then we need the police force to cast a larger net."

"Oh, so your fingerprint lead is basically like searching for a needle in a haystack."

"Exactly, unless the killer is a resident, which is precisely why I think we need help to crack this case, not to mention that people are dying. Dying, Brian!"

"I know, I know. Bring in help from the city, then, if you feel it's the best thing to do. If you're looking for advice, I won't be much help to you. You're the expert here, not me."

"Okay, okay. I'm gonna call them in, if we strike out with the prints. The CSI team will be at Silas' office around 8:30 this morning, but I don't think that they will be much help."

"Why is that?"

"Well, they didn't find anything at Pratt's house, and that was a far more elaborate murder. I'm afraid that we will have had three murders, in less than a week, without a single, solid lead to show for them, not to mention all the procedural rules that I broke when we first began to investigate the madman. Even talking to you about the cases is against policy, but I have no one else in this town to turn to."

"Whoa, whoa, whoa, let's not get ahead of ourselves. First of all, the CSI team might find something. We don't know that they won't. And, secondly, I'm still hopeful about the fingerprints. Try not to get discouraged. You're the only hope that this town has. At the rate the killer is going, he'll probably strike again, soon."

"My goodness, Brian, I hadn't even thought of that!"

If Fox's incompetence wasn't obvious before, it is certainly becoming more evident every time he opens his mouth. The young man is an absolute mess. He has no idea what he is doing, or what he should do next. He is calling *me*, a simple civilian, for help. How desperate! His ineptitude and despondency eradicates any lingering suggestions that he is the killer. By the shake and stutter of his voice, coming through the phone with crystal clarity, I can recognize that he is terrified. No hardened murderer has the wherewithal to feign a character as anxious and as distraught. I believe in his innocence. Thank goodness, too. It would be difficult to take him out. I think him a friend, more than anyone else, of late.

"So, what do you want me to do now?" I ask, wanting to get off the phone.

"Honestly? Just keep yourself and Miranda safe. Lock all the doors and shut all the windows. When the press releases the details of a second murder, I'm sure the entire town is gonna go into lockdown mode, anyway. Might as well get an early start."

"Okay, no problem."

"Oh, yea, when's the last time you saw the madman."

I think, for a moment.

"Wednesday, after Alaska's funeral. It was the third time I'd seen him. Miranda almost saw him too, but he dove into the water just as she got to the dock. It was ridiculously bad timing, as always."

"Alright, well, if you see him again, call me right away, and I'll go get the bastard! I've had enough of this guy running around my town. Anyway, I'm just about at the station now. Is there anything else I can do for ya'?"

"Yes, actually, now that I think of it, can you pay Jim and Helen a visit, to make sure they're alright? They have an alarm system but I'm sure they'd appreciate the gesture. Plus, I think they'll heed the warning more genuinely if it comes from you."

"Will do, Brian. I'll head over there when I'm finished with the CSI team. It might be a while, though."

"No worries, whenever you get the chance. Thanks, Vince."

"No problem. I'll update you when I can."

Normally, I would be worried about the threatening situation, a murderer at large, terrorizing my fair town, but I'll be damned if I'm going to succumb to "normal" any longer. To be honest, I long for the thrill of the battle. I can't help but think that, despite all the pretence that surrounds and distracts us, the game is rather simple. Pitted against the madman, it is a deadly, cat-and-mouse game of chess, intended for me and him, only. The stage is set for nature's most primal play to unfold. I am willing to bet that he will strike again, soon, perhaps today, at some point, and I am ready, and eager, to engage.

I'll have to talk to Miranda at some point, so I decide to get it over with. I gather my wits and make my way up the stairs, and into the kitchen. Miranda is cradling a cup of coffee in both hands, staring out over the lake. There is no reaction to my presence, although I am not sure she is aware of it. Her limp, brown hair hangs onto her shoulders, and she is in an unfashionable sweater, fit for a grandmother. Her expression is one of gloomy melancholy, and her body, lifeless. I step silently closer and softly place my hands on her shoulders. Words are absent, for both of us, as we take in the scene through the window. The morning sun streaks orange and gold across the waters. A small number of "cotton ball" clouds dot an otherwise clear, blue sky. Birds chase each other, spiritedly, in a horizontal number 8 pattern, totally unaware of the sinister infestation. Do I envy their ignorance? Not today, for today, everyone will see that I have shed any and all faulty pretences that keep me from my true self, and, like a butterfly breaking out from its cocoon, I will put my primal desires and instincts on display

As we both watch the lake, in silence, Miranda starts to cry. To me, her tears are nothing but liquid futility. She has not yet realized that dedication to living a socially-conditioned life pollutes her spirit, and destines her soul to eternal sadness. Her heart is poisoned, by her own hand, and has neither the ability nor the means to overcome her grief. Despair, the venomous snake that it is, does not feel pity or remorse, and is willing to attack even the most innocent of souls. Miranda, certainly, falls into that category, having never had an evil thought, or done an evil deed. Altruism, her lifestyle of choice, does not exempt her from the confines of pain and sorrow. Her tears are not able to rescue her, regardless of how many she offers up in petition.

I rest my chin lightly on her head, hoping to alleviate her misery. She closes her eyes, but tears still stream down her face. She seems to reject my tenderness as her entire body tenses up. I try, for a moment, to emulate her thoughts, but I cannot, and want not, for my stomach feels ill. The mind of a robotic humanoid is vastly different from that of an enlightened being, like me. She is under the strict control of her perception of normativity, and, because of this, my pity for her runs deep, and it is difficult to accept her as a superior human, and my partner.

"Look, Brian," she says, squeezing my hands. "I don't know what happened last night and I don't care. I don't even remember what we fought about. All I know is that I want us to go back to normal, again."

There's that notion of "normal" again. "Okay." It sounds more like a question than a statement.

"Please promise me that you'll never, ever, leave me at the side of the road again. I cried all night waiting for you to come home. I couldn't fall asleep until I heard you come in, and then I cried some more when you decided not to come to bed. What's going on with you, anyway? You've been different these last few days."

"Nothing is going on with me," I lie. "I just feel that I sacrifice so much for you, while you're not even willing to sacrifice an outfit to honour my feelings. I mean…what kind of relationship do we have if you won't do that for me? I'll tell you. We don't have one at all. Everything I do is in the name of your betterment, but I often feel like you aren't willing to reciprocate that ideal. Honestly, Miranda, it breaks my heart." I am lying.

Since last night's argument, I haven't given her a second thought. In fact, she is nothing more than a mere afterthought, and I doubt she has the ability to break my heart anymore. I do wonder, however, if Miranda and I will ever have children. Before now, I was never sure that I wanted children, but suddenly, it's of the utmost importance to me that I create an heir, suited to receive both my kingdom and my genes.

"I'm sorry," Miranda offers. "But, sometimes, I feel like you remove my autonomy, and replace it with your own ideals. Obviously, I think that's a problem. Don't you?"

"Frankly, I think you remove your autonomy all on your own. You cling, ever so tightly, to a flawed perception of what is acceptable and what is normal that you fail to properly discern what is just and what is useful. I, simply, try to steer you down the proper path. My intentions are not to strip you of your independence, but to liberate you from a life of dependency, from a life much too preoccupied with conformity."

"That all sounds much too convoluted, Brian. I just want us to be happy together."

"Happiness can be an effective trap, if achieved through improper means."

"What does that mean?"

"It means that you shouldn't necessarily strive for happiness. Happiness is a mere state of mind, and may not properly reflect the morality by which you live your life."

"So, what are you saying?"

"I'm saying that we need to live fittingly, that we should strive for a proper life, rather than a happy one."

"What if this "proper life" you speak of, results only in sadness and despair? Should we then continue to adhere to it, despite the loathing and misery it brings?"

"Of course! The greatest choice a human can make is to sacrifice happiness for goodness. Ethics over joy, Miranda, and, I think, therein, we will find all the happiness in the world."

"This is all much too complicated, Brian. Let's just start by treating each other with love and respect, always, and I need to you apologize for kicking me out of the truck last night. That was madness, and I will not accept being treated that way."

"Fine, I'm sorry."

Another lie. I want, more than anything, to be done with this dreadful conversation.

"Okay, then."

Miranda accepts my deceitful apology as genuine.

A few more minutes of silence go by before I turn to leave. I am sickened by the novelty of marriage, and by the idea that I must apologize for acting in simple accordance with my true nature, as

I did last night. I feel there has been some love lost between us. I go downstairs, into the man cave, close the door behind me, and separate myself from guile.

The couch is comforting and I relish the silence. Despite all that is going on in my world, my mind is blank. I am unconcerned with Silas' death, with Fox's investigation, Miranda, and even the madman, himself. I simply, am. My mind and my conscience are both clear, and I am, entirely, engrossed in a Zen-like state of peace. I count the seconds, as they pass; three hundred and six, three hundred and seven, three hundred and eight, three hundred and nine, and on and on, with absolutely no wish to do anything else.

The phone rings, but I make no attempt to pick it up. I can't be bothered with such things. I hear Miranda answer, but her words are muffled. I continue to count; five hundred and forty-one, five hundred and forty two, five hundred and forty three. My peace is shattered when Miranda loudly beckons me to pick up the extension. The receiver is within reach, thankfully.

"Hello?"

"Hey, Brian?"

"Yes?" I don't recognize the voice.

"Hey, buddy. It's Chuck. How are you doing?"

"Oh, hey Charlie Brown. I'm good, thanks. What's up?"

"Not too much. Just at home. The boys are covering the store. What are you up to today?"

"Today? Umm, don't have anything planned, I don't think. Yourself?"

"Oh, nothing at all, just gonna lounge around. I'm a little bit hung over after last night. Drank too much again. Dotty would have given me a stern lecture if I had come home to her in the condition I was in last night. I was right pissed."

Chuck laughs to himself. His giggles meet dead air.

"So, what can I do for you, Chuck?"

"Have you heard about Silas?" He pauses and waits for an answer.

"Yea, Fox called and told me this morning. A real tragedy. It's absolutely absurd, what's been going on lately."

"Yes, absolutely. I've been in a constant state of fear since I heard. I think the whole town is. We need to do something about this, before it gets any worse, don't you think?

"Yes, I agree, but what should we do? Neither of us are expert crime solvers. I mean, I wouldn't have a clue how to help catch the killer. What did you have in mind?"

"I think you and I should pay a visit to Jeff Bahl."

"The owner of the marina? Why? Fox already asked him if he had seen anything out of the ordinary. He said he hadn't."

"Okay, but I don't just want to ask him if he has seen anything, I want to see if we can set up some kind of security system around the lake. You say that the madman is living on the Hawkins' island, so maybe we can get some footage of him and identify him. We would need Jeff's help to pull that off. I don't mind even spending some of my own money on this, and I could get some of the most top of the line surveillance systems in the world. The store already has some basic ones."

"You know what? That's a great idea," I support. "When do you want to head over there?"

"Why don't we go in a few hours?"

"Perfect."

"Alright, Brian, I can pick you up, actually, save you the trouble of walking there."

"Yea, sure, that sounds good. Just give me a call before you leave. Thanks bud."

"No problem. See ya'!"

I hang up the phone, rather impressed with Chuck's idea. The possibility of setting up camera surveillance never occurred to me, but it seems like the perfect way to capture our man, and if Chuck thinks it possible, then, maybe it is. I also like the idea of imposing on Jeff. I don't think too highly of the marina owner, and it is time that he helped us with our investigation. I don't plan on simply *asking* him for his help; I intend to demand it, and if that fails, I will force his hand. Some issues are bigger than individual people, and this investigation is of vastly more importance than the safety of one imbecile. And if Chuck gets in my way, he will be dealt with in the same manner. It sounds harsh, but if we are to catch a ruthless madman, we must become ruthless, ourselves. There is no time for guilt, remorse, or weakness. "People are dying!" It seems as though the problem, in its entirety, falls squarely on my shoulders, and salvation is my responsibility. If I must adopt the embodiment of primal man, then so be it, and in doing so, I will put everyone in his place. Jim, Helen, and even Miranda, will fall at my feet in illustrious veneration, to finally understand my superiority. Any who seek to bring me down, will suffer, and ultimately, revere me as king! It is time.

CHAPTER 24

THE MIRAGE

I HAVE TAKEN CONTROL OF MY capacities, defied the social constraints, and mastered the sorrow serpent. I am finally comfortable with my position in this world, and the gods are looking down upon me with favour. They strengthen and guide my hands and feet. My chest puffs out, my fists tighten, and my arms swing back and forth like a king's foot soldiers marching into battle, as I conquer the stairs, the drawbridge, and occupy the kitchen, the castle courtyard. Having taken control of the tower, victory deserves repose. Chuck isn't going to be here for a while, so I make the decision to spend the time before he arrives, out on the dock, basking in the beautiful weather. The kitchen window frames the picturesque outdoor scenery. It would go well with a fresh cup of coffee.

The back door is the quickest way out, but as I open it, a forceful wind tries to push me back inside, almost as if Mother Nature, herself, is cautioning me against the move. Outside, I am met with a mysterious change of setting. The winds howl angrily, and the trees comply, swirling with a vengeance. The sun is nowhere to be found, and the sky has turned suspiciously grey. No clouds or birds exist. A dark fog rolls in over the lake which is absolutely still under the thick layer of vapour. It continues to darken in my presence, as an ominous mood takes a strangle hold on my entire world. An eerie feeling sinks into the pit of my stomach.

My eyes pan the menacing horizon. I feel as though a demonic curse is slowly consuming the vastness presented before me, banishing the majestic gold of the sun and the playful blue of the sky from this land forever. In their place, stands, what can only be described as, the manifest representation of a demon's soul. When I gaze upon the vista, I feel hatred, fear, guilt, and remorse; all the feelings that I promised myself I would avoid. It seems the madman is in control of nature, using it, quite skilfully, to instil fear, doubt, and despair in my heart, to weaken it.

My feet tremble with every step I take toward the dock. My thighs feel like sludge, and their muscles drain of strength, more and more, the nearer I get. I begin to think of Miranda. I do not know where she is, if she is still in the house, or if she has gone out. I feel a loving connection with her, and I am worried about her. A strong gust of wind hits me like a train, and I stumble back. Another warning from Nature, perhaps? After regaining my footing, a light rain begins to fall, with droplets so sparse, in fact, that they do not wet me, but so large that they hit like stones. I look up in amazement of the horrifying beauty of the falling rain, and accept the pummelling. As the sky cries epic tears of deep sadness, the ground discolours, darkening with each heavy droplet. I continue forward until my feet make contact with the wooden planks of the dock.

At the end of the dock, with my hands, I wipe the water from one the chairs, and take my seat for the imminent madman show. I am, suddenly and relentlessly, gripped by terror. Surges of self-doubt and insecurity flow toward me on the waves, penetrating my defences, and corrupting my inner being. I attend to the view across the lake, but am unable to pierce the fog. I am crippled by a fear that mocks my new found conviction and self-confidence. It screams at me, "You'll never be good enough for Miranda! You're an unfaithful cheat! Your in-laws hate you, you pathetic loser! Everyone looks down on you because you're an uneducated idiot! You'll never solve this crime!" In retribution for assuming a subordinate role, my very conscience cuts me to the core, like a harlot being stoned for her indiscretions. Panic sets in, and a tear streams down my face. I'm so scared. I'm so scared. I'm so scared. I'm so scared. Over and over, the words resonate, throughout my entire being and across the portrait of my entire life. I pine for the madman to appear, my soul calls out to him, for he is the rock I cling to in stormy seas. Each time he shows himself, I grow strong, brave, and assertive. I need him, now.

The fog begins to dissipate, in preparation for the madman's entrance, at last. Much to my delight, my fear washes away with the fog. Then, he takes the stage, in his traditional garb, but this time, there is another player. A small, young deer is trapped between the shore and its predator. The fawn is innocent, helpless, and instinctively afraid, and it tugs at my heart strings. It presses backward, closer to the water. The madman closes in on his prey, spear in hand, a sinister look in his eyes. Frantically, the deer prances to the right and to the left, but cannot escape. The madman licks his lips, savouring the taste of the kill, as well as, the meal to come. It's at this moment that the deer realizes his approaching demise and stops moving, stares at his enemy for an instant, and proceeds to lie down on the ground, in an admission of defeat. Immediately, the madman makes an aggressive forward lunge, swings his weapon with a ferocious thrust, and skewers the skull of the animal. Blood squirts from the wound, leaving a crimson stain on the sand. The deer flops and flails, impulsively, and eventually, lifeless, but afraid, no longer.

I watch the primal engagement in its entirety, intently, not with shock, awe, fear, excitement, pity, sadness, or guilt. I watch with a very cavalier stoicism. I do not weep for the innocent victim or guilt the hunter, as one might. It is a simple exercise revealing nature's way; it is not a moral battle between good and evil. Both beings are equally guilty of possessing a fragile life, one that can be taken away at any moment, and both are equally innocent in their desires to defend that life. I applaud them both; roles, well-played.

The scene reminds me that as long as I give proper veneration to my true self and primal instincts, I can rise above any problem and any person I face. I will be forever grateful to the madman for teaching me this hard-edged lesson, even if it equips me for his execution. The madman has hardened my spirit and built my confidence, and I will feel no guilt in winning the battle against him. It is simply the way of nature, and I will not compromise the integrity of our world by weeping its practices. I am as much a rudimental part of this world as the ocean and the grass. Its heart and mine are one. I am the world and I am man, and there is a blessed harmony between us.

The madman stands over the carcass, taking pleasure in the triumph. As he squats beside its mangled head, his thighs ripple with muscles and veins. His deeply-tanned arms surge with strength, as he grabs hold of his catch, lifts the animal high above his head, and howls, like a wolf, calling the pack for the feast. His stance widens in proud, primal glory, his head held high and his chest swelled. The madman's eyes are insanely wide, and he peers directly into my soul. Then, he slams the deer onto the ground with such force; blood splashes into the air, thunder echoes across the lake, and vibrations ripple the water. The mist begins to thicken again, and I try to hold on to the image, but I can barely identify the madman, dragging the dead animal toward the hut, before the fog conceals the island from sight. The lake is quiet once again. I am magnetized by the grotesque display of feral accomplishment. I feel reborn. A renewed spirit flows through me, and I grant it passage.

All of a sudden, I think of the family; Jim, Helen, and Miranda, and an unexpected intensity and frustration come over me. I envision scenes of violence *and* remorse, people, fighting *and* crying, but I am trapped on my thrown, unable to get off, let alone, intervene. They storm the castle and ransack my kingdom. My aching spirit calls out to the masses, in an attempt to calm them, but my efforts are futile, as my words fall upon deaf ears. I picture Miranda, crying over Alaska's dead body, holding a knife that drips with the blood of Officer Higgins. I see Jim, in black army boots and an intimidatingly-long trench coat, elbowing his way through the crowds, toward me. Casually, he steps over the body of Sergeant Fox, slain by his hand. He nears closer and closer, with heavy, threatening steps. I cannot see Helen anywhere. Mark Pratt, also, lay dead in the middle of the battlefield, blood all about. Silas Hammerstein is at my feet, lifeless, bloodied. I push at the arms of my throne, trying to get off. Strong from panic and horror, I bang, harder and harder, until one of the arms breaks. I whip the piece of wood into the lake; it explodes the surface of the water. I visualize Jim, still in pursuit; his eyes are as dark and hollow as the night. I flinch when steely-cold fingers wrap around my neck. Helen is holding a knife to my neck. I tremble violently, and the chair, also, rattles. I pull so fiercely at the remaining arm that it, too, is ripped from its support. I swing the board violently through the air, projecting it into the lake, farther this time. In my mind, I see Helen pull my hair, yank my head back, exposing my neck for the fatal slice. Jim closes in on me, and presses his hands on my chest. I think of the madman's deer, and, in similar fashion, I submit to my fate. I give up the fight, relax my head back, and keep my eyes locked on Jim, as he slides his hands around my neck, gripping tightly. I do not cry or beg for my life. I simply brace myself for a new world and a life beyond this one. Suddenly, and in glorious slow motion, a spear tip emerges from Jim's chest, stopping just short of my face. With a look of astonishment, Jim collapses in front of me, revealing the madman, in my line of sight, standing as epically as I have seen him, many times before. I turn my head to see Helen, her mouth, open in shock, and her eyes, wide with horror. She drops her knife, as she gapes, petrified, into the eyes of the madman. The madman, my rock, reaches over my head, grabs Helen by the throat, lifts her up, and with a flick of his wrist, breaks her neck. He, then, slams her violently to the ground, just as he had done with the deer. Life no longer exists for my in-laws. I glance at the madman, but when I return to where Jim and Helen lay, they are nowhere to be found. I look back at the madman and see that the battleground is clear; the players have all vanished.

I stamp my feet with such aggression and hatred that I break through the plank floor. I continue to pound the dock with my feet, smashing away at the floorboards, until shards of wood take flight. I stand, pick up my wooden throne, and smash it, again and again, hit after hit, fragments of wood spraying all around. I see the madman, hovering just above the ground, floating away from me, in retreat. I call for him to stay, but my words have no effect. I chase him, as swiftly and mightily as I can, but no matter how fast I run, the distance between us increases. Eventually, the madman disappears and I am alone. My pseudo-dream ends.

I survey the damage. A million floating splinters bob in the water, casually, with the ebb and flow of the tide. When I realize that I am still holding two wooden remnants, I abandon them, immediately. The chair I once sat in no longer exists, the remains, just bits and pieces, as if they never were a chair. In similar fashion, Alaska is no longer a dog, Pratt is no longer Pratt, and Silas is no longer Silas. Every person in the world will cease to be a person, when the reaper pulls its spirit from the body. I recognize that I am no longer part of this world, and in many ways, I never was.

CHAPTER 25

THE MARINA

I turn attention to the sound of Miranda's voice, calling me from the house. She is in the kitchen with Chuck Smith, who has come to take me to the marina. I greet my guest. Miranda has made him a coffee and he sips it, with a smile.

"Ya' ready to be a spy, there, James Bond?" Chuck jokes, spiritedly.

"Whatever it takes to catch this asshole," I snap, aggressively, welcoming Chuck with a solid handshake. "Finish up your coffee, there, and then we can go. Are you sure that Jeff is there today?"

"Yes, sir, I called him a little while ago and told him we'd be coming down for a visit. Didn't tell him what it was about, though. I thought I'd leave that to you." Chuck smiles, devilishly.

"Good thinking," I say.

I prefer to be the one to lay it all down for Jeff, so I am happy that Chuck leaves me the responsibility. I don't want Chuck talking to Jeff about our plans, without my being there, because I have the feeling that he is going to object. Miranda decides to say something. Evidently, Chuck has told her about our idea.

"So, Brian, you guys want to put up surveillance around the lake?"

191

"Yes, Miranda, Silas Hammerstein was found murdered last night, in his office."

Miranda's jaw drops. I continue.

"Yea, Fox found him dead, murdered, stabbed in the neck with his own pen. Apparently, he had been there for a few days. So yea, I think it's time we stepped up our game. People are dying."

"Oh my goodness, that's terrible," Miranda blurts out, shaking with terror. "But don't you think you should leave this up to the authorities? This is too dangerous for you guys."

"I think you're right, but Fox called, asking for my help. He can't handle this alone and it's gonna take some time until the city can mobilize a police force to help us. We have to do something."

Chuck nods in approval. Miranda says nothing. Her silence is approval enough.

"Alright, Chucky, let's head."

I make a move for the front door. Chuck follows eagerly, leaving Miranda alone in the kitchen.

"You, two, be careful, okay?" she warns, just as I open the door to leave.

Chuck and I both turn around to look at her. She scuttles up to me, puts her hands on my chest, and kisses my lips. Chuck looks at us, a warm smile on his face. He keeps his silent reserve.

"Come back to me in one piece, okay, dear?"

"Of course, honey," I return, walking quickly toward Chuck's pick-up.

Chuck hops into the driver's seat and fires up the engine, inciting a thunderous roar that eventually, melts into a throaty idle. He waves goodbye to Miranda, who is in the front doorway, her eyes, in concern, on me. I am not surprised by her look, considering my recent actions. She will learn, in good time, the magisterial importance of my new attitude and outlook on life. She will learn to understand it, accept it, and submit to it, by shedding her subscription to society's cruel system. Her enlightenment will be a difficult transition, perhaps, but one that must be completed.

Chuck and I ride in silence, most of the way. I am contemplating the defeat of the madman, and I hope that Chuck is doing the same. I look over at him. His expression is somewhere between serious and jovial. I cannot identify his mood, nor can I predict how he will deal with Jeff, or handle the madman situation, altogether. He handles the wheel calmly and seems relaxed, as he parks the car and gets out quickly. I am inspired by his adherence to efficiency. He heads into the marina, without hesitation, and I follow, closely behind. There is no one inside the structure, except Jeff, behind the counter, which is directly across from the front door. The building is relatively small, a simple square room with small windows on each wall. It's jam-packed with aquatic accessories, like life jackets, fishing rods, lures, and oars; a wide variety of products for the typical water sportsman. Chuck and I, however, ignore the displays and proceed straight toward Jeff, who does not offer us a smile.

"Jeff, my man, how are ya' doing?" Chuck cries, playfully, extending a hand in the name of diplomacy. Chuck knows, like I do, that we are asking Jeff for a rather large favour that may interfere with his business.

"Chuck, hi. Good, thanks," Jeff answers, as he shakes Chuck's hand, awkwardly. I nod to Jeff, he returns the same, and we shake hands as well.

"So, what can I do for you boys?" Jeff asks, keeping his words brief.

Chuck jumps in the lead.

"We need your help. Have you been following the murders on the news?"

"Yea, I've gotten wind of them. Why?"

"Well, we have reason to believe that the killer might frequent the lands around the lake. Sergeant Fox is having trouble procuring any significant leads, and has asked us to help out in any way we can. We're considering putting up some kind of surveillance system around the lake, but, since you own much of the coast, and part of the marina, we wouldn't be making much of a difference, unless we had your cooperation."

"So, what, exactly, are you proposing? What would you need from me?"

"We'd like to set up a series of cameras, connected by advanced, high-density cable that will send a live feed to an outpost somewhere close by. We would need to put a few on your property, and run some of the cable across your shoreline. Much of the other land is public domain, so we won't have an issue with that."

"You know what, guys? I don't think this is gonna work for me. The marina is a place of leisure, and I have many customers. I feel like this is a blatant invasion of privacy, not to mention the unsightly inconvenience it would cause. I'm sorry, but I don't think I can let you do it."

I allow Chuck to continue.

"Jeff, please. This may be the only way we can catch this guy and stop the killing. We're talking about killings, here, Jeff! This is serious stuff. Come on, it'll only be for a little while."

"You don't know that," Jeff interrupts. "Who knows how long this will go on for? Look, it's not so much a problem with me, but it certainly is an invasion of privacy for all marina customers. I can't allow that. I don't even think it would be legal. We'd have to place the cameras facing the lake, would we not?"

"Yes, of course."

"That means that we would be, inadvertently, monitoring our customers and their boats. I can't have that. I understand the importance of the situation but there has to be another way, a better way. I'm happy to help you guys out, but this, I cannot do."

"Listen, bub!" I roar. "Peoples' lives are at stake here. We have to do anything and everything we can to put an end to this. You cannot deny our request, or you're as bad as the murderer, himself."

"Excuse me?" Jeff says, smugly. He is not intimidated by the strength in my voice. "Don't you dare compare me to the murderer!

I can, in fact, deny your request. I already have. Do you understand or should I explain it to you again?"

My eyes are locked with Jeff's. I am about to explode, when I feel Chuck's hand rest, calmingly, on my chest. He takes over for the moment.

"Look, Jeff, we're not here to argue with you, or to fight. We know that you have every right to reject our request. We are simply asking you to think of the bigger picture here. With your help, we might save lives by catching this guy. There is nothing more important than that, is there?"

"Certainly not," Jeff admits. "But I simply cannot allow a camera system on the marina property that monitors the customers, intentionally, or not. I could get in big trouble for that, not to mention the moral sacrifice it would require on my part."

"How dare you speak of sacrifice!" I shout, in wild rage. I lunge over the counter, grip Jeff by the front of his shirt, and abruptly, pull him toward my face.

"Let go of me!" Jeff snarls.

"Brian! Stop!" Chuck tries to pull my arm away from the marina owner.

I tighten my grip, at the same time, kicking Chuck to the ground. Then, almost involuntarily, my left hand locks around Jeff's throat. He squeals out of shock and pain. From the corner of my eye, I notice Chuck rolling back to his feet, so I yank Jeff toward me and smash his face against the counter.

"You'd better do what we're asking you, buddy!" I yell, with a rhetorical hint of sarcasm. "Don't think for a second that I'm gonna let you sit idly by, while people die. Are you crazy?!"

At this point, Chuck runs toward me, and, with a powerful push, knocks me away from Jeff.

"Calm down!" he yells, with a reddened face and bulging eyes. He stands between Jeff and me, keeping us at bay with outstretched arms. "What is the matter with you? Why would you do that?"

"Come on, Chuck, this guy's nuts. He's helping the madman kill people! He must be stopped!"

"What are you talking about, Brian? You knew full well that Jeff might say "no" to our request."

"Yea, but I was never gonna let him. Jeff, you've got one more chance to change your mind," I warn, turning to face the pathetic weakling hiding behind the counter.

"Fuck off, Brian. No, I won't do it," he says, massaging his neck.

I am blinded by a red hot anger, as his words pierce my ears. With the speed of Bruce Lee, I leap over the counter and bash Jeff in the nose with my forehead. He falls to the floor in a bloody mess. Chuck grabs my shoulder, and, immediately, I spin around and crack him in the eye with a fierce right hook. Chuck goes down hard. As Jeff struggles to get up, I boot him as hard as I can, right in the mouth. Blood spurts from his lips, as he flails backward. I tear an oar from the wall and drive it into Jeff's skull. My arms fire like pistons, bashing, again and again, until blood flows from Jeff's head, his breathing stops, and he is unrecognizable. As I reach back for one more thrust, I feel Chuck bind my arms from behind, like a boa constrictor. I can't break free. Running out of options, I flip Chuck to the floor, hold him down with one hand, and pummel him with the other, in a fit of rage. He attempts to block my punches, but I continue my flurry of punches. When I am done, Chuck's face is a mangled, bloody mess, but he is still breathing, albeit with much difficulty.

I go to the bathroom, wash the blood from my hands and face, stare in the mirror, taking the time to collect myself. As the adrenaline subsides, I stop shaking, and I start to feel pain in my knuckles. I cackle in delight at the reflection that accompanies me. What a good fighter I am! I haven't been in many fights, but I seem to have a natural talent for it. I am tickled with pleasure and pride. I have destroyed two grown men with my bare hands, and don't have a mark to show for it. I have been blessed with so many talents that I didn't think I deserved one more, but here it is. The two bloodied bodies on the floor, clearly, serve as evidence of the fact that I am a tough, brute of a man. Perhaps now, people will pay me the respect I deserve. I vacate the marina, thrilled with myself, and, with a precocious smile, I begin the jog home.

CHAPTER 26

THE MADMAN

IT ONLY TAKES TWENTY MINUTES to jog home from the marina. I enter through the front door and glide into the kitchen, to get myself a drink of cold water. I listen for sounds that indicate Miranda's presence, but detect none. The water refreshes me, as I gaze out at the lake. The fog has lifted and the sun is shining brightly. The blue sky has returned to watch over the playful birds that fly within its expanse. I spy the dock, to see the damage I did, but the trees obstruct my view. No matter. I have no intention of fixing it, or covering it up. I'm not sure why, but I am, simply, unconcerned with the destruction, much like my unconcern with the recent havoc I caused at the marina. In fact, I forgot about Jeff and Chuck by the time I got home. I have no concerns or worries about anything, right now. If I am to face consequences for my actions, then, so be it. I am not bothered by any judgement by the pawns around me. I am beyond them, passed them, above them. Gone are the days when I worried about the rulings that others imposed on me. I welcome such adversity, and I will stomp on them, like cockroaches. I exist, and that's all that matters at the moment.

I pace the kitchen floor for a while. I am bored and unable to come up with something to satiate my time. I am sick of the man cave, I am sick of my bedroom, I am sick of the dock, I am sick of the kitchen, and I am sick of the television. It seems I am sick of everything. The sole affair that engages my interest and passion now is to identify and apprehend the madman, although at this point, I consider him more like a brother, or a long, lost relative with mental issues, than a criminal. Does one love a troubled brother any less because he is troubled? Certainly not! I truly sense a kinship with the madman, and his demise remains the only preoccupation worthy of my thoughts. Everything else that manifests within the confines of society's mundane structures is completely blasé to me.

Suddenly, the phone rings. I turn in its direction. It rings again, piercing my ears. On the third ring, I hear quick footsteps upstairs. It must be Miranda. She is home after all and en route to the phone. I reach for the phone, and place it, quietly, to my ear. Miranda answers first. I hold my breath, cover the receiver with my hand, and make myself perfectly silent.

"Hello?" She answers.

"Hi there, is this Miranda?" a man's voice asks, with composed uneasiness.

"Uh, yes it is. Who's this?"

"Hi, Miranda. It's Sergeant Fox."

"Oh, Sergeant Fox. Sorry, I didn't recognize your voice."

"That's quite alright ma'am. I'm sorry to bother you, but I really do need to speak with you. Unfortunately, these aren't the best of circumstances, I must admit."

"What do you mean? What's the problem?"

"First of all, is Brian with you?"

"Uh, no, he's not."

"Is he home?"

"No, I don't think so. He left for the marina with Chuck a few hours ago---"

"The marina? Why?"

"Well, he and Chuck were going to talk to Jeff about setting up surveillance around the lake. You know, because of the murders and the madman."

"Oh, dear," Fox gasps.

I don't understand Fox's reaction. Why is he alarmed that Chuck and I were going to the marina? It doesn't make any sense to me. It's not like there's any danger. I listen as the conversation continues.

"What? What's the matter?" Miranda asks, frantically. "Is Brian okay?"

There is a sincere tone of concern in Miranda's voice.

"No, Miranda! Nothing is okay. About an hour ago, I got the forensics report back from the CSI lab in the city, regarding the pen that was used to murder Silas Hammerstein. There were only two sets of fingerprints on the pen, Silas', and your husband's!"

The conversation dies, seemingly, for an eternity, until Miranda manages to emit a weak response in my defense.

"Ok, well, Brian went to see Silas earlier this week, which must be why his prints are on the pen."

"Fair enough," Fox replies. "That's exactly what I thought, too. I thought we were at another dead end, but, as it turns out, we aren't."

"What do you mean?" Miranda questions him, suspicion in her voice.

"Did Brian tell you that he and I spoke on the phone, this morning?"

"Yes. You told him you found Silas Hammerstein dead."

"Right, I did, and then he asked me to check up on your parents after I was finished with the CSI team at Silas' office."

"Okay, well that was thoughtful of him. I don't see what this---"

"Miranda," Fox interrupts, solemnly. "Your parents are dead. They were murdered last night."

The morbid silence that follows is deafening. I absorb the Sergeant's words with a mixture of disbelief, shock, and admission. The madman strikes again! I told Fox he would!

Miranda is only able to cry out, "What?!" She sobs in anguish.

"I'm really sorry, Miranda, but it gets worse," Fox waits until she composes herself. "Your parents have a security system with a video camera at the front door. It's connected to a live feed on your dad's computer. I took the hard drive to the station and an IT expert on the CSI team went through the footage. Your parents got home last night around 11:00. The footage shows Brian entering the house at 2:43 in the morning and leaving at 3:16. The examination report says that's the exact time of the murders."

Fox sighs deeply.

"I'm really sorry, Miranda. I'm on my way to the marina right now, to see if I can find Brian, but then, I'll come by to see you."

What?! I am very confused. I don't remember going to the Cranston's house last night, let alone murdering them. It was the madman! I was framed! I am innocent! I am not worried, because I am sure that the truth will be exposed, after I have the chance to explain myself. I wait for Miranda to respond but she does not.

"Miranda? Miranda!" Fox yells, in futility.

I hear a thud upstairs. Miranda has dropped the phone. I run to the top of the stairs. Her face is as white as a ghost, her body tense, and her mouth and eyes, open wide in horror. She collapses to the floor, as the agony consumes her. Her weeping cuts to the core of what is left of my humanity. She clutches her knees, assuming the fetal position, and begins to rock, instinctively, back and forth; a babe, in total misery.

I run to her, offering words to defend my innocence, but pure terror captures her face, and she erupts with a very primal coping mechanism. She begins to swing her fists, like a crazed boxer, making connection with shots to my face, my chest, and my ribs. I back off, and Miranda returns to the solace of the fetal position. With all the power that her voice can muster, she screams, "Get away from me! Get away from me! Get away from me!" Her wails are unending. Her face swells to a dark shade of crimson, and her body continues to tremble.

"I'm innocent!" I announce, loudly, although I doubt that she hears my declaration.

Suddenly, and faster than I have ever seen her move before, she scrambles to the bedroom and slams the door in my face.

"Get away from me! Get away from me! Get away from me!" she goes on screaming.

I push the door open to see her curled up in a ball on the bed. I dash to her side, but, as I pass the window, I am stopped dead in my tracks. It's as if I am being beckoned to look out, across the lake, at the Hawkins' property. I see the madman, at a great distance, yet, easily identifiable. He just stands there, chest out, head up, as per his usual posture. His presence gives me a wonderful idea. I will show him to Miranda and prove my innocence.

"I can prove it to you! I can prove it to you!"

I shout with excitement, but it seems Miranda is in another dimension, oblivious to my words. I embrace the fetus that is my wife, and carry her downstairs. She is numb to the act. She doesn't stop crying, and her body doesn't stop quivering, violently.

Passing through the kitchen, I grab a knife from the wooden knife holder that Jim and Helen got us for our anniversary a few years ago. The metal blade sings as it is extracted from its slot. The sweet high-pitched twang is music to my ears. I decide, once and for all, that I will hunt down and kill the madman, no matter what. With Miranda, still secure in my arms, I open the door, and rush across the lawn, toward the dock. Out of the corner of my eye, I notice Chuck, staggering around the side of the house. He is shouting, but I cannot make out what he is saying. My eyes are fixed on the madman, even as his image bounces up and down with every bouncing step I take.

Finally at the end of the dock, having avoided the hole I made earlier in the day, I put Miranda down in one of the vacant chairs. The madman is on the edge of the island, reaching out for me. His presence is crucial to proving my innocence. Before I can say anything to Miranda, I feel Chuck's footsteps hit the wooden planks of the dock. He is badly injured, but hikes toward me, obviously, with a very real purpose.

"Get away from her!" he shouts. "Get away from her, you demon!"

My mind is racing in search of clarity, understanding, and my next move. Chuck finds the strength to charge at me.

"I didn't do anything!" I roar, hoping he will stop, but he does not.

He advances, with his head, low, like a taunted bull trying to gore me with powerful horns. When his hands are only inches from my body, I promptly, crouch, causing him to topple over me, landing chest-down on the dock. I take hold of the hair at the back of his head and yank it backward, thrusting his face upward, and exposing his neck.

"Brian, Brian," he struggles to whisper my name, as I hold my blade at his throat, lightly pressing against his skin. "Brian, please," his raspy voice continues to be heard. "What have you become?"

I freeze for a moment at his question. What is he talking about? We are here to stop the madman, aren't we? Has he truly lost sight of the greater good? He charged after *me* out of a violent aggression. Why he is incriminating me is a mystery. I am not the bad guy. I am not the bad guy. I push my knife harder against his neck and with one swift motion, I slit his throat. Blood, immediately, paints the floorboards, as Chuck's life and spirit drain from his eyes.

Miranda is curled up on the chair in a catatonic state, unaware of the violent act happening just behind her. She has stopped shaking and her eyes are closed. I look beyond and see the madman, his arms still reaching out for me, as if to extend a warm embrace. I roll Chuck's lifeless corpse with my foot until it flops into the lake. I take a deep breath, wipe the sweat off my brow, and straighten up. My back cracks a few times and I feel much better. Maybe I will see a chiropractor this weekend, if I have time. I still want to finish painting the garage doors. I take another deep breath and walk to Miranda's side.

"Miranda? Miranda?" I utter, but my words yield no change in my wife's state.

I nudge her and repeat her name until her eyes flicker and turn toward me.

"There she is," I sigh, happily. "Look, Miranda. Look across the lake. Do you see it?"

"See what?" she whispers, faintly.

"My innocence; proven!" I jest. "And the madman, of course. He's standing right there, on the Hawkins' island. He's the killer, Miranda. I haven't hurt anyone. Look at him. Isn't he grotesque?"

Miranda leans forward and squints.

"I don't see him. I don't see anyone."

"Look, I'll show you."

I drag her chair to the edge of the dock and squat down to her eye level. I point directly across the lake to where the madman stands. His position is the same; his arms extended in welcome.

"There's no one there," Miranda says, calmly. "There's no one on the island, or anywhere else, Brian."

"Look, he's right there," I reiterate, my finger pointing, rigidly, at the barbarian.

"There's no one there, Brian!" Miranda roars at the top of her lungs. Her voice echoes across the lake, scattering the birds into flight.

"What are you talking about, Miranda. He's right there, staring back at us," I claim, rising back to my feet.

I can see the madman quite clearly. His hair, his arms, his legs, his clothes, his posture, and the look on his face are all very familiar; they are all as they have always been. His muscles are rippling, his expression is stoic, his shorts are tattered, his hair is long and greasy, and he stands, upright, with an epic grotesqueness that I both fear and admire. He is absent of any and all devotion to social civility and normativity, existing only as pure, bare masculinity. He emanates primal instinct and desire, pursuant only to the will of his nature. He is man's true nature. He is impassable, he is immutable, and his essence fills my heart, my spirit, and my soul.

Then, a peculiar thing happens. Right before my eyes, the madman begins to slowly disappear, feet first. I watch in pure, horrified amazement as his flesh fades, more and more of him, with each passing second. His shins, and then, his thighs, are removed from visibility, like bubbles that pop from visibility, leaving nothing but empty space. The scourge continues, proximally, toward his torso. His hands and arms experience the same gradual obliteration. Never, during his eradication, does the stoic, emotionless expression leave him. His penetrating glare remains poised on me, until he is gone, completely erased from sight. I stare at the spot where he once stood. Perplexed and confused, I ask myself, "Had he ever existed at all?" The island is silent and void of any sign of the madman.

I hang my head in despair and see my reflection in the water below. My mind is suddenly flooded with thoughts, images, and sounds that I have blocked out up to now. I remember killing Alaska. The memories are vivid of my bare hands at her throat, squeezing, until her lifeless body hung in my grasp. I recall staring into the blue of her eyes, watching life escape them. I remember stabbing Silas in the neck with his pen and eyeing the stream of blood that squirt from the wound. I stole the life from him, as well, in a ferocious rage. I remember slaughtering young Mark Pratt, just to see if I could. I can still hear his screams of terror, and see his blood smeared across his bed sheets. I remember butchering Jim and Helen, and cackling, as I smashed their bodies into blood-soaked oblivion. At the mercy of a demonic force, I slew my terrible in-laws, and felt good about it. I can finally put my paranoiac fears to rest.

Fear is the cause of it all. Fear is the source of my madness. Fear, turned into primal hatred, and stripped me of all civility and conformity, reducing me to a mere slave of man's inherent essence. It eradicated all righteousness my heart possessed.

The parasite overtakes me, once more, and I welcome its possession. I am host, again, to the evil that flows through me without restriction. My memories are suppressed, yet again. I give way to the malicious whims of primal nature and therefore, must give up my right to exist, autonomously.

I look at Miranda, a woman I no longer connect with. She makes no movement. Suddenly, I hear footsteps creeping up behind me. I spin around to see Fox and Higgins, guns drawn, coming toward me. I grab Miranda and, using her as a shield, I hold my knife up to her neck. They beg me to release her, but my grip only tightens. I want to slaughter them all and escape this wretched town. I imagine slashing each of their throats and riding off into the sunset. I lick my lips at the prospect of more bloodshed. Evil has an unrelenting grip on me, and it taunts, commanding my hands to kill, destroy, and hurt. *I must obey.* Just before making a violent move, I detect a soft voice.

"Brian," Miranda whispers.

I lean an ear closer to her mouth. This moment of silence owns the whole universe.

"I want to go home."

Miranda's words cut deep, ripping out my insides and tearing out my heart. They manage to fan a remaining, infinitesimally-small ember of goodness in my heart into an all-consuming inferno that singes the fear within. It forces my hands, more powerfully than evil ever could, to raise my knife, and back away from Miranda, away from Fox and Higgins. I have let Miranda go. I have let her live.

The momentary spark of decency hastily burns out, and once more, I am possessed by evil selfishness. I can do nothing to thwart its control as both of my hands tightly grasp the knife. I watch as the knife pierces my chest, slowly, and with unrelenting force, it penetrates deeper. My hands do not shake, nor do I cry or tremble, as the blade enters my heart. With one final thrust, the team of Hatred and Fear pushes the steel as far as it will go. I start to fall backward, in, seemingly, slow motion. My feet still touch the dock, as my body is parallel to the water. Finally, I hit the water with a great splash. As I sink below the surface, I can see blood, swirling with the water about me in cascading shades of red, twirling playfully. I begin to die.

As my vision grows dim, and my grip on life grows weak, I am swamped with so many emotions that my brain cannot process them all. My deeds, my regrets, my loves, my hates, victories, defeats, hopes, dreams, joys, and sorrows, all saturate my mind. I contemplate who I am, and as I drift out of this realm, I have a final linear conclusion; I am primal, I am savage, I am uninhibited, and I am ruthless. *I* am the madman!

Printed in the United States
By Bookmasters